DATE DUE

IRIS
in WINTER

Also by Elizabeth Cadell in Large Print:

Around the Rugged Rock
The Cuckoo in Spring
Enter Mrs. Belchamber
The Golden Collar
Honey for Tea
I Love a Lass
Out of the Rain
Shadows on the Water
The Toy Sword

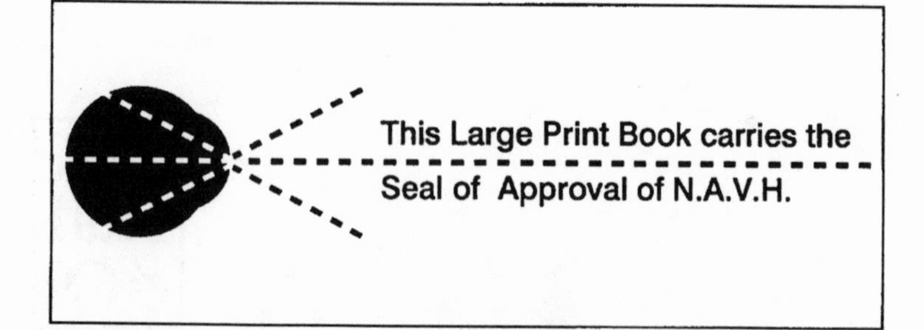

IRIS in WINTER

ELIZABETH
CADELL

**G.K. Hall & Co.,
Thorndike, Maine**

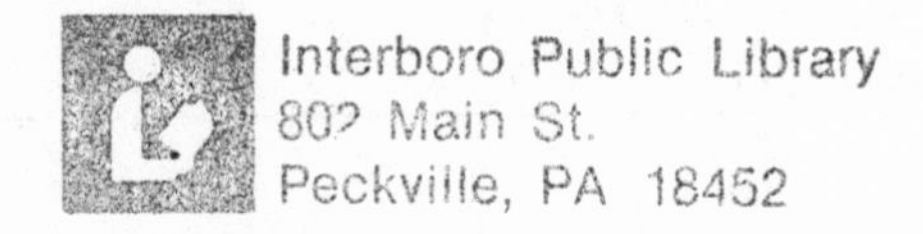

Published in 1996 by arrangement with
Brandt & Brandt Literary Agents, Inc.

G.K. Hall Large Print Romance Collection.

The text of this Large Print edition is unabridged.
Other aspects of the book may vary from the original edition.

Set in 16 pt. Bookman Old Style by Al Chase.

Printed in the United States on permanent paper.

Library of Congress Cataloging in Publication Data

Cadell, Elizabeth.
Iris in winter / by Elizabeth Cadell.
p. cm.
ISBN 0-7838-1860-2 (lg. print : hc)
1. Large type books. I. Title.
[PR6005.A225I75 1996]
823'.914—dc20 96-19597

IRIS
in WINTER

CHAPTER ONE

Iris Drake added a few lines to the sketch on which she was working, and studied them critically, her head on one side. The result did not appear to please her for, with an impatient movement, she left her sketch-board and, walking to the window of the small, bare room, stared out moodily at the uninspiring view.

It was the beginning of September, but there was nothing outside to remind the watcher of the passing of summer. A heavy sky, a steady drizzle, and fallen leaves on the pavements seemed rather to lay undue stress on the more unpleasant aspects of autumn.

Iris turned away. It was not a sight to cheer anybody, and her spirits were already low. With a recollection of the tonic effect attributed to the counting of blessings, she leaned against the table and proceeded to enumerate her own.

There seemed to be, she admitted, a lot of blessings: youth — some people thought twenty-two quite young — and beauty. Everybody said that she was beautiful and, on days when her hair didn't give trouble and when she couldn't detect any lurking blemishes on her skin, she thought so herself. It counted, she thought, for very little — her beauty hadn't really done much beyond insuring her escorts for everything that went on. Talents? Oh well, she could sketch hats and she could write a pointless and vapid daily column in — well, it was, in a way — a leading newspaper. She had a well-paid job and a pleasant flat at Knightsbridge. But who, reflected Iris dismally, forgetting her blessings and concentrating on her woes, who wanted to sketch hats?

She didn't. Here she was, with half her ambitions realized and the other half as far away as ever. She was in Fleet Street; but she hadn't wanted a job sketching hats. She had expected . . .

Her gloomy meditations were interrupted by the cautious opening of the door. A head appeared round it and the owner, finding Iris alone, stepped into the room. Iris looked at the newcomer without any perceptible brightening of her expression.

"Hello, Ted," she greeted him.

The young man dropped into a chair, crossed his legs comfortably on the table, and looked at her with pleasant brown eyes.

"I say, Iris," he said, "I popped in to ask whether you'd marry me."

Iris, back at her sketchboard, gave the hat a slightly larger brim and answered absently, "No, Ted. Thanks awfully, all the same."

"You had your whole mind on that answer, did you?" questioned Ted Harris anxiously.

Iris looked up. "My mind, my whole mind and nothing — I say," she broke off to inquire, "I thought you told me you had an important session with the Chief this morning."

"I did. I had," answered Ted. "I've had half of it, but there was an interruption. I saw it coming — at least, I didn't exactly see it — but I heard the scraping of chairs outside as flustered junior reporters leapt to their feet; I heard the creaking as elderly reporters bowed from the waist. Then the door was thrown open and there he was."

"Who was?" inquired Iris.

Ted smiled at her indulgently.

"Dear Iris," he said, "sometimes you don't quite merit the brilliance and the wit I shower upon you. Who, think you, would throw the main body of this organization into confusion? Think, now. It couldn't have been old Ernest, because he was with me — that is, I was with him. So that — "

"Oh — you mean Sir Kenneth Harfield? What did he want?" asked Iris.

"I can only guess," said Ted. "He owns this newspaper, but he doesn't tell me anything. Never confides in me. Ernest gave me a look which I could only interpret as one of dismissal, and told me to shut the door after me. And so here I am. . . . Did you really mean what you said about not marrying me?"

"Yes. And the look on my face," Iris informed him, "is one of dismissal. If Ernest finds you here — "

"Why should he come here?" asked Ted. "I mean, I know this room's the setting for one of Nature's brightest jewels and so on et cetera, but you also happen to be a very junior member of the staff. If Ernest wanted you, he'd have you fetched, wouldn't he? . . . What's making you so pensive?" he inquired.

Iris threw a glance of distaste round the room. "It's this rathole," she said gloomily. "And look at the view."

Ted looked.

"It's pretty bleak," he said sympathetically, "but you won't be looking at it long. When's the second bit of your vacation coming up?"

"End of the month," said Iris. "But my Swiss tour's fallen through."

"So one of the boys told me," said Ted. "What're you going to do?"

"Dunno," said Iris listlessly. "I keep looking at the Travel section but I can't work up any enthusiasm about any of the offers. I'm going to wait and see what my sister's doing. She's just taken a cottage in a place I've never heard of, and when I can find out where it is, and whether it's in a nice spot with all the amenities — "

"Meaning three cinemas and a pier?" put in Ted.

"Something like that. It doesn't sound promising."

"What's it called?" asked Ted.

"High something — yes, High Ambo," said Iris. "As far as I can — "

"Half a minute," broke in Ted. He was looking at her intently, a puzzled frown on his forehead.

"High — ?" He paused.

" — Ambo," supplied Iris. "Know it?"

Ted spoke musingly. "Funny," he said. "That's the second time I've heard that name this morning. Ernest mentioned it. It's the scene of the rumpus — the site of — "

"What rumpus?" inquired Iris.

"The rumpus that my session with Ernest was about. The rumpus that's brought our Chief's Chief up from his landed estate. What *is* a landed estate, can you tell me?" he asked.

"Who cares?" asked Iris. "We can't be talking about the same High Ambo. The one Caroline my sister's going to is about six hours' journey from London and — "

"Well, this one's God-forsaken, too," said Ted. "Cumberland or Westmorland or one of those bleak outposts. Must be the same place. What's your sister going there for?"

"Well, to escape, in a way," said Iris. "It's a long story."

Ted arranged himself more comfortably and tilted his chair back at a dangerous angle.

But just then the door of the room burst open and the Chief, Ernest Reed, an ominous frown on his forehead, stood on the threshold. Ted swung himself to his feet in a lightning movement and, straightening his tie, turned to face his employer. Ernest Reed pulled a watch from his waistcoat pocket, studied it, and looked up at the young man towering above him.

"Half-past eleven," he informed him. "Your day's work, I presume, is over?"

"Er — not quite, sir," said Ted.

Mr. Reed spoke with rasping finality. "If you want to put your feet up and talk to young women," he said, "you can do it at your own expense. Get out of this room and stay out of it."

He moved aside. Ted walked past him and, with a backward glance at Iris behind Mr. Reed's back, closed the door quietly.

"You," said Mr. Reed, opening it again and glaring at Iris, "you come along and see me. Got something to say to you."

Leaving the door wide, he turned and walked away and Iris stared after him moodily. Perhaps, she reflected, he was going to sack her, and in her present mood she didn't care much. If this was Fleet Street, they could have it.

Well, the sooner it was over, the better.

With a glance at herself in the mirror behind the door, she went through the maze of offices which led to Ernest Reed's room. She knocked on the door and, entering, confronted the stout, irritable man at the desk.

Though unmarried and leading a bachelor existence, Ernest Reed nevertheless gave the impression of being a man oppressed by numerous family cares. He had a harassed, almost a hunted expression which gave strangers a feeling that he was being bullied.

Any bullying that went on, however, was done by Ernest. He disliked women and had never — until he met Iris's sister, Caroline Drake — felt the smallest desire to take one to his bosom. He had met Caroline too late — she was already engaged to be married to his neighbor, Jeffry West. But four years later, she was back — a widow, free and making arrangements to live in the big house standing next to his own. Ernest had been uncertain as to what length of time should elapse before widows could, with propriety, receive fresh advances. He waited six months and then began to call regularly, but he was dismayed to find that his visits were made, not only to Caroline West, but to several of her late husband's relations who seemed to have attached themselves to the household.

The wooing seemed to be making very little

progress. Caroline was not, he told himself, quite like other women; she had a quiet aloofness — elusiveness — Ernest could hardly find a name for the quality which gave her an almost absentminded air and made him feel that she scarcely knew, sometimes, who he was.

She had asked him to give her sister a position on the paper, and Ernest had done so — reluctantly, grudgingly, but still, he had done it. His kindness, he reflected bitterly, had done him little good. Caroline was as elusive as ever, and he was stuck with one of the kind of young women he hated most — the kind he considered pert, modern, made-up, over-dressed hussies.

He studied the hussy before him and spoke abruptly.

"This Harris fellow," he said. "I suppose he's told you about the visit from Sir Kenneth Harfield?"

Iris felt a little surprise, but her air was composed. "Yes, Mr. Reed."

"He told you where the trouble was?"

"Trouble?" Iris echoed.

"Don't be stupid," said Ernest testily.

"Yes, Mr. Reed."

"Place called High Ambo," said Ernest. "Know anything about it?"

Iris hesitated. He lived next door to Caroline, but she had no means of knowing whether her sister had told him of her plans.

She decided that it would be better to know nothing.

"No, Mr. Reed."

Ernest directed a keen glance at her, and Iris met it calmly. He toyed irritably with the papers on his desk and then leaned forward and addressed her.

"Listen to me," he said. "I'm going to give you a job."

A curious expression flitted across Iris's face. She had come into the room prepared to lose one; instead she was being offered one. She waited warily.

"When you joined this paper," Ernest continued, "you wanted to be a reporter — a damn silly idea that a lot of girls have nowadays. In my day they wanted to go on the stage; now they want to be reporters — pah! But that's neither here no'there. You wanted to be a reporter," he went on. "If you'd made as good a reporter as you did a columnist, then God help the paper — but that's beside the point. I'm going to — " He broke off, gave a shiver, and looked malignantly round the room. "Where's the damn draught coming from?" he demanded.

Iris wondered. Every window in the room was hermetically sealed. Mr. Reed, having ascertained this, directed her attention to the door.

"Push that mat under there," he directed. "No, not that one, not that one — the big one.

That's it. Right against the bottom of the door — that's it. Nothing but draughts," he grumbled under his breath. "Whistling all round me and getting on m'chest." He settled himself in his chair and came back to the subject in hand. "Now listen t'me," he said. "Listen carefully, because I don't go over anything twice. If you don't get it first time, then you can't follow good plain English. Now." He pointed a fat forefinger at his listener. "Up at a place called High Ambo there's a school — a prep school and a good one. I know, because I was there m'self once, when it was even better than it is now. They've got fine grounds, but near them there's a large property belonging to Lord Fellmount — a bit of an eccentric who lives by himself with an old manservant and likes privacy. There's a lake in his grounds, and he has a good bit of trouble keeping the schoolboys away from it. He complains to the School, and the authorities do their best, I take it, to keep the boys off. But they won't keep off, and so the old man — Fellmount — takes the law into his own hands and deals with offenders as and when he catches 'em. Well, he caught Sir Kenneth Harfield's son, and he threw him into the lake — to teach him. He didn't know who the boy was, and he didn't care — he threw him in. I suppose you've got all that?"

"Yes, Mr. Reed."

"Very well. Now comes the trouble — blast that draught! Get up," he ordered, "and see if that window fastener's properly shut. That's better. Now this boy Harfield was thrown in on the last day of the summer term; he fished himself out and nobody — so he says — knew anything about the incident except himself and the man who threw him in. He didn't want to be seen at the School, so he hung about until he was dry and then went back. The other boys had gone — the train contingent, that is. Harfield was to go home by car with his parents.

"Well, they came to fetch him. They took him home, and the next thing he's down with a serious chill and misses pneumonia by a hair. They make inquiries when he's better, and it all comes out and his parents don't like what they hear. In fact, Sir Kenneth liked it so little that he wants me to print the story — delicate boy, large fees, school guilty of gross neglect and breach of contract. He wouldn't have a case in court, of course, because the boy was out of bounds, but the parents feel that no boy ought to be left in the position of being able to run himself into serious trouble in that way. And he insists that the School — somebody in the School, anybody in the School — had a good idea of what had happened but said nothing because they were frightened they'd have to give up a bit of their summer holiday to keep the boy at school for a few days to see if any trouble developed. They let him — the father says — they let him do the long drive home and said nothing. Those are all the facts — have you got 'em?"

"Yes, Mr. Reed," said Iris.

"All right. Now I'll tell you what I'm going to do. I've seen Sir Kenneth this morning and we've had it out. He's got the story and he'd like to see it in print — but I wouldn't. I was well looked after when I was at school there and I've got a feeling for the place. Print a story of this kind and bang goes the School. If the School doesn't face up to its responsibilities, if they've got people on their staff capable of neglecting their duty to the boys, then I'll print the story and be glad to. But I want to give the School a chance — and I've got Sir Kenneth round to agreeing to let me do it my own way. My own way is to send somebody down there to keep their ears open. I want somebody there who will get to know the School and who could do a little discreet questioning. Then we'd get at the root of the trouble. If we found that the School wasn't to blame, Sir Kenneth's prepared to drop the matter; the boy's all right and clamoring to go back. But we've got to do a little investigating. And — " Ernest Reed leaned forward and glared at Iris — "and I'm going to send you to do it."

"Me?" In spite of herself, Iris spoke in a squeak of surprise.

"You. Don't imagine," Mr. Reed warned her, "that I've any confidence in your intelligence or in your discretion. Far from it — but that's neither here no'there. But High Ambo is a hamlet of — well, apart from the school, which is some distance above the village, there's a mere handful of people. No stranger could go there without having every eye fixed on him and every yokel asking questions about him. Nobody'll ask any questions about you. You're merely going to spend your holiday with your sister — that's all."

"With — "

" — your sister. Don't try," directed Mr. Reed, "to look as though you hadn't any idea she was going there. If you don't know now — which I'm convinced you do — then you'll know pretty soon, because she *is* going there. I saw her last Friday and, when I heard where she was going, I was naturally interested. Now I've an even greater interest. I want you to get her up to Town for a talk with you. Tell her what I've told you and make arrangements for going to stay with her at High Ambo. You'll get an increase in salary and your expenses, and you'll send me a report every week — understand?"

"Yes, Mr. Reed."

"And don't sit there and say, 'Yes, Mr.

Reed,' 'No, Mr. Reed.' Get back to your work and think about what I've told you. When you've seen Ca— when you've seen your sister — let me know the date you're joining her. Now out and shut the door properly behind you and draw that rug back as you go out — closer now, closer — that's it."

The door closed behind Iris.

CHAPTER TWO

Caroline West stepped off the bus and, watching it drive away, prepared herself for the dangerous business of getting herself across a London street.

She made her way to a point from which she could carry out the operation in two parts. A little island in the middle of the road — if she could get to it safely, half the ordeal would be over.

She watched a knot of people as they left her side and performed the swift yet unhurried series of twists and turns by which Londoners — to Caroline's deep admiration — threaded their way through stationary traffic. It was perfectly easy. People did it without fuss every moment of the day and Caroline, rooted to her spot opposite the island, was deeply ashamed of her hesitation. At twenty-eight, slim and active and in the best of health, to cower before the splendidly regulated London traffic was, she felt, nothing short of idiocy.

It would have been better to have crossed by the subway. But she was at Piccadilly Circus, and she had once tried the subway and, following the directions as well as a total lack of knowledge of the names of the streets permitted, had found herself above ground on a pavement far removed from the one she had intended to reach.

She pulled herself together and, waiting until a group of people had gathered, made her way — gently, but with the firmness of desperation — into the middle. The traffic stopped; the group moved, and Caroline, amply protected on both flanks, was conveyed safely across to the other side.

She waited for a moment to get her breath and look about her. Iris had said round the corner and down the little street and then it was the building with the green door. . . .

Caroline found the green door without difficulty and studied the brass plate upon it: Willow Club. It looked pleasant and Caroline had a feeling that it would be well heated. Though it was only the beginning of September, the air was chilly and she was beginning to feel cold and hungry.

She entered the building and, still following her sister's instructions, went up a beautiful old staircase and found herself on a large, well-carpeted landing across which women, who all seemed to Caroline to be extremely well-dressed, passed at intervals.

Caroline waited for a few moments and looked round in the hope of seeing her sister. Iris was usually late for appointments. At last she heard the sound of swift footsteps and it seemed to her that the room had suddenly grown brighter. With the feeling of pride and pleasure that the sight always aroused in her, she watched her sister coming across the room to greet her. She rose and took a step forward to meet Iris and, as they met, the likeness — and the difference — between them was at once apparent. It was as though an artist, working with the same model, had produced two works — one painted in quiet, sober hues and the other glowing and brilliant. The difference was more than superficial: Caroline was calm and dreaded emotional upheavals; she avoided if she could, anything controversial, violent, or even mildly disturbing. She would concede most points without argument — which, indeed, she considered mere waste of words. She accepted, without resentment, the knowledge that many people thought her humdrum and even dull, and she paid as little attention to these labels as to her friends' urgings to do more, see more, move more, and generally to behave in a way quite foreign to her nature. Iris, on the other hand, was eager, impulsive, and determined to go through life at a speed which she felt to be in keeping with the swift pace of modern living. Pace, to Iris, was synonymous with Progress, and if she had been asked to define the word "movement," she would have said that it meant going forward.

Caroline stood before her and listened to

the rush of words — so swift as to be, at times, almost unintelligible — that her sister called conversation.

"Darling, I'm late," said Iris. "Hours and hours, but I had a mad rush and I couldn't make it earlier. Have you been here ages?"

"No, I haven't. I've only just come," said Caroline.

Iris raised her eyebrows. "But — didn't your train get in at eleven or eleven-five or eleven-something?" she asked.

"Yes, it did," said Caroline, "but I took a — "

"You took a bus, and the bus put you down on *that* side of Piccadilly, and you stood for forty minutes waiting for the traffic to run out of petrol, and you got across between the prams — isn't that it?"

"There aren't perambulators in Piccadilly," pointed out Caroline. "How are you, Iris?"

"Fine," said Iris. "I've got a lot to talk about, as I told you in my letter. We'll tackle it at lunch."

"Tell me," Caroline queried the straight young back preceding her down the corridor, "have you seen Robert lately?"

"No, and I don't want to," said Iris. "At least — yes, I did. He came to the flat with a frightful woman and stayed until I froze her out. Nothing could freeze Robert out, of course, but I did manage — in the most delicate way — to convey to the creature that I thought she had a damned nerve to dare to — to darken my doors. Glacial, I was. Her drink — I had to offer her a drink — but it must have practically frozen as it went down her throat. I wouldn't care sometimes, Carol," she declared earnestly, "if I never set eyes on Robert again — even if he is my only beastly brother."

"It must be harder for you, living in London," sympathized Caroline. "He only came down to Folker once, and he didn't finish the week end — he said the house was ghastly and the heating grisly and he was awfully rude to my mother-in-law, who was staying with me at the time. But isn't he," she asked, "going abroad again? He isn't often in England for the winter, is he?"

"He'll be leaving in January," said Iris. "Opening one of his Sailing Clubs at a place in I can't remember whether it's Australia or New Zealand — somewhere a long way away, thank goodness. Sit here," she directed Caroline to an empty table to the right of the dining-room entrance, "and we'll have lunch and get it over and do some talking."

Settled in the quiet corner with a good meal before her, Caroline looked round her with interest. She was unused to scenes of such bustle and variety, and the people at the neighboring tables were of a type seldom seen in the quiet little town of Folker in Sussex. "There are lots of men," she noted in surprise. "I didn't know men came here."

"Men'll come anywhere," said Iris, "for a free lunch. And this is a Club for Press women, not purdah women." She looked across at her sister in amusement. "Carol darling," she informed her, "you're looking just like the little boy paying his first visit to the Zoo!"

Caroline attempted to fix her attention on her stewed steak, but she had seen something to which her eyes had, perforce, to return.

"What particular animal," inquired Iris, "have you spotted now?"

"That hat," said Caroline. "Don't turn round, but it's an extraordinary one — it's a black and white sort of tortured-looking one, and it's got something that looks like celery round the brim."

Iris turned and gave the hat a keen, professional glance. "Not bad," she commented, going on with her food. "I'll make a sketch of it in a minute and use it." Then she leaned across and addressed her sister with solemn earnestness: "Carol, I've got it at last!"

"Got what?" Caroline, with a stern effort, withdrew her attention from the table manners of a stout lady dealing competently with a plate of spaghetti.

"Got the job I wanted, the job I always knew I could do, the job I've waited for for nearly two years while that foul Ernest kept my nose to his dirty little job of drawing hats and writing tripe. I'm going to — " Iris broke off and stared at her sister blankly — "Carol, you're not listening!"

"I'm terribly sorry, Iris — honestly. I'm sorry, but — well, it was all hanging off her fork in strips about ten inches long, and she just took a deep sort of inward breath and — "

"I'm giving you," said Iris, "an extremely important piece of news."

"Tell me," begged Caroline.

"I've got — " Iris paused and brought out her news with a dramatic flourish — "I've got my first assignment. After two years old Ernest relented. Carol — " she frowned anxiously across at her sister — "Carol, you do realize, don't you, that he still has some romantic ideas about you?"

Caroline tried to picture the stout, irritable Ernest Reed having romantic ideas about anybody, and found it impossible. "I think he's put the romantic ideas aside," she told her sister placidly.

"No — you're wrong, Carol," said Iris. "Simon Gunter was waiting outside the office for me the other day and when Ernest saw him, he leapt three feet in the air and — "

"Ernest," said Caroline, "couldn't leap three feet."

"Well — two feet," said Iris. "And next day he came to my room when I was working and stood over me and tried to find out whether you ever saw Simon nowadays. I knew he was trying to sound casual, but when he's interested he always goes 'Hm, hm' — you know that irritating way he has of breathing out through his nose — and then he — "

"I," pointed out Caroline, "breathe out through my nose." There was a pause. Iris knitted her brows and looked across at her sister in bewilderment.

"You know, Carol," she said hesitatingly, "I don't want to seem — well — critical, because I love you and I think you're wonderful, but — but sometimes it does strike me that for a woman of twenty-eight, who had four years of marriage, who's been about the world and had an upbringing that would have made most people — that made Robert and me, anyhow — pretty independent, you do behave in a — a sort of rather naïve way sometimes. I mean — you can't cross a London street, and you refuse to make the best of a lovely face and figure, and you — you don't seem to make yourself have any — any *presence*, and you never get worked up or excited, and you come to what is, after all, a perfectly ordinary lunch and look round as though — well — " she paused helplessly — "Do you see what I mean?"

Caroline helped herself to another potato. "Well, yes," she said, "I think I do. But I can't help keeping calm. I don't see that there's anything to be gained by trying to look excited when I don't feel excited. And I haven't been about the world. I've only been to Nigeria, and then only to a part which had no streets and which didn't in any way give one practice for darting underneath the buses in Piccadilly Circus. And I didn't mean to — well — gape, but you must remember that I only see ordinary people as a rule, and never run across women with what looks like celery in their hats, or who suck up long tails of spaghetti, or who dye their hair a sort of dark green color, like that dreadful woman over there."

Iris, glancing at the dreadful woman, identified her casually. "That? That isn't dark green," she said. "It's the new olive shade, if you like your hair an olive shade, and that woman happens to be the one who came to the flat the other night — Robert's latest."

Caroline, horror-stricken, could only stare across the table at her sister, and Iris looked amused. "I know," she said. "You've never imagined that Robert could so forget his boyhood training — only he never had any boyhood training — and you're shocked to discover that — "

Caroline had found her voice. "She must be at least thirty-five," she said in an awed tone, "and she looks like a — like a — "

"Careful!" warned Iris. "I'm only twenty-two and I live in London and work in Fleet

Street and you can't use that word in front of me. But you're quite right. She's exactly what you're trying not to say, and you needn't be squeamish about it. Robert isn't. Now that you've seen the worst," she went on, "I'll tell you why old Ernest told me to get you up here."

As briefly as she could, she told her sister the story of what she called the Harfield immersion. It was difficult to get Caroline past the part at which the victim had contracted the chill, for with deep sympathy she begged for details of the duration of his illness and the steps taken to insure the patient's complete recovery.

"Young Harfield," Iris assured her, "is as right as rain. But you do see, Carol, don't you, what Ernest's driving at?"

Caroline looked doubtful. "Well, yes, I think I do," she said. "I'm glad you're coming to stay, anyhow. I never dreamt you'd be able to manage it before Christmas, and now I can put you into Sue's room and — "

"Who's Sue?" asked Iris.

"You ought to remember her — Sue Stannard," explained Caroline. "I got rather friendly with her the last year at school and it was through her that I first went to High Ambo. Her aunts own this place — Lilac Cottage — they and their brother used to own the School, too — "

"Lilac Cottage! You mean this place I'm

"I don't think so," said Caroline and Iris in nison. "Well, here we are," went on Iris as e taxi drew up. "I'll come to the train and ıt you in."

Caroline found an empty carriage and set-d herself in a corner.

Thanks for coming up," said Iris. "I'll see ı at High Ambo. It sounds, if you don't nd my saying so, a pretty cheesy sort of ce."

t isn't bad," said Caroline. "You have to nge going up," she went on. At Norbor-h Junction. The other train goes from form Five and you can have a nice sleep ause High Ambo's the terminus and so can't go beyond your station."

ce sleep — Who on earth wants a nice ?" asked Iris. "Is there any scenery?"

ell — yes," said Caroline. "It's flat at orough and then you begin to climb t gets higher and higher and — "

and bleaker and bleaker. It isn't quite me of year," commented Iris, "to land illage in the dales or fells or whatever ll them. Cinema?"

n't think so," said Caroline. "But the oys are very nice. They wear green ith white lines — you often meet them."

ooked dejected. "No diversions? No ?" she asked.

don't know whether the place would s if it could," said Caroline, "but they

coming to," asked Iris, "is called Lilac Cottage?"

Caroline nodded.

"Gosh," commented Iris. "Doesn't sound quite my setting. But I can quite see that nobody'd suspect anybody from Lilac Cottage of being a newshound. You see — " She broke off and looked at her sister. "What's wrong?" she asked.

"That woman — you know — Robert's one," murmured Caroline under her breath. "She's standing up and she's looking in this direction. You don't think she'll — you don't suppose she'll come over and talk to us, do you?"

"No, I don't, my pet," said Iris reassuringly. "As I was saying — "

"She's coming," said Caroline. "No — she isn't. It's all right. She's going to talk to the woman in the celery hat." Her eyes returned reluctantly to Iris. "Do go on," she said. "I'm listening. But I think you ought to tell Robert that his lady friend is being awfully friendly with that foreign-looking man she's just joined. He — "

"He isn't foreign-looking," said Iris. "He's perfectly ordinary-looking. His name is Smithers and he comes from Bristol. To come back to the not uninteresting subject of ourselves," she went on, "when do you plan to go off to this High Ambo place, Carol?"

"In ten days," replied Caroline. "There was rather a lot to be done once I'd made up my mind to go."

"I suppose the in-laws kicked a bit at having their nice free hotel crumbling under their feet," said Iris.

"Well — at first they didn't seem to care about the idea," said Caroline. "Then my mother-in-law admitted I needed a rest, and after that things were easier. One of my brothers-in-law is buying the house and he's going to pay me something for the use of the furniture. It's all much easier than I thought it was going to be." She gathered up her bag and gloves and, looking at her watch, rose reluctantly. "I'll have to go, Iris," she said. "This early train suits me much better."

"I'll come to the station," said Iris. "We've got a lot more to say."

The two women made their way out into the street, and Iris hailed a passing taxi.

"We'll share it," she said, ushering her sister in. "It's easier to talk in this than in a bus or the Underground."

"How soon can you come?" asked Caroline as they were driven in the direction of Waterloo.

"Second week in October," said Iris. She paused for a moment and then spoke with some hesitation. "About Simon Gunter, Carol — "

She stopped and Caroline, who was fish-

ing in her handbag collecting silve
the cabman, looked up. "Simor
about him?" she asked placidly.

"Well, I told you I saw him."

"Yes — and Ernest breathed th
nose."

"Yes," said Iris. "Well — are yc
marry him, Carol?"

Caroline looked surprised. "Er
mean?" she asked.

"Ernest? Good Lord, no!" sai
sively. "Who in the world wou
nest? No — I was talking abo
keeps sending his love whene
and he — well, are you going t

"I don't think so," said Carc

"Well — I don't want to poke
you don't want it, but — well
awfully long time," pointed
remember Jeffry West muc
"because he was a bit befo
do remember thinking at
it was odd you'd choser
Simon. Simon's so nice, a
I'm sorry to call Jeffry
wasn't, but he certainly
you — I mean couldn't y

"I don't think so," said

" 'I don't think so, ye
so,' " mimicked Iris n
Carol, you won't ever
will you?"

aren't allowed to have any cinemas or cafés or anything of that sort."

"Not allowed? Who does the not-allowing?"

"Lord Fellmount. He owns most of High Ambo and the part above it," said Caroline, "and he wants to keep things as they are. He doesn't like progress."

"And he doesn't like little boys," added Iris.

"But there is Blakely," Caroline added as an afterthought.

"Another peer?" Iris asked.

"It's the neighboring village and I'm sure you'll like it. They've opened cafés and inns and they've a cinema. . . ."

The whistle blew and Iris banged Caroline's door and moved back.

Ten days after her meeting with Iris, Caroline was on the train to High Ambo.

She really expected to find things much the same as they were in her childhood when she used to visit Sue Stannard. Sue, of course, was now married and no longer lived there, but her great-aunt still held court for the village.

The School had long since passed out of Stannard hands. When Major Stannard died, High Ambo College had come to an end, and Castle Ambo had been born, under the direction of Mervyn Clunes, a young, brilliant, eager young man, and one of a line of famous schoolmasters. What had been a flourishing family concern for Major Stannard became a well-known, academically sound enterprise. Fees were high, the school prospered, the scholarship list grew to imposing lengths; more and yet more parents walked round the spacious grounds on Speech Day.

The village, too, might have prospered from this influx of parents willing to pay high prices for accommodation or food, but — Lord Fellmount didn't allow it. The two remaining Stannards, Miss Louisa and her sister, had been gently retired from teaching activities and lived in Ambo Lodge, an imposing mansion not far from Lilac Cottage.

Indeed, the first person Caroline saw when she stepped from the train was the short, stout form of Miss Louisa herself. It was as though she had only been away a week. Even Miss Louise's rough tweed suit with the faint mustard-colored line was the same, the battered felt hat, the shining shoes . . .

She advanced sturdily upon Caroline and held out a hand. "Welcome, m'dear. Welcome from us both. Glad to see you, very glad indeed. Both are. Come 'long — taxi waiting."

It was the same economical conversation. It was the same taxi — a sadly scratched affair owned by the son of the postmistress, and the village's one example of private enterprise.

The drive to the cottage was short, and Miss Louisa spoke, on the way, of the preparations she had made. "Didn't change any furniture, m'dear. Susan's piano still there. You still sing?"

Caroline smiled and shook her head.

"Pity," said Miss Louisa. "Nobody any accomplishments nowadays. They look at football matches, listen to the wireless, sit inside the dreadful cinemas. All critics — no performers. It used to be so good for young girls, all the useful practice. Discipline. Now none. I've aired your bed, put some eggs and milk and bread into your larder. Place very clean. Very, very. But no maid for you. All working up at the School. None over for anybody. Mustn't do too much, remember. So many women far too much to do, far too much, far too much."

The taxi drew up before a plain, square-built house and Miss Louisa, getting out, kept a stern eye on the postmistress's son as he lifted out the suitcases and carried them up the path. She inserted a key, opened the front door, ordered him to wait for her, and, turning, ushered Caroline into the house.

"Won't stay, m'dear," she said. "I'll leave you to settle in. Ask at once if you want anything. Tradespeople calling tomorrow.

New people in the cottage over there, anxious to help you. Colonel Brock — not young, but the right sort, quite the right sort. Lives with housekeeper. Ill-tempered woman. Sour face, very sour face. Good-by, m'dear. My sister sent you her love. Come and see her. Good-by."

Caroline, with a little murmur, glanced out at the taxi and half-opened her bag. Fearing to offend Miss Louisa, she hesitated.

"Three shillings and sixpence," said Miss Louisa, and watched Caroline count it out. "Used to do it for one and sixpence, but if people call a College a Castle, prices soar. Naturally. Everything three times what it was. Good-by, m'dear, good-by."

She was gone. Caroline looked after her with affection. Dear Miss Louisa . . . She must go and call on the Misses Stannard. Hat, gloves, and the very best behavior . . .

She closed the front door, which opened straight into the pleasant living room, and stood looking round her. The one comfortable chair, the other uncomfortable ones, the dining table near the window, the glossy grand piano — she remembered it all.

She walked through the door which, situated exactly opposite the front door and leading directly into the kitchen, made the living room a draughty place on cold days. Beyond the kitchen was the coal shed and a place for the gardening tools which, as far as Caroline knew, nobody had ever used.

She walked once more into the living room and up the staircase at the far end. She went into the largest of the four bedrooms and saw that it was arranged just as she remembered it; she was grateful for the flowers on the dressing table. Going across the landing, she looked into the bedroom which had been Sue's. Though smaller than Caroline's, the room was of a prettier shape, and Caroline thought that Iris would like it very much.

She opened the doors of the two smaller bedrooms. One was a pleasant room with a view over the hills; the other was rather dark, and was papered in an unpleasant shade of green which gave the place an almost underwater look. Caroline smiled. She and Sue, she remembered, had called it the aquarium. . . .

She shut the doors and went downstairs. It was not, perhaps, a particularly pretty house; the furniture, with the exception of the best chair and the piano, was poor. But it was compact, it was easy to run, it was quiet, and it was friendly. Caroline decided that she was going to be very happy.

And, in a fortnight, Iris was coming.

CHAPTER THREE

Iris threaded her way through the crowds on the main line platform, tiptoeing now and then in an attempt to keep her porter in view. She had not his advantage in being able to carve a way through the throng with two suitcases and a typewriter, and she wished she had asked him to go slowly.

He looked round and waited for her; she caught him up and walked beside him down a flight of steps, along an underground passage, and up some steps at the other end. A little breathless, she reached the top and looked round her.

Platform Five. It was a great change from the scene of confusion and bustle which she had just left. Here was no scurrying; there were scarcely a dozen people in sight and the shabby train standing alongside looked as though nothing would ever get it to move.

"Leaves in 'bout fifty minutes," said the porter. "Nonsmoker?"

"No. And an empty one, if possible," directed Iris.

It was gratifying, after the crowded conditions of the main line train, to have an almost unlimited choice of corner seats. Iris, now in the lead, moved with firm steps along the platform, looking into the carriages. Two women . . . a man and a woman . . . one woman . . . one man . . . ah! She stopped and indicated the empty carriage but the porter, with a jerk of his head, moved her on.

"Fill up later," he warned. "Better near the engine if you want to be by y'self. Here."

He opened the door of the last carriage and ushered Iris in. Swinging her suitcases to the rack, he received his fee and departed.

Iris relaxed. This, she felt, was the way to travel. No crowding forms squeezing her elbows, no clumsy feet ruining her stockings. She leaned back in her seat and watched idly the forms of passengers appearing at the top of the steps, noting the contrast between their plain, country appearance and the elegant travelers she had left behind in the express.

The train filled slowly, but nobody disturbed Iris's privacy. She glanced at her watch: thirty minutes to go. She would get out a book and . . .

There was a slight clatter, a minor disturbance which would have been unheard on the other platforms, but which made a distinct ripple on the serenity of Number 5. Iris, looking at the steps, saw on the topmost a small boy. He was carrying so many parcels that it was difficult to see how he managed to get up at all, but he had achieved the ascent, and only one parcel had detached itself and clattered down again.

An aged porter, following with a Gladstone bag and an armful of parcels almost as numerous as those carried by the boy, attempted to retrieve the fallen one and found it impossible. The boy turned, and a kindly woman following with a large basket picked up the parcel and, holding it, walked beside the boy, who smiled at her gratefully.

A stray puppy entangled itself in the boy's feet and two more packages fell onto the platform. A burly countryman picked them up and added himself to the little procession and Iris saw, with horror and dismay, that the entire party was directing its steps — guided by the boy — toward her carriage.

They came nearer. There was a pause, and Iris had a moment of hope. It was only, however, a short halt to pick up another package; then nearer and nearer . . .

"Blast!" said Iris.

The old porter wrenched open the door. The boy was in, filling the rack with his assortment of luggage. He leaned out, relieved the man and the woman of his property, and dragged off a green cap with white lines.

"I say — thanks," he said.

The man and the woman, Iris saw with thankfulness, were moving away. But the boy remained, and, with a feeling of dismay, she remembered Caroline's words regarding the boys' school: green caps with white lines

— Castle Ambo. There was no hope of his getting out earlier; the boy's destination was her own.

The last parcel was disposed of, and the boy, with a sigh of relief, thanked the porter and explored first one pocket and then another in an attempt to find his purse. He discovered it at last in the inner pocket of his jacket and, sitting down, poured the money into his cap. Iris saw that there were three ten shilling notes, some half crowns, and a few pennies. He hesitated, and she knew that he was feeling that half a crown, was a good deal to pay for a mere transfer from one platform to another.

He gave the porter the half-crown and watched him wistfully as he departed. Then, after directing a keen glance at his luggage to assure himself that it was all there, he looked at Iris a shade doubtfully. Iris saw that his ears were set at an extraordinary angle, flaring out almost at right angles to his head and giving him an attractively gnome-like appearance.

Drawing her gaze away with some difficulty, she got out a book and was about to open it when a strong smell of cheese came to her nostrils. She looked up to find that the boy had opened his Gladstone bag and taken out a battered package of sandwiches. He looked at them, hesitated, and held them out to Iris.

"I say — would you like one?" he asked.

Iris declined with thanks and tried to look grateful, but the paper surrounding the sandwiches had burst open and several inedible articles had added themselves to the food. The boy extracted an India rubber, two studs, and three pen nibs and replaced them, crumb- and cheese-covered, in his bag.

"I s'pose," he said, "you had lunch on the other train?"

Iris nodded, and put a question in her turn. "I thought school terms usually started in September," she said. "Aren't you a bit late?"

The boy nodded energetically and swallowed his mouthful of food. "Measles," he said. "I think the School's got them now, prob'ly, 'cos Winter was staying with me for part of the hols and he went back to school and he didn't know about the measles until afterwards, so I expect he's sort of got them now. I only got them a bit," he went on, "and I did an awful lot of carpentry. All that — " he nodded toward the parcels filling the racks — "all that's mostly what I did. Mostly in the summer hols there isn't much time 'cos you're out all the time and can't do much, but I couldn't go out and I got an awful lot done. Would you," he asked, "like to see some?"

Iris hesitated, trying to frame a sentence

which would, without offense, convey her complete lack of interest in any form of woodwork. The boy, taking her hesitation for joyous consent, placed his sandwiches carefully in his cap, in which were also three pennies which he had forgotten to put back into his purse, and in a moment Iris was surrounded by a sea of parcels.

"This," said the craftsman, stripping brown paper from the first, "is a mousetrap. There's lots in our dorm — mice, I mean — and I fixed one up last term — a mousetrap — and it worked jolly well, but I sold it to Winter and made another one."

Iris admired the mousetrap, a model ship, two boxes with crude attempts at carving — at which, the boy explained, he had not had very much practice — a pencil box, a stamp box, a cash box, a collar box, and a tool box. On one seat were arrayed the articles neatly in a row, while on the other was a growing pile of paper and string.

The exhibition over, the boy sat down and resumed his lunch, to which was now added a large amount of sawdust and some string. The show had increased the comradely spirit in the carriage, and Iris learned that her companion's name was David Carruthers; that he lived in Yorkshire, detested soccer, played scrum half on the School rugger team, collected Empire stamps, and had been to Belgium with his father and mother last spring. He reviewed the wonders of Brussels, dwelling upon the varied richness of the confectionery, the melting qualities of the cream cakes, and the extraordinary desire of shopkeepers to supply customers with anything they wanted, but he seemed a little disappointed at the unlikelihood of the visit being repeated for some time.

"My mother," he explained obscurely, "won't be able to sort of travel for a bit, my father says."

Iris assumed that another pair of ears was to be added to the family of Carruthers, and hoped that they would be of more orthodox pattern. A woman, she reflected, could hardly do that twice. It must have been a difficult matter to decide whether to have small bonnets which left the ears free, or large bonnets with escape hatches.

She saw David pushing up his sleeve to examine a watch far too large for his wrist.

"Ten minutes to go," he announced. "Mr. Sheridan's leaving it a bit late."

Iris, on inquiry, found that Mr. Sheridan was the French Master at Castle Ambo. He was to meet Master Carruthers and act as escort for the remainder of the journey.

"We could easily go ourselves," said David, "but we're only allowed on main line trains by ourselves. Nobody comes with us except on this last bit. Once," he explained, "some of our chaps did an awf'ly good train robbery — not a real one, 'cos they gave all the money and jewel'ry back, but they climbed along the train and sort of frightened people. I wish," said David wistfully, "I'd been there. And after that Mr. Clunes — that's the Head — had to give a guarantee that there'd always be a master in charge, and so there is, but we all think it's a pretty good swizz, and so do the masters."

There was only five minutes to go, and there was still no sign of Mr. Sheridan. David finished his sandwiches and, leaning out of the window to question a passing official, learned that the train would be delayed for a quarter of an hour. Seating himself once more, he gazed upwards for a time to examine the labels on Iris's suitcases.

"You're going to High Ambo too," he told her finally. "Have you been there before?"

Iris shook her head.

"I'm going to stay with my sister," she told him, "at a place called Lilac Cottage."

"Lilac Cottage!" David's face expressed surprise and pleasure. "If you're going to Lilac Cottage," he said, "then we'll be awfully near you, 'cos we're in Holly Lodge and that's just near."

"But I thought," said Iris, "that you were up at the Castle."

"No, we aren't," said David. "Not all of us. We've been put into houses — some of us, I mean — 'cos the School's got bigger, it's got more boys, I mean, and we can't all get in very well, and until the new part's ready, a lot of us have got to live out of the school. I'm with Winter and Stuffy Hume — we're sort of friends — and Mr. Sheridan's with us, and Mr. Swintzchell — he's the Music Master. First there were only a few boys at the school, and then it went up to a hundred and fifty and the Head said he wouldn't have any more but then he did, and now we're a hundred and seventy-two — at least, it was a hundred and seventy-two last term, but I think Clifton Secundus isn't coming back. I think he's gone to another school 'cos he didn't like being with his brother 'cos his brother's cleverer than him and — "

The history of Clifton Secundus came to an abrupt end. A young man stopped, glanced into the carriage, and opened the door.

"Hello, sir," said David.

The French Master nodded and threw a glance round the scattered papers. "On the rack," he ordered briefly.

"Yes, sir." David, scrambling up, moved his handiwork to one side and proceeded to wrap the articles and place them once more upon the luggage rack, leaving a space for the leather-encased camera which the master had brought with him. Mr. Sheridan took a seat in the corner farthest from Iris, opened a newspaper, and began to read. It was clear that there was to be no more conversation.

The engine gave a sudden heave and a series of jerks.

"Mayton," caroled a porter, banging doors as they went past him. "Mayton, Newing, Connorfell, Dale Underby, Dale Overblow, Blakely, and High *Am*-bo!"

They were on their way. David, feeling his way among crumbs and miscellaneous articles, produced from his bag a highly colored paper and opened it at a page headed "Bleached Bones." Mr. Sheridan put up the window, resumed his seat, and went on with his reading. Iris was left to read her book or study the scenery.

She chose, instead, to study as much as she could see of the newcomer. This was a schoolmaster, and she knew very little about schoolmasters, but there were several points about this one which entitled him, she felt, to her interest. He was, she guessed, about twenty-five or six; he was tall, and he looked athletic, in spite of the horn-rimmed spectacles he was wearing. He would have looked better, she reflected, in a well-tailored suit instead of that sports coat and flannel trousers, but perhaps well-tailored suits weren't the thing in High Ambo. He was good-looking — if he'd come out of his newspaper she could see what color his eyes were and whether his mouth was as attractive as she had thought at first.

The French Master, lowering his paper in order to turn the page, found the eyes of the girl opposite fixed upon him in frank and unembarrassed scrutiny.

For a moment they stared at one another, and then Mr. Sheridan folded his paper calmly and unhurriedly and resumed his reading.

Odd, some girls, he mused. Most of them looked exactly alike. Same kind of clothes, same hair, same everything. It was hard for a fellow to tell one from another. This one was good-looking and looked intelligent, but they all wore that air of I-know-everything. Those poor devils of fellows — if there were any nowadays — who had remnants of knight-errantry, must have a poor time. . . . Young Carruthers was looking a bit peaked — ought to have had a bit longer at home, perhaps — or perhaps not. His mother wouldn't be really up to looking after him. The Head had written himself, he remembered, to advise the boy's early return. . . . Here was this article, second of the series. The fellow could write, and he knew what he was writing about. . . . Mr. Sheridan settled himself more comfortably and began to read what the fellow had to say.

David paused in his perusal of "The Vultures' Vigil" to put a question. "Sir," he asked, "has Winter got measles?"

Mr. Sheridan answered in a low, slow, calm voice — almost, thought Iris, the male counterpart of Caroline's.

"He hadn't," he said, "when I left this morning."

David looked disappointed. "He ought to have, sir, 'cos he was with me. P'rhaps," he suggested in more hopeful tones, "he's a sort of carrier and gives them to other people and doesn't get them?"

"Perhaps," agreed Mr. Sheridan.

"This lady, sir," went on David, indicating Iris, "is coming to High Ambo, and she's going to Lilac Cottage, and that's quite near us."

Mr. Sheridan acknowledged this introduction with a slight bow and appeared to be returning to his newspaper. Iris put a question. "I understand," she said, "that the school has overflowed."

"Hundred and seventy-odd," said Mr. Sheridan. "Do you know anybody there?"

"No — well, at least," said Iris, "I did meet the sister of a boy named Coates — no, Clowes — and I promised I'd take him out one day. Perhaps — " she turned to David — "perhaps you'd come and see me one day, and bring him along?"

There was a brief silence, and Iris felt a certain tension in the air. David's ears, she saw, had turned a deep red. He spoke in a tone of embarrassment.

"Well, you see, as a — as a matter of fact," he faltered, "he's — he's Head Boy."

Iris realized that she had made a grave error and murmured something to the effect that perhaps some other time. . . . She glanced at Mr. Sheridan, bracing herself to meet derision behind the horn rims, and found the French Master deep in his newspaper once more. Really deep, she acknowledged with rising chagrin. He wasn't pretending. He was easy and relaxed and deeply interested — in his newspaper.

Iris had a feeling of having stepped with bare feet onto an unexpectedly cold stone floor. She knew a great many young men, but she had never met one who, in her presence, had been easy and relaxed and deeply interested in anything but herself. The man opposite, she assured herself after a further scrutiny, was young, healthy, and completely normal-looking. She didn't want him to spend the entire journey making conversation, but they were to pass more than two hours together, they were bound for the same destination, and there would be, in all probability, future meetings. And he sat there and read.

Mr. Sheridan, finishing his article, put aside his newspaper, and took up the country magazine lying by his side. Glancing casually at Iris, he found that she was still studying him and noticed that her glance was less friendly.

Wanted to talk, he decided. Well, she could chat to Carruthers when he came out of that disgusting little paper he was reading. He'd have to watch him, or he'd try to smuggle it into the school. Nobody could stop boys from reading under the bedclothes with the aid of torches, but one could at least insure that they read decent print and not that sight-destroying type young Carruthers was peering at. . . . Lilac Cottage that girl was going to. That must be why the Head hadn't been able to get it for the Science Master and the four boys trying for Eton. The Stannards had practically said he could have it, and then told him they'd had an appeal from a previous tenant. This didn't look like a previous tenant, but he remembered hearing that the cottage was already occupied, so this girl must be a friend or a relation coming on a visit. Pity the Head couldn't have used it — it made things difficult for him; but once the school buildings had been enlarged, all this business of being parked out would cease, though in some ways it wasn't bad to be away from the School. It was quieter, for one thing, and the boys enjoyed the home atmosphere. He was lucky to be at Holly Lodge. It was a decent house, and old Swintzchell was a good fellow. Pity one had to listen to the choir practices, but it was natural of the Head to put the three Choir leaders in with the Music Master. . . . Wonderful photographs, these. Look at that greenshank, and that reed bunting at nest. His own photographs had been disappointing, but now that he'd got the good camera back, it would be all right. . . . Blakely already — it was getting a bit crowded and overdoing its prices. Old Lord Fellmount had been right to hold out, although he'd only done it out of cussedness. Mean old devil — if he'd keep all the rest of his estate and let the school rent that grand bit of water in the summer, they could get a bit of model yacht sailing well out of sight and sound of his lordship, and wouldn't make the smallest difference to his privacy. But the old man wouldn't hear of it, and it was no use persisting — he'd only become really unpleasant. . . . This was a magnificent photograph of a wheat ear. Winter's brother had written from Cornwall to say they'd spotted some down there last week, but that wasn't unusual — they'd been observed as late as December. What did this chap here say about it? He hadn't much more time — nearly Blakely now. The journey seemed quite short.

Iris flipped the pages of her book and stared out at the flourishing little town coming into view. Blakely. Thank goodness, the journey was nearly at an end. Next time anybody told her she was irresistible, she'd try to forget the occasion on which a man had traveled with her and kept his eyes riveted on pictures of sparrows. And next time she traveled with a schoolmaster, she'd try the other approach — spectacles and a bun and sensible shoes. This man was obviously charm-proof. He had to be, or how could he go month after month seeing nothing but desks and little boys with ears?

David Carruthers rose and began the task of assembling his luggage. The train slowed and drew into a tiny station.

"All change," sang the porter. "All change. High Ambo." Iris stood up, waited for Mr. Sheridan to carry her suitcases onto the platform, followed him, and gave him a nod of thanks. Mr. Sheridan returned to the carriage in time to observe a swift and stealthy movement on the part of his pupil.

"Out with it!" he ordered.

David opened his jacket reluctantly and pulled out the creased copy of the paper he had been reading. Mr. Sheridan took it and tossed it on the seat.

"Fifty lines by Saturday," he said calmly. " 'It Pays to Be Honest.' "

"Yes, sir." David followed the master onto the platform and stood for a moment in indecision. He flexed his knees tentatively and felt a distinct slipping. . . . It'd be sure to fall out when he got into the school car, and then he'd have twice fifty lines and there wouldn't be any free time before Saturday.

He began a series of convulsive wriggles, and Mr. Sheridan, turning, watched him with calm expectancy. After a great deal of effort, David plunged a hand inside his shirt, produced an even more battered paper of the same type as that which the master had confiscated, and held it out.

"I had another, sir," he said.

"I see," said Mr. Sheridan, taking the paper and tossing it into the empty carriage. "Thirty lines. It pays to be honest."

David's eyes became round with horror. "T-thirty, sir? You m-mean thirty more?"

"I mean twenty less. Get all those things along to the car," directed Mr. Sheridan.

David hesitated. The August and September issues had gone. There wasn't much point in keeping October. Nobody'd know what had gone before in all the serials and anyhow, there wouldn't be any more until Christmas unless Stuffy's mother brought some down at half term. . . .

"I've got October, sir, in my bag," he informed the master.

"Well, keep it there and bring it to me tonight," said Mr. Sheridan. "Is that all your stuff? Run it along. I'll bring these and my camera."

He turned and found, to his annoyance, that a porter, clearing the pile of luggage at his feet, had removed not only the girl's suitcases but also his camera — his best, his most expensive camera. There it was. The fool had carried it across and left it with her cases. . . .

But she was standing and looking at it, Mr. Sheridan saw, and she had done nothing to disclaim ownership, and she was letting the man pick it up and — by gosh — she was going to let him carry it away with her things and . . .

Mr. Sheridan reached Iris in a few long, swift strides. "Excuse me." His voice was cold. "I think that's my camera you've got there."

Iris gave him an impatient look. There was Caroline just coming along the platform, looking friendly and welcoming, and this Sheridan had emerged from his absorption and was looking at her as though she'd got designs on his property. She glanced carelessly at the camera and addressed the porter. "That isn't mine," she said.

The porter detached the camera, handed it to Mr. Sheridan, and moved away with the rest of Iris's luggage. Iris, glancing at the man beside her, found that he was still regarding her with dislike and something like suspicion. She raised her eyebrows and spoke lightly.

"Jolly journey, wasn't it?" she said. "Hello, Carol darling. How are you? That's my luggage over there, but it's an awful shame: I picked up the most wonderful camera because I thought the owner was dead and wouldn't notice, but I — "

Her voice died away in the distance, and Michael Sheridan, regaining his habitual calm, turned and walked to the waiting school car.

Dead or not, he'd got his camera back. And he wouldn't have to go to Lilac Cottage for it, either. . . .

CHAPTER FOUR

Iris's comments on the cottage, its rooms, and its furniture were terse and uncomplimentary. She had expected, in spite of Caroline's description of the place, something rustic and picturesque, and the ugliness of the house proved an unpleasant surprise. She was willing to admit that the view was magnificent, but complained at the lack of comfort in the house.

Caroline listened to the complaints with unruffled calm, and Iris looked at her with wonder.

"For a summer cottage, yes," she said, "but for a long winter spell, how *can* you, Carol? Good Heavens, there isn't a decent thing in the house except that chair and that piano — and who wants a piano? Why couldn't those two old girls have swept out the piano and put in some comfortable sofas and things? Can't you go and *ask* them? They must be practically shouldering their way through spare furniture in that huge place of theirs."

"There's nothing wrong with this," said Caroline calmly. "We'll take turns at sitting in the big chair and you'll soon get used to the look of the house."

"I won't," said Iris. "And if I put my typewriter on any of those tables, they'll collapse." She threw a glance round the living room and looked at her sister. "How could you ever like it?" she asked.

Caroline led the way upstairs.

"Come up and I'll help you to get unpacked and settled in," she suggested, "and then you'll feel more at home. I don't *like* it, exactly," she went on, ushering Iris into the bedroom she was to occupy. "I mean, I know it's full of drawbacks, but you're judging it from a Londoner's angle and I'm comparing it with the dreadful place I've just been living in. Three flights," she said slowly, pausing in her task of opening a suitcase and staring at her sister. "Three flights of stairs and eight bedrooms. It was torture, in the end, just to go up and down them. It took eighteen steps to get from the front door to the drawing room, and fourteen — "

"Oh, look, Carol — how sweet!" Iris bent down, one hand outstretched invitingly, and looked at a beautiful cat which had just come into the room. "Puss, puss," she coaxed.

"Oh — don't touch it!" cried Caroline.

It was too late. Iris, with a yelp of pain, had snatched her hand away from the spiteful claws, and, with a handkerchief, was wiping the blood from her hand and calling down maledictions upon all cats.

"I'm so sorry," said Caroline. "I ought to

have warned you. It always does that. It does it to me if I get too near."

Iris looked with loathing at the cat, now seated on the floor engaged in washing itself. It looked mild, placid, and very friendly.

"It came in one day," said Caroline, "looking terrible — all draggly and thin and I felt sorry for it and gave it some warm milk. I didn't try to touch it until it had got a bit used to me, but the moment I put a hand out, it put its claws in — and it does it to everybody. I hoped it would go away, but it didn't, and — "

"You can make it go," broke in Iris, sucking the back of her hand resentfully. "Throw the thing out."

"I can't help feeling," said Caroline, "that if it sinks its claws into you when you're giving it a home and food and kindness, it won't stop at anything if you try to send it away. It knows its name now — I called it Solly. I don't know why — I suppose because there was a cat called Solly at school once. It rubs itself against your leg and ends up by digging a piece out of your ankle. It's odd, isn't it?"

"Let him try it again, and he'll find out whether it's odd," said Iris. "Supposing it jumps up on my bed tonight and scratches my face?"

"I don't think it'll do that," said Caroline, a shade doubtfully. "It hasn't done that so far.

It's a pretty thing, isn't it?"

Iris's emphatic opinion of the cat was interrupted by the sound of firm footsteps sounding on the gravel path. Iris raised her eyebrows inquiringly at Caroline, who moved to the window and peered out cautiously.

"It's the Colonel," she said.

Iris brightened.

"Colonel old type or Colonel new type?" she inquired hopefully.

"Indian Army, last century," said Caroline.

"Golly — a museum piece," said Iris. "I thought they were all extinct. I needn't come down, need I?"

"You'd better," said Caroline. "It would be kind, I think. You might like him. He's a V.C."

"Siege of Lucknow," guessed Iris.

Caroline was already half-way downstairs, and in a few moments Iris followed her reluctantly. She went round the turn of the staircase and saw a tall, snowy-haired old man standing in the middle of the living room. He came to meet her, and spoke without waiting for Caroline's introduction.

"This is Iris," he said, taking her hand and studying her. "Dear me, dear me, all those poor young schoolmasters up at the School are going to have a hard task keeping their minds on their pupils, aren't they now? Very disturbing thing, beauty, when it's in the form of a young woman. Sets all the young fellows thinking about primroses and daffodils and makes 'em restless, poor fellers. I'm very glad to welcome you, my dear. I hope you'll let me come and see you sometimes. Your sister's very kind to me — lets me come in and chat, come in and sit, and it makes a pleasant morning for an old feller like me. Nice people here, but not young, you'll find — unless you climb up the hill and peep at the M.A.'s and the B.A.'s and the B.Sc.'s and what-all. Clever lot, they are, and full of high-sounding letters after their names, and all to teach a lot of little shavers how to make two and two into four. My father used to coach boys — hundreds of them, hundreds, and never a letter after his name, but he stuffed their heads full, I can tell you, and what he once got into 'em never got out again. Funny thing — I used to have fellers coming up to me all over the world and saying, 'You any relation of old Crammer Brock of Winsley?' and when I said I was his son, b'Jove, you should have seen 'em! Never forgot him, never. Old Crocker of the 54th even remembered the way the old man used to pronounce his name. Never remembered names, the old man, and called him Croaker to the end of his days. Used to say to me, 'Ever come across old Croaker these days?' Never Crocker. Never. Always old Croaker."

"Really?" said Iris.

" 'strorodinary old feller, my father," went on the Colonel with pride. "Straight as a ramrod at eighty. People used to take him for half his age. When I came back on my first furlough I looked at him and said, 'B'Jove, sir, I've aged twenty years and you've dropped twenty and now they'll take us for twins, ha ha ha!' Pleased the old feller, but it was true. Straight as a ramrod and full of spirit, right up to the last. He always hated a sloucher."

"Really?" said Iris.

"Hated 'em. I can't help wondering what he'd say if he could see most of 'em now — young men, too, most of 'em, but no figure and no carriage. Slouchers. Badly cut sports jackets, uncreased flannel trousers, and slouching along. I look at 'em and say to myself 'B'Jove, young whippersnapper, I'd like my pater to have you under his eye for a week or two — you'd stop your slouching then, I'll wager.' And the women, too. When I saw Mrs. West there, first thing I said to myself, 'There's a woman who knows what shoulder muscles are for. No slouching.' Nice slow-timed walk, too, and none of that teetering along on spikes. The fellers who makes shoes ought to be made to wear 'em. Only wonder is why all the women aren't crippled."

Caroline, who had been doing her best to break into the Colonel's discourse with an invitation to sit down, now gave up the attempt and, grasping the best chair, turned it in his direction. The movement arrested the flood for a moment.

"Thank you, thank you, but no — I didn't come to stay. Miss Iris only this minute arrived, I said to myself. No time to drop in and keep the ladies from their unpacking and settling in. They'll be anxious to chat, too, I said to myself. Couple of girls away from each other for a week and you'd think they hadn't met for donkey's years. Chat chat chat chat chat. Fairly go at it, they do, bless them, and you'd think their tongues'd never cease wagging away. Nothing like women for tongue-wagging, eh? Ha ha ha."

"Ha ha ha," echoed Iris hollowly.

"When you're settled in, I'd like to come over and have a nice chat. Give you time, I will, to get your own exchanges over and done with and then there'll be room for an old man to put in a word or two, eh? And, remember, any time you want anything in the town, just let me know. I'm always popping over to Blakely and it'll be a pleasure, a pleasure. Any time. You just tell me what you want, give me the size and so on, and leave it to me. Pleasure. Is there anything," he asked Iris, "you'd like me to get for you when I'm in there tomorrow?"

"No, thank you — nothing," said Iris.

The Colonel looked disappointed. "Cottons, ribbons, notepaper, envelopes, library books . . . ?"

"No, thank you," said Iris. "Oh! — yes."

"Pleased to do anything," said the Colonel.

"I don't suppose you'd be able to get them in a G — in an out-of-the-way place like this," said Iris, "but I need two typewriter ribbons. I forgot them before I left London."

"Get anything in Blakely," the Colonel assured her. "Very progressive little town, sell anything. Typewriter ribbons. I'll go to that new stationers on the High Street just past the big chemist's. Size, color?"

"They're for a portable typewriter," said Iris. "Black, please."

"And how much," asked the Colonel, "do you suppose they'll come to? Five shillings, ten shillings?"

Iris felt a little surprise. She had been about to mention payment, but she had not expected the matter to be brought up by the Colonel. Seeing a movement past his shoulder, she glanced beyond him and saw with astonishment that Caroline was pulling her usually placid countenance into a series of grimaces. Iris, after a moment's bewilderment, interpreted the signs to be an indication that the Colonel was very poor, was living on a small pension, and could not be expected to advance even a few shillings for the purchases he had so kindly offered to make. She went upstairs and brought down her purse and the Colonel made some calculations.

"About three or four shillings each, you say? Well, things go up every time you ask for them, nowadays. Suppose we say five shillings each, eh? If you give me ten shillings, that'll do for the two and we can settle up later. Always best to get these things straight — no muddle or misunderstanding afterwards."

Iris gave him ten shillings and noticed with surprise that Caroline was still making faces. She decided a little irritably that if her sister expected her to offer the old boy another ten shillings to buy himself some ice cream, it was too bad. Let him buy his own treats.

The Colonel — and the ten shillings — went away and Iris threw herself into a chair with a long sigh of relief.

"Well, that's over, thank Heaven," she said. "Forever. Next time he comes I shall be hiding behind the bookcase." She sat up and looked at Caroline. "Why on earth," she asked, "were you standing there screwing your face into knots?"

"The money," said Caroline. "You oughtn't to have given it to him."

Iris, her expression one of bewilderment, could only stare at her sister.

"Not given it?" she said at last. "But I thought you meant that he was poor and — "

"I don't know anything about his finances," said Caroline. "I only know that you'll never see that ten shillings again. Or," she added, "your typewriter ribbons."

There was a long silence. Iris, a frown on her brow, wrestled with the implications of this statement. She spoke at last in her usual quick, decided tones. "Look, Carol," she said, "that's a pretty mean remark to make about that old boy. I mean, I hope I never see him again — except when he brings my things — and if I ever have to listen to one of his monologues again I'll scream loudly in the middle of it, but he is, after all, the son of old Crammer Whatnot and — "

"I don't care," said Caroline placidly, "whose son he is. I'm only telling you that you'll never see that money again. I tried to make some sort of sign but — "

"You mean you were screwing up your face to indicate that I mustn't give the old boy money because he'd pinch it? Good Heavens, Carol, what a rotten suggestion — and from *you*, of all people."

Caroline remained unmoved. "I'm not making suggestions," she said. "If I'd known he was coming, I might have remembered to warn you and I'm not using any ugly terms like — like pinching and so on. I only know that when I came here, he offered to shop for me, and I gave him the money. Nothing happened — I didn't get the things and I didn't get the money. The next time I — "

"Next time! But next time," cried Iris, "you should have *reminded* him. You should've said, 'Look, old son-of-a-ramrod, it's all very well to stand there offering to get my laces and library books, but what happened to that ten bob that passed between us on our last meeting?' You could say that, couldn't you? Then you pin him down to producing it or producing the goods. Don't tell me you didn't even mention it!"

"I did mention it," said Caroline, "but — "

"You leave it to me," said Iris. "How you've got so far through the world, I can't imagine. *Of course* people will forget. Some of them can't help it, and some of them find it more profitable not to remember. You leave me to deal with the old boy."

Caroline expressed her perfect willingness to leave Colonel Brock to her sister.

The next day was cold and wet and so unpleasant out of doors that Iris spent the day helping Caroline with housework and putting her own things in order. Her type-writer was put in a corner near the fire, and she wrote a brief letter to Ernest Reed telling him of her arrival.

Before the breakfast things were cleared on the following day, the Colonel made his appearance. Iris, with a bland look at Caroline, indicated that her methods of jogging the old man's memory would be worth study.

She took the breakfast things into the kitchen and left Caroline to listen to the Colonel's comments on the weather of the previous day, his description of monsoon conditions in Seringpatee in '99, his mother's indifference to all kinds of weather, the impossibility of obtaining shoes which resisted damp, and the skill of a Chinese bootmaker at Bhongi who could glance at a sketch, run his hands over a customer's foot, and produce in less than a week a perfectly fitting boot. Not until the Colonel had risen and broached the subject of his expedition into Blakely did Iris re-enter the living room.

"Iris," said Caroline, "Colonel Brock wants to know if you'd like any shopping done."

"Very progressive little town," said the Colonel. "Sell anything. Cottons, laces, notepaper, envelopes, library books — "

"Didn't you go in yesterday?" inquired Iris.

"Yesterday?" The Colonel raised bushy eyebrows in surprise. "Yesterday! My dear young lady, even the bus didn't go in yesterday. There was a nasty bit of water across the road about three miles out, and that's as far as the driver'd venture. Very sensible feller — no need to get water into the engine."

"Well, I gave you ten shillings day before

yesterday," said Iris. "If you could bring back the — "

"Ten shillings?" The Colonel's eyes, of a faded but pleasant shade of blue, opened wide. "Ten shillings? What on earth," he asked, "did you give me ten shillings for?"

"For two typewriter ribbons," said Iris. "Black. Portable. Remember?"

The Colonel lifted a hand and shook a gnarled forefinger at her. "Ah! Now *that,*" he said, "is what I always tell people. I always say to them, 'Don't have any misunderstanding. Get it all straight in the first place, and then you'll always know where you are.' Remember that, now, and it'll stand you in good stead when you're older. Can't be too careful in money matters. And I'm only too pleased to help you out when I can. You just tell what you want, size, color, and I'm only too pleased. Typewriter ribbons, you said? One? Two? What price," he asked, "would you say they'd be? If we said four shillings and I got three — that's twelve — let's say fifteen shillings to be on the safe side. Fifteen shillings. If you give me fifteen shillings now, there won't be any confusion later. It's always best to keep things in order from the start. I'll do my best for you, my dear. Three. Black, portable — was that what you said? Very well. I think fifteen shillings ought to do it."

He paused, expectant, confident. Iris

looked up and gazed straight into the calm blue eyes, and the Colonel, thin, tall, upright, the embodiment of candor and honesty, met her gaze with one of unswerving kindliness.

Iris opened her mouth and closed it again. If she had been asked to make a sketch of a fine, straightforward British gentleman, here was her model. It was impossible to meet that direct gaze and to harbor for an instant a thought that he was — that he could be . . .

"What did we say — fifteen shillings?" asked the Colonel.

Iris, without a word, went to her bag and extracted fifteen shillings. She looked at the money for a moment before handing it to him, and Caroline knew she was bidding it a silent farewell.

"There!" Iris put the money into the old man's hand and a moment later the erect figure was out of the house and striding along the path.

"There," said Iris gloomily, "goes my fifteen bob."

There was a short silence, and Caroline spoke thoughtfully. "It's odd, isn't it?" she said. "Perhaps the Indian sun was a bit too much for him. Perhaps it made his head a bit dull."

"Or his wits," suggested Iris, "a bit sharp."

CHAPTER FIVE

The afternoon, though bitterly cold, was fine, and Iris sat down to lunch announcing her intention of setting off immediately after it to explore the neighborhood and to get her bearings.

"I'll walk up as far as the school," she told Caroline. "I might even go as far as Fellmount and try to find out something."

"What sort of something?" asked Caroline.

"How do I know? I've never been a reporter before," said Iris. "And I'm not going to be one now."

Caroline looked at her in surprise. "But you're here to — " she began.

"I'm here," said Iris, "on this Harfield case. That's what *I* thought. When Ernest talked to me that morning, I was almost convinced I was getting a reporter's job at last. But then I thought it over and I saw old Ernest's game. All he's doing," she went on calmly, "is marking time. 'Yes,' he says to Sir Kenneth, 'you leave it to me and I'll have the matter investigated. I'll put one of my best reporters onto it and send him down there and we'll have the facts of the case in no time.' Then Sir Kenneth goes away, satisfied; Ernest sends me to High Ambo and tells me to keep my ears open. While I'm keeping them open, Sir

Kenneth's wrath gradually cools and he drops the whole thing and the School's reputation is safe." She sighed. "No, Carol," she said, "I don't think this is an assignment, after all. But I'm drawing extra salary and expenses, so why should I complain? I — "

"I wouldn't," advised Caroline, "eat too much of that butter if I were you."

Iris looked at the small pat of butter reposing in the yellow dish. "What's the matter with it?" she inquired.

"Nothing's the matter with it," said Caroline, "but you finished off my week's supply at breakfast and now you've started on your week's supply — and this is only your second day."

"Well, why," demanded Iris, "didn't you tell me?"

Caroline finished a mouthful of toast and margarine and spoke placidly. "Well, I always think that when it's gone, it's gone," she said.

"There's something in that," agreed Iris, taking the last of the butter. "But surely, bang in the middle of the country like this, there's piles and piles of butter and milk and eggs and so on?"

"I don't think so," said Caroline. "I did think of going round to a farm or two and seeing what I could get, but it's an odd place. The farms are miles apart, for one thing, and though I did suggest to one or two farmers' wives, when I first came, that I'd be only too glad to buy any sort of extra they felt they could spare, nothing happened. They all looked awfully pleasant and I waited, thinking there'd be a regular tramp of country boots up the path, but — "

"No boots."

"No nothing. I tried again and they looked even more pleasant, but that's as far as it's gone."

"About housework," said Iris. "I'll do what I can, Carol, but I'm not much use. Somehow there always seems to be so much to *do* in a beastly house, and when I think about it, I get a dreadful sort of creeping paralysis."

"I get a creeping, paralysis, too," said Caroline, "but I have to creep out of it."

"Well, I'll do my best," promised Iris, "but don't bank on me. I'll do — "

Her words came to an abrupt stop, and Caroline, looking up inquiringly, saw that her sister was staring out into the road with an expression of the utmost astonishment.

"What's the matter?" she asked.

"Come and look," said Iris rising and going to the window. "It's the most extraordinary sight — the Wizard of Oz and four dogs."

"Oh — Lord Fellmount," said Caroline, carrying plates into the kitchen. "He always goes past at this time. He's on his daily walk."

There was no reply. Iris, her eyes round,

her mouth open, was following his lordship's progress past the house. She spoke at last in an incredulous voice. "You must be wrong," she said. "I mean, it — it can't be."

"Why can't it?" inquired Caroline from the kitchen.

"Well, for one thing," said Iris, craning her neck to catch a last view of the procession, "for one thing, he's too rickety. He wouldn't have the strength to throw a boy into the lake."

"You don't need strength," explained Caroline. "All you need is to come up behind and catch him off his balance. One finger can do it."

"You mean," asked Iris, still incredulous, "that that little bag of bones is the — the High Ambo autocrat? And his clothes! Who'd believe he was a peer out for an airing?"

"What did you expect?" asked Caroline. "A coach and four?"

"I don't know," said Iris. "I didn't expect a spindle-shanked old fossil with a hat that looks as though it fell under a steam roller and a coat that a self-respecting tramp wouldn't turn out in, and a face with an eagle's beak and a vulture's expression. Where's your *dignity?* Where's your nobility, your — your proud lineage and your centuries of greatness and your — " She broke off, sensing a lack of response. "Carol, where are you?"

"I'm up here," came a voice from upstairs. "Tidying my room. Did you want me?"

"No," said Iris. "Not at all. I suppose I'll soon get used to seeing the audience walk out in the middle of my performances."

She walked upstairs and made herself ready for her walk. Caroline walked to the front door with her and looked doubtfully at the sky.

"It looks all right at the moment," she said, "but I don't really trust it. Haven't you got an umbrella?"

"I have never," Iris informed her, "had an umbrella in my life. I hate the things. But if I did have one — " she threw a contemptuous glance toward an object standing in a corner — "I wouldn't have an appalling thing like that. Gosh, Carol, that isn't yours, is it?" she asked.

"Well, no — as a matter of fact, it isn't," said Caroline slowly. "I — well, I lent mine to Colonel Brock."

There was a long silence. Iris looked from her sister's face to the umbrella and back again. She tried to speak, but for a few moments seemed to find some difficulty in finding her voice.

"He can't use a — a lady's umbrella," she said at last.

"It wasn't a particularly ladylike one," said

Caroline, "and he does use it. I met him in the Post Office the last time it rained and he had a little difficulty opening it as he went out. I went up and said, 'Let me help you.' "

"And — and what did he say?" asked Iris in awed accents.

"He said, 'Ah, thank you, thank you,' and then he told me that it had always had a very awkward catch," said Caroline.

Iris closed her lips in a firm line. "Look, Carol," she said, "he can't do this to us. We've got to *do* something." She frowned thoughtfully for a moment and then asked a question. "Where," she inquired, "does the old boy live?"

"I don't know the name of his house," said Caroline, "but it's one of that group of four that you can see from your window. The School has one of them and I think the biggest one is Colonel Brock's. Why?" she asked.

"Because I'm going to call on him," said Iris. "Just a friendly call, and when I'm leaving, I shall look up into the sky and say it looks like rain — and then I'll ask him to lend me an umbrella. Can you see any flaw in that?"

"Well — no," said Caroline. "Supposing he's out?"

"If he's out, his housekeeper'll know where he keeps his umbrella," said Iris. "He won't have it with him on a day like this. You wait and see, Carol," she promised. "When I re-enter this house, your umbrella re-enters with me."

"Well, it would be nice to have it again," admitted Caroline, looking distastefully at its substitute. "Good-by, darling. Don't get lost."

Iris left the house and set out in the direction of the cottages. In spite of the piercing wind, she found herself enjoying the walk. She passed through the village and, hesitating at a fork in the road, chose a route which took her up a steep hill, along a wind-blown ridge, and past the Castle in which one hundred and seventy pupils were pursuing knowledge.

She turned off the path to avoid a rush of boys engaged in something that looked like a paperchase. She watched green caps, pink cheeks, and red ears dash by, and recognized a pair which, by reason of their exposed position, were even redder than those of the rest of the group. She acknowledged David's hurried but polite greeting and, returning to the road, followed it round the hill and left it for a path which she saw would take her almost directly down to the group of little houses among which she would find Colonel Brock's.

She came upon the cottages from the

back, and stood for a moment in indecision. Remembering Caroline's conviction that it was the biggest of them, she turned to the largest of the group and walked slowly toward it. It looked well-kept and had a larger garden than the rest, and Iris, looking at its plain unadorned exterior, felt that it was just the place in which one would expect to find Crammer Brock's son.

She went round the house and looked for a moment at the front door. It was closed, but a long window leading from a room at the side of the house into the garden stood invitingly open. Iris decided that this would be the one to try. She would knock and inquire if the Colonel was at home. The housekeeper was reputed to be fierce, but she could scarcely, Iris felt, deny her the loan of an umbrella.

She walked round to the window and, raising a hand, knocked gently on one of the panes. Hearing no sound, she knocked again a little more loudly but, though she waited and listened, no sound or movement came from within the house.

She felt a little dashed. She had prepared several opening speeches; it now looked as though nobody was going to listen to them. Somebody, thought Iris impatiently, must be in. Nobody would go out on a day like this leaving a door open. Knocking once again and receiving no answer, she wondered whether the sour housekeeper was deliberately keeping her waiting.

The woman might, of course, be deaf. Iris accepted this explanation unhesitatingly; only a deaf woman could live with that ceaseless monologue. She was stone deaf, and the thing to do, Iris decided, was to go inside and find her.

She stepped over the threshold and stood for a moment looking about her. The room was scarcely one in which she had expected to find herself; it was neither the usual drawing room nor the trophy-hung retreat of an Indian veteran. The floor was bare, save for two rugs which looked as though they had seen long and hard service; there were two large sofas, three chairs, and a number of small tables covered with deep scratches.

Iris walked across the room and, opening the inner door, found herself in a large, square hall. There was a fire and a general air of comfort. There was a carpet, chintz-covered chairs, a desk with papers . . .

And, in the corner, an umbrella stand.

Iris drew a breath of triumph. If she could see something that looked like Caroline's umbrella, there would be no need for her to encounter the housekeeper; grasping her prize, she could bear it triumphantly homeward. Moving cautiously, she walked across the carpeted floor but, as she passed the desk, her eyes fell on the photograph of a woman. The thought of Colonel Brock married was a new one, and Iris, pausing, picked up the silver frame and studied the picture within it.

She saw a sweet, rather worn face, white hair and quiet, kind eyes, and a feeling of surprise swept over her.

This? It couldn't be! Gentle, well-bred, faintly smiling. No woman married to the Colonel could have looked so tranquilly out on life. It couldn't be his wife, and it couldn't be the ramrod's wife. It might be . . .

"My mother," said a voice.

With a gasp of terror, Iris dropped the photograph. It fell with a clatter onto the desk and she spun round, her heart pounding violently, her eyes searching wildly round. There was nobody to be seen. Save for herself the hall was empty.

"My mother," said the voice again — calm, low, unhurried like Caroline's, only a man's . . .

Iris lifted her eyes to the landing above. She had not been mistaken. Tall, laconic, horn-rimmed . . .

"Oh — it's you," said Michael Sheridan.

Iris tried to speak, but the emotions of the past few minutes seemed to have robbed her of breath. She made an effort to steady herself and succeeded in achieving at least an outward calm.

"Good afternoon," she said.

"I didn't," said Mr. Sheridan. "hear the front door."

"I came in," said Iris, "the other way."

"Why?"

The query was brief, cool, and unfriendly. Iris realized that she was at a serious disadvantage and made an attempt to sound convincing. "I'm sorry," she said. "I knocked, but nobody heard me. I waited for some time and then came in. I wanted to ask the — "

She stopped, unwilling to enter into details. She was in the wrong house and she was in an extremely awkward position. The French Master was waiting for an explanation, and though his textbooks might dwell upon *plume-de-ma-tante,* Iris very much doubted whether they would introduce the *parapluie-de-ma-soeur.*

"Why," inquired Mr. Sheridan, "did you creep across the hall and pick up that photograph?"

Iris felt her cheeks growing hot with anger. "Why," she inquired, "don't you join the Boy Scouts and go in for tracking in a big way?"

"I was working upstairs," said Michael Sheridan calmly, "and I saw you from my window. You studied the house for some time and you didn't go to the front door. You didn't knock at all loudly and you crept into the hall — I saw you — and you went straight for that frame."

"I — "

"Solid silver," said Mr. Sheridan reflectively.

Iris opened her mouth, but rage choked her utterance. "You — you — Come down here, you — "

Mr. Sheridan came, with no appearance of hurry, down the stairs, and Iris confronted him with blazing eyes.

"Say that again," she demanded.

"Solid silver," said Mr. Sheridan. "Not as valuable as my camera, of course, but all the same, a — "

"Your camera !" Iris's tone was bewildered. "Your camera! Do you seriously imagine that I — I wanted your — ?"

"I didn't say you wanted it," said Mr. Sheridan. "I only said you took it. I can't think what you'd do with a photograph of my mother, but — "

Iris moved toward the front door and Michael stepped in front of her.

"Get out of my way," said Iris furiously. "Get out of my way and let me pass."

"I won't," said Mr. Sheridan. "I certainly will not. If you can't explain your extraordinary behavior to me, I shall telephone to the Headmaster and he can deal with the matter. I'm in charge of three young boys; this isn't school property, and I can't have young women coming in and — "

"Don't you young-woman me," choked Iris. "If you were a normal man instead of a cold-blooded professor type full of stuffy ideas and as good as dead and — "

"You said that before," pointed out Mr. Sheridan coldly. "On the station. I'm sorry you don't care for schoolmasters, but I assure you we're nothing like dead. Not quite alive, perhaps, to your beauty and charm, but perfectly capable of dealing with young women who take things which don't belong to them, creep into houses without an invitation, and tell lies when they're caught. Will you please sit down," he ended, "while I telephone the Headmaster?"

Iris, scarcely able to believe her eyes, watched, as if fascinated, his progress across the hall to the telephone. He had reached it; he had taken it off its old-fashioned hook; he was —

"Don't!" she cried.

As if she had not spoken, Michael Sheridan remained still, the receiver to his ear, waiting for the operator's voice. Iris, with a swift rush, crossed the room and put a hand on his arm.

"Wait a minute," she said.

Michael Sheridan replaced the receiver and waited, calmly, for her to speak. Iris, swallowing her rage, humiliation, and dislike, looked at him and spoke steadily.

"You needn't yell for the Headmaster," she

said. "My name is Iris Drake and I'm staying with my sister, Mrs. West, at Lilac Cottage. We're tenants of Miss Stannard, and the Stannards have known my sister for years and know all about us. If you've got any fantastic ideas that I'm what you'd no doubt term an adventuress, then go and call on Miss Stannard and ask her to put your fears to rest so's you can enjoy your usual unbroken night's sleep."

Michael Sheridan was looking at her with unshaken coolness. His words were, as usual, unhurried.

"You won't," he told her, "have the smallest effect on my night's sleep. Or — if you'll excuse me now — on my day's work. May I show you out — by the front door?"

He turned, but before he reached the door, there was a rustle, a clatter, and the sound of a key being turned. The door opened and an old man, white-haired, bespectacled, and extremely stout, stepped into the hall.

"Here I am — I am here!" he stated, in accents so guttural than Iris was reminded of an incompetent amateur attempting to impersonate a German professor. "A little early, because on so fine a day I — "

His blue, beaming eyes fell upon Iris and an expression of delight overspread his countenance.

"Ah! See — a pretty girl!" he exclaimed in rapture. Dropping his hat to the ground, he came forward and, taking Iris's hand, patted it enthusiastically. "Good afternoon, good afternoon, welcome, welcome," he said. "This is the only time. Never — never before have I come home to find a pretty girl. There is here an old professor, a young professor, three little boys who sing — but no pretty girl." He looked from Iris to Mr. Sheridan in happy expectation. "You are staying?" he asked her.

Iris shook her head. "I'm just going," she said.

"Oh!" The exclamation was one of deep and genuine disappointment. The old man put his hands together and wrung them; his spectacles became crooked and his hair drooped disconsolately on either side of his soft, loose cheeks. In a moment a happy thought struck him and he became a picture of glee.

"If you are going," he proposed, "then I am early and I have much time. I shall be your cavalier, your gentleman, your escort. For see — Michael has not introduced us. I am the Music Professor and I teach the little boys to sing. If I ask the Headmaster, he will say that you have permission to come and hear the boys sing in the Chapel. My name is Swintzchell — that is not a pretty name."

He paused and looked inquiringly at Mr. Sheridan.

"This," said Michael, "is Miss Drake."

"Drake. That is easy to remember — Drake," said Mr. Swintzchell. "Miss Drake." He looked at Iris with his head on one side. "Miss Anna Drake? Miss Elizabeth Drake? Miss — "

"Iris."

"Ir-is. Ah! Miss Iris Drake. Michael, you will come with me and we shall walk with Miss Iris to — "

Michael shook his head. "Busy," he said briefly.

"Busy, busy, busy," repeated Mr. Swintzchell, his head going from side to side and his lips pursed reprovingly. "What is so important to keep you from walking with a pretty girl? What are you doing that is so busy?"

"Finishing off those nuthatch articles," said Mr. Sheridan.

Mr. Swintzchell's expression changed to one of respect and understanding. It was obvious that the articles were of primary importance. Without further persuasion, the old professor ushered Iris through the door and waved a genial farewell to his colleague. He banged the door behind him and, turning again with an exclamation, beat upon it an energetic tattoo. The door opened, Mr. Sheridan handed out the wide-brimmed felt hat, and the old gentleman, dusting it with his sleeve, put it on.

The two went on their way. Iris, after a

short time, gave up the attempt to suit her steps to her companion's short stumbling ones. She gave his eager and unceasing monologue half her attention, the other half being employed in guiding his unwary footsteps. The professor traveled with a happy disregard of the road's pitfalls, and Iris, after making several saving clutches as he tripped over stones, splashed through puddles, and squelched through muddy patches, grasped his arm firmly and steered him clear of obstacles.

"This is pleasant — so pleasant," he told her delightedly. "On this good afternoon, to be walking with a pretty girl, so suddenly. We must know," he told her, "the business of each other. I am a professor of singing, but at the school I teach the boys other things — piano, violin. You will not know the name of Swintzchell — Karl Swintzchell — Karl Hermann Swintzchell. You will not know it, but your mother, perhaps, or even your grandmother since you are so young — they will perhaps know me. When you say that you talked with Karl Swintzchell, they will say 'That name I know!' "

Iris let her thoughts wander, and was recalled to the present by hearing the sound of Mr. Sheridan's name. Mr. Swintzchell, having apparently brought his own history up to date, had embarked upon that of his colleague. While not in a position to give his hearer details of Mr. Sheridan's early life, he had a good deal to say of the present. Iris learned that the French Master, in addition to his normal duties, was an authority on bird life, and had contributed much-discussed articles to the *Bird World* and *Wings and Feathers.* His essay on the nuthatch, Mr. Swintzchell assured Iris, was extremely informative, and the photographs accompanying it, obtained only after long and patient waiting, were the finest to be seen.

Between French lessons and bird photography, Mr. Sheridan had organized a school riding party. The Headmaster's only part in this enterprise, Mr. Swintzchell averred, was to add several guineas to the bills of any boy expressing a wish to ride; on Mr. Sheridan had fallen the task of searching, in an almost horseless countryside, for some four-footed beasts which would reasonably approximate to horses and carry enthusiastic novices in comparative safety. It was not ideal riding country, for those paths which did not go steeply up went steeply down; there was a good deal of loose stone on the scant open ground and a great deal of mud in the narrow valleys, but Mr. Sheridan's object seemed to be to get his pupils upon the horses and let the horses worry about the terrain.

"The horses," said Mr. Swintzchell, looking at Iris with a shake of his head and making straight for a pile of stones by the wayside, "the horses are not good. Some big, some small, but not good. The little boys fall off, but Mr. Sheridan says that it is good for them to fall off because it teaches them how to ride. To learn to ride," said Mr. Swintzchell thoughtfully, "is to learn to sit on top of the horse and not fall off. But everybody is happy. The Headmaster is happy because he gets the guineas, and Mr. Sheridan is happy and the boys are happy, and when they fall off they do not tell their fathers and mothers and so the fathers and the mothers are happy. They are all happy."

On this pleasant note the gate of Lilac Cottage was reached. Iris halted and her companion looked at the little house with an unmistakable air of expectancy.

"This is your house?" he inquired.

Iris shook her head, told him that she was staying for a time with a sister, expressed her thanks for his escort, and smiled her most charming farewell.

"You have a sister?" asked Mr. Swintzchell. "If we go inside, she will be inside and I can see her?"

Unable to deal with this unusually direct approach, Iris led the way through the gate and to the front door. Opening it, she stepped inside and called her sister. "Car-ol!"

Caroline appeared from the kitchen, and

Iris, ushering Mr. Swintzchell into the drawing room, performed an introduction. The visitor appeared to be delighted with Caroline, with the room, with the view, and, most of all, with the sight of the piano standing in a corner. He dropped Caroline's hand, which he had been patting in a fatherly manner, and moved eagerly toward the instrument, pausing in the act of opening it to look at Caroline.

"You permit?"

Caroline nodded.

Mr. Swintzchell prodded with a forefinger at first one note and then another. He struck a chord and, head on one side, listened critically to the sound.

"It is not so bad," he pronounced. "You play?"

Caroline shook her head.

"The piano," Mr. Swintzchell told her, "is not my instrument. My instrument is the voice." He opened his mouth to its widest extent and pointed down his throat. Caroline and Iris having had the privilege of glancing at his larynx, he closed his mouth again and resumed. "At one time," he told them, "it was thought that I might be as great a teacher as Verino, but it was not so. Nobody could be as great as Verino. He was the greatest and, when he died, there was nobody. Nobody. He was the greatest of them all." Mr. Swintzchell paused and gave a heavy sigh. "I have a photograph," he added reverently, "with his name written by himself."

Caroline's lips widened in an affectionate, reminiscent smile.

"Yes, I know," she said. "He gave one to everybody."

"That is — " Mr. Swintzchell stopped and his expression became puzzled. He looked at Caroline with a frown. "I speak," he said, "of Emilio Verino. The great — "

"Ricardo Verdi Emilio Fachioni Verino," said Caroline. She gave a little sigh. "He was a pet."

There was a long silence. Mr. Swintzchell bent upon her a suspicious and searching gaze and seemed to be sifting evidence. "You," he questioned at last, "are a singer?"

"No," said Caroline. "People said I ought to be, but I — well, I didn't agree."

"You studied?"

Caroline nodded. "For two years," she said. "Under Verino. Then I gave it up."

Mr. Swintzchell seemed to have some difficulty in getting out his words. "You studied," he said, "under Verino. And you — you gave it up!" He looked dazed for a moment and then rallied. "No" he said decisively. "People did not give up Verino. Verino gave *them* up."

"I got married," explained Caroline simply. "and I went abroad."

Mr. Swintzchell drew a deep breath and leaned on the piano for support. "You could have sung," he said, "under Verino, and you — you got married? You gave it up? You threw it away? You — you went abroad?"

To each of these questions Caroline gave a little nod. At the end of them, Mr. Swintzchell was silent for a long time, staring at the slim, charming woman confronting him. When next he spoke, his voice rang sharply through the little room and made Iris jump.

"Come here!"

Caroline found herself walking across the room.

"There! Stand there!" commanded Mr. Swintzchell as she came up to the piano. "Now!" He struck a chord with his left hand, repeated it once or twice, and, with his other hand raised, looked at Caroline. "Now!" he repeated. "Ah-oo and afterwards Ee-oo. Come!"

Caroline's mouth opened slowly to the master's irritated "More, more!" and from her throat issued a note, at first uncertain and then gathering tone and clearness. Mr. Swintzchell changed key, struck three more chords, and issued another command.

"Koo koo, kah kah, ko ko, kay kay!" he ordered.

"Koo koo, kah kah, ko ko, kay kay," sang Caroline.

Mr. Swintzchell played an arpeggio and, with a scoop of his right hand, directed Caroline's notes downwards and upwards. There followed a scale, a series of staccato notes, and a clear, beautiful, long-drawn note which left Caroline breathing shortly and unevenly.

There was a long silence as the note died away. Mr. Swintzchell was staring at Caroline, his expression earnest and absorbed, and, when he spoke, his tone expressed a bitter regret.

"Once," he said slowly, "there was a voice. And you left Verino and you took a husband!" He gave a deep, prolonged sigh. "Ah! that was sad," he went on. "For anybody can have a husband; anybody can have children. Any woman," he qualified. "But the Almighty God, who gives many husbands, does not give so many voices like yours. No. And it is a pity that when He gives it, it is wasted for a husband. And where now," he asked, "is this husband?"

"He's dead," said Caroline.

Mr. Swintzchell seemed to be on the verge of pointing out that this made the matter even more wasteful. Instead, he plunged his hand into first one pocket and then another, producing finally a small, battered notebook.

"Monday, Tuesday, Wednesday," he mused, going through the pages. "No.

Thursday — yes." He looked at Caroline. "On Thursday, if you permit," he said, "I shall come to give you a lesson."

"Oh — but — " Caroline began a swift protest, and Mr. Swintzchell raised a large, fat hand and waited for silence.

"Please," he said. "It will be a great pleasure. I teach only little boys now, and their voices — sometimes — are good, but it is only hymns in the Chapel. To take a voice like yours, to bring it back to you, to make it perfect again — this will be a great happiness."

"But — "

"Please — on Thursday," said Mr. Swintzchell once more. Caroline tried desperately to think of something that would turn the visitor from his purpose. Before she could voice any of her objections, Mr. Swintzchell had looked at his watch and uttered a loud exclamation. Dashing his hand against his forehead and pulling despairingly at his white locks, he hurried to the door.

"Your hat, Mr. Swintzchell, your hat!" cried Iris.

"My hat — yes, thank you, thank you," panted Mr. Swintzchell. "Thursday — Thursday — good-by, good-by!"

He had gone. Iris shut the door and, turning, leaned on it and faced her sister. Caroline, still a little dazed, looked back with a frown of bewilderment.

"You went out," she said, "to find my umbrella. How — I mean, where did you find this — ?"

Iris broke into her sister's question with one of her own. "Have you any idea, Carol," she asked thoughtfully, "what a nuthatch would be?"

CHAPTER SIX

After reviewing Mr. Swintzchell's kind proposal for a night, Caroline rose the next morning determined to write a letter to the professor in which she would point out that it was not practicable for her, at present, to resume her singing lessons. She tore up several beginnings which were either, she thought, too regretful or too indecisive, and finally showed the result of her labor to Iris.

Iris scanned the letter and looked dubiously at her sister. "I'm absolutely with you," she said, "but I think the old boy'll be upset. He gave me the idea — I don't quite know why — that running into a Voice with a capital V had somehow stirred him up."

"I don't think I can help that," said Caroline. "I'm sorry about it in a way, but I don't feel it's a very sensible scheme, and I'm not really an artist. Verino used to tear his hair out — you could see the bits in his hand — because I had the voice but not the — the — "

"Passion, fire, temperament — "

"None whatsoever," said Caroline. "I used to do my best, but if you haven't got that sort of sensitiveness or artistic perception or whatever they call it, you haven't and that's all. And sometimes," she confessed, "I used to feel rather glad, because some of Verino's pupils were really, apart from their singing, awfully difficult people. It was like being with a lot of Roberts, and you can imagine how awful that was. I couldn't help feeling that if that was the artistic temperament, I should be much more comfortable without it. Shall I send the letter?"

"Yes, send it," said Iris. "I'm rather relieved in a way because it would have been rather trying to have you koo-kooing when I'm trying to send a report off to Ernest. I didn't say anything at the time, but I do think that if there's one row that's worse than a violin being practiced, it's a voice being shunted up and down those do-mi-sol-dos. It sounds so pointless.

She stopped in astonishment. With a glance at the window and a muttered exclamation, Iris leapt from her chair and, with as much speed and as little noise as possible, darted up the stairs and out of sight.

A knock at the door and the voice of Colonel Brock soon enlightened Caroline as to the cause of her sister's rapid disappearance. Caroline rose, arranged her face in an expression of welcome, and invited the old gentleman inside.

His visit was brief, and he was disappointed that neither Caroline nor Iris — who, Caroline told him, was busy upstairs

— needed any cottons, lace, envelopes, notepaper, or library books.

When he had gone, Iris came cautiously downstairs. "Safe?" she inquired.

"Yes. Are you going to do that," asked Caroline, "every time he comes?"

"No — only every time I see him coming," said Iris. "I really can't go through all that again, Carol. After all, he's your neighbor, not mine."

"He borrowed some of your nice shiny magazines," said Caroline. "Do you mind?"

"He can borrow anything," said Iris, "so long as I don't have to meet him. Soon the sisters Stannard are going to find their way across and start up some Edwardian conversation, and that's going to be more awful still."

"You oughtn't to judge," said Caroline, "until you've seen them"

"I have seen them," said Iris. "I saw them in the Post Office. Isn't it *fantastic*, Carol, to think that they taught Ernest! They're an odd pair: short round one with wash-leather gloves and tall thin one with wash-leather gloves, and both exactly alike. No difference but their shape. The tall one looks exactly like the small one run over by a steam roller."

Caroline thought this a summary description of the appearance of the two sisters, but when she went to the door a little later in answer to a knock and admitted Miss Stannard, she felt that her flat face and long, thin appearance might mislead a stranger into thinking that she had, indeed, been rolled out.

She greeted the old lady with pleasure and invited her in, and Iris, who had been in the kitchen and was unable to escape, came out with a reasonable appearance of cordiality. Miss Stannard extended a hand.

"How do you do? We're very pleased to welcome you," she said. "How like your sister you are."

"You think so?" said Iris.

"Anybody who has eyes at all," said Miss Stannard, "would think so. The likeness is unmistakable. No, thank you — I'll sit in this chair, if I may. I would like a straight back."

Iris would have liked to tell her that she already had a poker-straight back, but there was something about the old lady's bland and unreadable expression which made her wary. She saw the pale blue eyes studying her and wondered how she was faring by old standards.

"You live," asked Miss Stannard, "in London?"

"Yes."

"We used," said Miss Stannard, "to have a house in Town. Clonmel Square — Belgravia. You know it, perhaps?"

It was obvious that Iris had never heard of Clonmel Square.

"London," said Miss Stannard, "isn't what it was."

"You mean bombs and things?" asked Iris.

Miss Stannard crossed her hands on the long, thin umbrella she held before her. "No," she said. "I mean far more irretrievable damage. One can repair a shattered building, but one cannot rebuild the old ways of life. . . . You like living there?"

"Yes, I do," said Iris.

"Do you live far from your work?" asked Miss Stannard.

"Half an hour," said Iris.

Miss Stannard nodded her head. "Distance, nowadays, is time," she said. "When my friends were urging me to go to Oslo, they all said, 'Oh, do go — it's only three hours.' And when my niece — I'm speaking of Susan, Caroline, my dear — when she was proposing to go off to America and I said I thought it was a long way off, she said, 'Of course not — it's just seventeen hours.' " She turned to Caroline. "I think you told me," she said, "that your sister is on Ernest Reed's staff?"

"Yes, she is," said Caroline.

Miss Stannard turned to Iris, a warm, reminiscent smile on her lips. "Dear Ernest, she said. "He was such a charming boy."

Iris did her best to look as though she

believed this statement.

"And so full of promise," proceeded Miss Stannard.

Iris wished it was possible to say that he was now full of self-importance. She refrained, however, and smiled attentively at the visitor.

"Will you please," requested Miss Stannard, "give him our love? We so often speak of him. He used to give us a little anxiety sometimes — his chest, you know. We used to put him into special waistcoats."

Iris, with an effort, brought her mind back from an entrancing vision of Ernest in a special waistcoat and heard Miss Stannard addressing Caroline.

"Caroline, my dear," she said, "you must let us see something of your sister while she is here. We would like her to come and have tea with us on Thursday. Are you free on that day?" she asked, turning to Iris.

Iris tried desperately to think of a series of engagements which would prevent her from attending. Nothing, however, came to mind, and she was forced to smile gratefully at the old lady.

"Thank you, that would be very nice," she said.

"Thursday, then," said Miss Stannard.

"Thursday," smiled Iris.

Miss Stannard rose. "We shall not, of course, be a party," she said, "but I always send an invitation to the School. The masters are glad of a change, and they feel a little left out of things if we neglect them."

"I'm sure they do," said Iris.

With a gracious inclination, Miss Stannard went toward the door. Caroline accompanied her up the little path to the gate and returned to find Iris in a state bordering on frenzy.

"If she comes again, if *any* of them come again, I'm *out,* Carol. I'm away, I'm ill, I'm dead, I'm anything you like, but I won't be caught again to listen to conversation that makes me feel as though I've been shut into a museum for the afternoon and can't get out. I'm sorry to sound a pig, but I do feel that life doesn't leave you *time* to sit and listen to this antedeluvian drivel about old Crammer Brock and three hours to Oslo and where do you live and do you like it, and — and — "

"Oh — do look out!"

Caroline's cry of warning came too late. Solly, watching with limitless patience from the window sill, had followed every movement of the angrily waving hand. Crouching lower as Iris, with an impatient flow of words, moved nearer and nearer to the window, Solly watched for the exact moment and struck. Iris, with a cry of pain and rage, dived toward the attacker, but Solly, in an instant, was behind the china cabinet and beyond reach.

"Oh, I'm so sorry!" Caroline's voice was remorseful. "I saw him waiting and — Where are you going?"

"Out," said Iris. "A nice, long walk before I get trapped by any more neighbors or ripped to shreds by that man-eating tiger. I'll try to get as far as this Fellmount place. Ernest'll be pleased to know I've started on my investigations. . . . Don't wait tea if I'm late, Carol. I might be fleeing round the lake pursued by the old boy."

"Do you know the way?" asked Caroline.

"No, but I can find it easily," said Iris. "I can't very well miss it, can I?"

"It isn't as near as it looks," said Caroline. "There's a dip which you can't see. Will you drop Mr. Swintzchell's letter at the Post Office as you go by? There's a special delivery up to the School about now, and it might go by that."

Iris took the letter, handed it in to the Postmistress, who informed her that the School post was leaving immediately, and walked briskly through the village toward the snow-covered hills.

It was a damp, raw day, and Iris wished she had tied something round her hair. There had been a light fall of snow during the morning, and there were puddles of melted snow — sometimes large enough to be called pools — on the rutted path along which she was walking. She was on rising ground and could see, as she climbed, more and more of the wide, unpopulated country-side. She could see no sign of a human being, and she tried to calculate how many people would have been living in a similar space in London. She decided that it was pleasant — at any rate, for a change — to have the world, to all intents and purposes, entirely to herself.

She walked steadily, stopping now and then to look at the lovely scene from a fresh viewpoint. She thought it a fine stretch of country, but felt that if she had been consulted, there would have been more woods and more water. That narrow, winding strip of water down there was scarcely worthy of the name of river.

She had not, she found, the world entirely to herself. Approaching her on horseback was a small figure — whether boy or girl, Iris could not as yet tell. She walked on; it was a boy, a small boy on a rather large horse. Iris edged off the path. The horse appeared to want more than his share of it, and she had no wish to be forced up a bank or into a field.

The horse came to a division in the path, and Iris saw that there was also a division in the wishes of horse and rider. The boy wanted to take the right fork, but the horse had other and stronger views. Ignoring the appeals of its rider, the animal came steadily on toward Iris. She looked again at the boy and saw a large and familiar pair of ears.

"Well, well," she said, as he came up and pulled the horse to an unwilling stop. "We travel, don't we? Train, horse — "

"Good afternoon," said David. "I'm sorry I can't make him give you more room. He's not very good at doing what you want him to."

Iris studied the big, bony animal with wonder and David read her expression correctly.

"He isn't a — sort of thoroughbred, quite," he said. "We haven't got very good horses, but it was awfully hard for Mr. Sheridan to get any at all. This one's called Lazarus, because they were going to kill him off for old age and then Mr. Sheridan got it for us, but he's awfully full of life. You can see, can't you?"

"Yes, I can see," said Iris. "Are you out by yourself?"

"Well, just at present I am," explained David, "because I got ahead of the others because I couldn't stop Lazarus, and I think I must have missed them because I waited at Mossop's pond and they didn't turn up."

"Weren't you intending to go *that* way?" asked Iris, pointing to the fork of the road.

"Well, yes, but Lazarus knows we usually come this way and go down there and cross the river," said David. "He seems to like jumping, though he isn't really awfully good at it."

"Well — " Iris prepared to move on — "it was nice to see you. Come to tea one day, and bring some friends."

"Thank you," said David. "I'd like to come and bring Winter and Stuffy if possible, because we live together. We're all in the Choir but Stuffy isn't now because his voice broke. I say, please — " he reined Lazarus in with difficulty — "if you meet the others, please could you say that I'm going to wait for them at the last farm?"

"Which last farm?"

"They'll know. It's just the one we wait at if we get separated," explained David. "Good-by!"

Lazarus, Iris saw, was making up for lost time. With a great deal of splashing and slithering, he was making for the wide path which led to the river. Iris walked on for some distance and then turned to look once more at the horse and rider.

Lazarus appeared to be making for the stream. It was not wide and Iris felt that the horse ought to manage it without difficulty, but she was not so sure about the boy. Iris saw his preparations for the jump and remembered her school riding master's instructions: "Up to it, one, two, three, steady, h'up and over."

Not quite over, she saw. Only the horse's forelegs had reached the opposite bank. The rest of the horse, and the whole of David, were in the water.

Iris took an instinctive step forward and then stopped. David had surfaced. He took two strokes and made a successful snatch at the horse's tail and in this manner reached the bank and scrambled up it. Releasing the horse's tail and securing its bridle, he shook himself, wiped his face with his sleeve, and mounted once more.

Iris walked on. He was a nice little boy, she mused. He was natural and friendly and he had an attractive smile. She must remember to tell Carol in case he turned up one day — he and Winter and Stocky, no, Stuffy. Why Stuffy? Perhaps he overate; perhaps he wore too many clothes, or liked all the windows shut. He . . .

Iris looked into the distance, frowned, and looked again. Horses. Four, six, eight — coming toward her. She saw that they would soon pass her, and remembered that she had a message to deliver, but so great was her interest in the approaching animals that she found it impossible to fix her mind on anything else. She looked at them incredulously.

Horses large and horses small; a pony

dancing in rings round an apathetic animal which was proceeding at a donkey trot. A boy, the smallest boy of all, astride an enormous animal, and a red-headed boy imperturbable on a wicked-looking mount which had its ears back and its teeth showing. A skittish chestnut glanced contemptuously round at the rider on its back, pivoted on its quarters, and came down to gaze contemptuously at its rider on the ground. A rough pony came up and nuzzled Iris and was pushed aside by a big, black, bullying animal. Two more ponies, a shambling mare, and, last of all, Mr. Sheridan on the smallest pony of all, his feet dangling almost to the ground, his whole appearance ludicrous and his manner as cool and unmoved as on the first day Iris had seen him.

She stood aside to allow the cavalcade to pass, stepping closer to address Michael Sheridan as he drew near. "Good afternoon," she said. "I was asked to tell you — "

"Whoa!" called Mr. Sheridan to his charges. "Steady on, there."

Those who could, whoa-d; the others steadied on as well as they could, but it was plain that the horses were on their homeward way and saw no reason for whoa-ing. Mr. Sheridan turned to Iris.

"Sorry," he said. "You were saying?"

"I met David Carruthers," said Iris. "On a

so-called horse called Lucifer or Lazarus or — or something."

She paused, but Mr. Sheridan made no comment.

"He said he'd lost the rest of you," went on Iris, "and asked me to say he'd wait for you at the last farm — or somewhere of that sort."

"Thank you," said Mr. Sheridan. "When exactly did you see him?"

"Well, I — I don't carry a stop watch," said Iris. "A quarter of an hour ago, roughly, and exactly four minutes before he landed in the river."

"Did you fish him out?"

"He fished himself out," said Iris. "I was several hundred yards away. Lucifer— Lazarus — took him halfway across and then gave up trying."

A brief grin passed over Mr. Sheridan's countenance. "Wet mud," he commented. "That's the second today. The school laundry doesn't like it."

"Corker's coming, sir," came a chorus of voices. "There, sir — over there."

Iris was unable to decide whether Corker was a boy or a horse, and was prevented from pursuing the subject by a sharp shower of rain. She turned up the collar of her coat and shook her wet hair out of her eyes.

"No hat?" asked Mr. Sheridan.

"Neither have you," observed Iris.

"That's different. I haven't got all those wet wisps hanging round my face," said Mr. Sheridan, with more accuracy than tact. "If you were coming so far from home, why didn't you bring an umbrella?"

"I haven't got an umbrella," said Iris.

"Where're you making for?" asked Michael Sheridan. "There's nothing in this direction except Lord Fellmount's property and if he sees you on that, he'll throw you off personally."

"Let him try," invited Iris cordially.

"Well, you've chosen a bad day and a bad time," said Mr. Sheridan. "It isn't open to visitors and, anyhow, you're on the wrong path."

"Well, I've come so far, so I'll finish the trip," said Iris.

"Have it your own way," said Mr. Sheridan. "It's the wrong way, but walking's good exercise." His eyes went to the boys. "Come on, you fellows. Bellinger, tighten that rein, will you? Winter, keep that animal still if you can."

"Yes, sir."

Iris, with a nod into which she put as much dignity as her wet hair would allow, went on her way. It was, she knew, foolish to go on in spite of this sudden change for the worse in the weather, but as she had come so far, she would go on. It was a pity she had been held up by boys on horses and masters on horses, if they called them horses. . . . What a life, with nothing but small boys and birds and a lot of French grammar and nothing that could be called real living. It was a pity to think of a man, young, good-looking — because he *was* good-looking: he had a nice mouth and his eyes were gray and he didn't look white like most scholars but was a nice dark tan as though he lived in the open, which of course he did, mostly, what with birds and horses. If he only had a more approachable manner and if . . .

Iris brought her mind back with a jerk from Mr. Sheridan's shortcomings to the path in front of her. It had never been broad, but it had been shrinking steadily for the past few hundreds yards; now it had narrowed to a width scarcely sufficient for Iris to walk upon. At every step becoming fainter, it led straight to the edge of a stream and died away.

Iris turned back. She was wet and she was beginning to feel tired out and, worst of all, she soon found that she was making little progress. Far from finding her way back on her original route, she was brought up by obstacles which she could not remember having passed before, and it was not long before she was forced to admit that she was, if not lost, then taking a very long time to get a relatively short way. She set her teeth and quickened her pace.

She rounded a hill and saw that she was once more moving in the wrong direction. Before her, at some distance, was Castle Ambo, and just ahead of her was the school riding party.

Michael Sheridan glanced over his shoulder, saw Iris, called the boys to a halt. He waited until Iris drew level and then addressed her. "You seem," he said, "to have lost your way again."

"I haven't lost my way at all," answered Iris. "I'm — " she hesitated, and realized that she was defeated. "I'm — going back to Lilac Cottage."

Mr. Sheridan ran his eye over the cavalcade and called to one of the riders. "Winter!"

"Yes, sir."

"I'll take your horse," said Mr. Sheridan. "You go with this lady and put her on the right road for Lilac Cottage."

"Thank you, but I don't want anybody to come with me," said Iris.

She spoke firmly and young Winter hesitated for a moment. A glance at the master, calm and unmoved and holding out a hand to take his reins, made him dismount with a promptitude which ought to have moved Iris to admiration for the school discipline. In a moment Winter was beside her, and the riders, with Mr. Sheridan in their rear, were drawing rapidly ahead.

Iris walked silently beside her escort, listening with outward interest to his explanations as to why she had lost the path, when she should have branched off it, and where she ought to have got back onto her original road.

"It looks easy," he said, "but it's not. When we're out sometimes we nearly get lost, but we've got kind of landmarks. You need landmarks," he added, "in a big sort of stretch of country like this."

"You do," agreed Iris politely.

"Sometimes we get lost when we're riding," went on Winter. "And sometimes when Mr. Sheridan brings us bird-spotting. Corker didn't come back until nearly suppertime once. We were going to organize a search, but we didn't in the end."

Corker, decided Iris, was probably a boy. It was unusual for a horse to go bird-spotting.

"Mr. Sheridan takes us out at about four in the morning," went on Winter. "Not now, I don't mean, but in the summer. We built a hide-out and we watched a nest for two days, not all at once, I don't mean, but in sort of batches. Mr. Sheridan got some pictures and sent them to the paper. He sends lots of bird pictures to the papers," he informed Iris proudly. "He knows all about birds."

French grammar. Horses and birds. . . .

A girl would find herself a little crowded out. . . .

"Mr. Sheridan," she said, "appears to be very busy."

"Yes, he is," agreed Winter eagerly. "He does an awful lot, and he does it jolly well, too. He's going to write some essays about birds for a magazine, he says. He told Miss Bellingham about it on Friday and — "

He broke off and pointed to the right.

"That's the way you ought to have gone to Fellmount," he said. "But it's a good thing you didn't go there," he went on. "Lord Fellmount watches out all the time and, last term, he caught Harfield and he threw him in the lake. And Harfield hasn't come back yet, 'cos he got ill 'cos he fell in the lake."

Winter glanced up and saw that his companion was looking at him with a curiously intent expression. He felt gratified; he was an intelligent boy, and he knew when grown-ups were really interested and when they merely pretended to be. He liked Iris and he was glad to be carrying his conversational weight. She wasn't, he told himself, just being polite. She was listening, and she was jolly interested in what he'd been saying, too.

He met Iris's eyes and saw in them a question. He waited expectantly and, she spoke.

"Who," she inquired, "is Miss Bellingham?"

CHAPTER SEVEN

About the time that David Carruthers disappeared into the stream, Mr. Swintzchell, with an angry gesture, flung open the gate of Lilac Cottage, marched with firm steps up the path, and banged in a peremptory manner on the panels of the front door.

Caroline opened it, and Mr. Swintzchell, answering her greeting by a mere grunt, stepped into the house, removed his hat, and searched in its lining, producing at length the note which Caroline had written and waving it before her.

"This — what is this?" he asked angrily.

"Won't you sit down?" invited Caroline.

"No," said Mr. Swintzchell. "Thank you, but no. I am angry and I am disappointed and I prefer to stand. I prepare work for you, passages for you to practice, songs for you to sing, and you write to me and you say — " Mr. Swintzchell gave the note a contemptuous flip — " you say, 'I am sorry, but no singing, it cannot be done.' Why," demanded the speaker, "can it cannot be done?"

Caroline considered the question and spoke unhurriedly. "I'm so sorry," she said. "You see, I have to work in the house. I have to buy things and cook them and dust and clean and polish and — ”

“Still,” interrupted Mr. Swintzchell impatiently, “I wait for the work.”

“Well — I'm explaining,” said Caroline. “Cooking and — ”

“Fft!” Mr. Swintzchell expelled his breath in a manner expressing profound contempt. “Fft! Look — ” he threw his arms wide in a gesture which embraced the room — “Look at the work! The chairs, the tables — with one blow I can blow off the dust. One woman, two women, living in this so-small place, with no man who eats a great deal, with no rooms, with no grand staircases, with no children to make dirtiness, with no need for the big reception, for the many guests, with no food to cook because so little there is to have — where is the work? I wait. Where? If you have husbands, children, if you must be a *hausfrau*, then there is work, but here you have only chairs and tables. Cooking — what is that? For your break fast, coffee, bread. Fft! It is finished. For your lunch, what? A taste, a piece which you make ready in ten, twenty minutes. Fft! It is done. For your tea, a drink; for your supper, something on a plate. Where is this cooking? Where is this work? Here you have nobody who sees what you do. Here is no neighbor who will peep and see what you are working and what you are leaving. Here there is no Mrs. One and Mrs. Two who will point and say, 'Look, that Mrs. Caroline does not every day scrub and clean and polish!' Here is only you and a good piano — and your voice. *That* is the work which God has given to you. When He sees you, will He say, 'What did you cook each day for the pretty Iris?' No! He will say, 'I gave to you, Mrs. Caroline, a great gift. What did you do with it?' And you will say, 'Dear God, I threw it away.' And who will care, up There, that you dusted and polished these so-hard chairs of no value? It is your *voice* that you must dust; it is your *voice* that you must polish and take away the cobwebs, so that soon out of your throat will come sounds so pure, so of Heaven, that the angels will look and say, 'There is Mrs. Caroline doing her proper work at last.' "

Mr. Swintzchell came to an end and, taking out a large handkerchief, wiped his brow. Caroline looked at him with gratitude and affection, but said nothing in answer to the old man's look of questioning.

"Well?" asked Mr. Swintzchell at last.

"There's Iris to look after," said Caroline slowly. "I have to — "

"I have seen," said Mr. Swintzchell, "the pretty Miss Iris. I have looked at her, and I see that she is not sick, not weak, and I see that she is able to look after you and do what you call this work and this cooking for you. It is not all the day. It is only for the time that you practice."

"But Iris has to do her own — "

"That is so; she has to work at her machine, and when she is doing that, you cannot sing, so you see that it will be turn and turn; first her turn, now your turn, and so you will each have time for your work." Mr. Swintzchell came a step nearer and took Caroline's hands in his. "See, Mrs. Caroline," he said. "I am an old man and now I only hear the voices of little boys. They sing, they grow, they go away, and then more come. It it not what I thought I would do, years before. We have met by chance; I have knowledge and you have talent and together we can make your voice what it should be, and when you go away from here you can say, 'Karl Swintzchell has made my voice in good repair and I shall keep it so. I shall go on singing and this time I shall not let my voice go into rust.' " He paused for a moment and then spoke quietly. "Is it," he asked, "that we shall sing?"

Caroline looked at the large, kind face, the lank white hair falling over the bulging forehead, the beseeching look behind glittering spectacles.

"Please!" said Mr. Swintzchell once more.

"Well, I — "

"Ah, Gott! That is good, that is so good!" cried Mr. Swintzchell exultingly. Releasing Caroline's hands, he pressed his own together, walked agitatedly to the piano and back again, put his hands on his stomach and beamed at Caroline. "I am so happy, so glad, I am so thankful. We shall work together and you will sing — how beautifully, you do not yet know. This house will be full of song, and the little village, and when the boys at the school sing at the Carol Service, I hope that you will sing for me the solo I have prepared. Perhaps already you know it." Mr. Swintzchell hurried to the piano, opened it, and played an air with one finger. "You know this?"

Caroline shook her head.

"We shall learn it. It is beautiful," said Mr. Swintzchell. "I do not play the accompaniment they give. It is too much, too heavy, too *important*, I think, and it takes from the singer. I shall play my own interpretation. One day you shall come to the school and I will play it for you on the organ, but not now, not until you have learned to sing it. Look — " Mr. Swintzchell opened his coat and, fumbling in an inner pocket, produced some sheets of manuscript music. "See — here is what I have prepared for you to practice. Shall we begin now?"

"Won't you have some tea first?" asked Caroline.

"No, not first — after," said Mr. Swintzchell. "First you will sing, and then I will help you to make the tea."

The lesson began without delay and at the end of it, Mr. Swintzchell, true to his promise, followed Caroline into the kitchen and, seating her firmly on a chair, proceeded to prepare the tea.

"You shall sit there," he said, "and tell me where is this and that, and I shall do everything."

The professor did, indeed, do everything. He boiled water, laid cups and plates, cut bread, buttered scones, hummed a gay air, and, occasionally, trod a measure in time to it. He was thoroughly happy and expressed his appreciation of Caroline's restfulness.

"You are so good," he told her, "because you do not look at me and say, 'This is the way to do this' and 'This is the way to do that.' You do not jump up and down, you do not make a scene of confusion, you do not agitate yourself, you do not say, 'These dishes are not mine to break, you must be careful.' You sit quietly and you let me do it. Now see! Everything is here. Two cups, two plates, milk, sugar, the pot of tea, the bread and butter, the scones, the little sponge cake. Now we shall push the little wagon so — into the little *Wohnzimmer* and put it before the fire. There!"

"That's lovely," said Caroline. "Only we need another cup because I see Iris coming."

"Another cup — " Mr. Swintzchell hurried into the kitchen and came back bearing an extra cup and saucer and plate. "There! Now we shall have the party."

The door opened and Iris entered, and at the sight of her wet and bedraggled hair and bespattered shoes, Mr. Swintzchell gave an exclamation of distress.

"See — you are wet," he said, pulling a chair close to the fire and throwing on a large proportion of the coal which Caroline had hoped would last for the whole evening. "Come — give me your coat and take off your shoes and sit here. You are so wet and cold and here is the hot tea which I have made all by myself."

"It was a horrid afternoon for you," said Caroline. "Did you see the place?"

"From a distance of a mile and a half — yes," said Iris.

"What is this place?" asked Mr. Swintzchell, pouring out a cup of tea and handing it to Iris with a fatherly air.

"The ogre's castle — Fellmount," said Iris. "I went to look over it and I lost my way and all I saw was a boy in a stream and a lot more boys on a collection of horses all looking like that one of Don Quixote's, only much worse. And all in charge of your friend, Mr. Sheridan. I don't know how many guineas get tacked on to the parents' bills for riding lessons, but before writing the next check, the parents ought to come down and have a look at the — "

"Wasn't it Rosinante?" asked Caroline.

"Wasn't what?" Iris asked in her turn.

"Don Quixote's horse," said Caroline. "I just remembered that it was called Rosinante."

"Thank you, darling," said Iris. "I'll make a note of it."

"The horses," said Mr. Swintzchell, "were so difficult to get, and there was not much money, not enough to buy good horses. But the boys are happy and Michael is happy and — "

"Yes, I saw them," said Iris. "When does Mr. Sheridan find time to put in a French lesson here and there?"

"All this that he does," said Mr. Swintzchell, "is extra to his teaching. He likes the boys to swim, to ride, to learn about the birds, even to sail little toy boats, but there is no water, not enough water, only the so-pretty little lake which belongs to Lord Fellmount, who does not let the boys go there. Twice Michael asked him, and once the Headmaster himself, but no — always the answer was no. It is a pity, for the little Carruthers has made a little ship that sails — so well he made it, so well he makes everything with his hands. We called it the *Humming Bird* but there is nowhere for the *Humming Bird* to sail. It is a pity. The boys would have been happy."

"They'll have to fall back on French grammar," said Iris. Mr. Swintzchell studied her gravely. "You do not," he said after a time, "like Mr. Sheridan?"

"I don't *know* Mr. Sheridan," said Iris. "I don't see how anybody could get to *know* him even if they wanted to. What does he do with his friends — sandwich them in between French lessons and swimming and riding and sailing and bird-watching?"

"You should not say it like that," said Mr. Swintzchell, "because it is not only bird-watching. You say, 'Bird-watching, fft, fft, what is bird-watching?' but it is more than that. It is waiting with long patience, and finding out what others do not know, and getting beautiful photographs which are put into papers for everyone to read."

"Which papers?" inquired Iris.

"I do not know their names," said Mr. Swintzchell. "They would pay for more photographs, and they ask for writing, but Michael only makes a scribbling in his notebooks and does not make the notes into neat ones just as you can do on your machine over there. You cannot send a scribbling book to the papers or to the magazines who ask for the writings. I say, 'Come, Michael, and copy your scribbles so that they can be read,' but he says, 'No, some other time.' But the other time does not come. But see — " Mr. Swintzchell took out his watch, looked at it, and rose hastily — "see,

I sit here and speak of time, and time is going and I have work to do."

He looked round for his hat, and Iris, padding across the room in her stockinged feet, picked it up from under one of the chairs and handed it to him.

"Always it drops," said Mr. Swintzchell. "Thank you, thank you. And for my tea, Mrs. Caroline, thank you also. Please to practice diligently, and on Thursday I will come. Good-by, good-by."

The door closed behind him and Iris turned and looked at her sister in surprise. "I thought," she said, "that you wrote and called the lessons off."

"I did," said Caroline. "But he said that I could quite well go on with the lessons. All I have to do, he says, is leave everything to you, and when you're doing your work at your machine I can put in a little work for you."

Iris was standing in front of the fire, one foot tilted up to the warmth. "It's these beastly reports that make things so difficult," she said. "I did suggest to old Ernest that it would be better not to send reports until I'd made some progress, but he said no, he wanted a weekly summary of what I'd been doing. You can't pad — he's like a sieve. Lets all the padding go through and then has a look to see what facts he's got left. And the fact that I've walked ten miles on a wet afternoon won't interest him in the slightest. *'Facts,'* he'll say, 'where are the *facts?*' Well," she ended, "where are they? I might as well — "

She stopped. Caroline was looking out of the window, her expression apprehensive.

"What's the matter?" asked Iris. "Ernest coming to take over?"

"Well, no," said Caroline slowly. "It's a — it's a boy with a telegram."

Iris's face went white. "The sack," she said. "What did I tell you? One dud report and you're out on your ear. Go on, open the door, Carol, and let's get the thing read and done with."

Caroline took the telegram from the boy and, after a glance at the envelope, spoke with relief. "It's all right," she said. "It's addressed to me."

She slit open the envelope and read the telegram, and Iris, watching, saw that it contained bad news. Caroline looked up and spoke a brief sentence to the boy.

"Thank you," she said. "There's no answer."

She closed the door slowly and turned, staring at the telegram in her hand.

"Bad news?" asked Iris gently.

"Terrible," said Caroline.

She handed the telegram to her sister and Iris read the brief message:

ENGAGED. COMING WITH FIANCÉE.
ROBERT.

CHAPTER EIGHT

The first few hours after the receipt of their brother's telegram were spent by Caroline and Iris in an effort to ward off the threatened blow. There was no telephone in the Cottage, but Iris spent a chilly hour in the Post Office telephone booth in an attempt to get through to her brother's flat in London. When, after exasperating delays, she was connected, there was no answer, and an appeal to the operator at the block of Service flats in which Robert lived elicited the information that Mr. Drake had left for the country and would be away indefinitely.

With this depressing news, Iris made her way back to Caroline.

"It's no use," she said, attempting to warm herself by the low fire. "He's away and they don't know where. Probably on his way down here with his lady love." She turned and faced her sister gloomily. "Gosh, Carol," she said, "it's going to be too awful for words."

"Well, yes," agreed Caroline, "I think it is."

"Imagine," said Iris, "*both* of them. Robert by himself would have been bad enough, but Robert and his creature — because she *will* be a creature, you can take it from me. I don't care a damn about the people here, but they'll take one look at her and then we shall be outcasts. Everybody'll run a mile every time we go into the village."

"Do you think," asked Caroline, "it'll be the one we saw when I was lunching with you?"

"No, it won't. It'll be something even worse," said Iris. "Why would Robert come all the way to a hole-and-corner place like this unless it was going to give him some real amusement? All he's coming for is to watch our faces when he walks in and says, 'Girls, meet your new sister' — or something poisonous of that sort."

"He may," suggested Caroline hopefully, "have got hold of somebody quite nice."

"Have you ever," asked Iris, "seen Robert with anything quite nice?"

"Well, no, I haven't," admitted Caroline.

"Men stick to type," said Iris, "and I've seen Robert's. And I don't care, much. I mean, it's never been any use caring what Robert did, because it was his own show and, after all, we're all free to muck up things as we please. But this is different; this is bringing it too close. I haven't the least interest in how many women he ties himself up with, but I do feel it's going over the limit to mix us up in it."

Caroline said nothing. She had lost the thread of Iris's remarks and was lost in a mental preview of what life in the Cottage would be like when her brother arrived. Nothing in the picture did anything to raise her spirits, but she felt disposed, as always, to remain calm until the worst was upon them. For the moment, she and Iris were alone, and it was more than probable that something would prevent Robert from arriving at all. She tried to put this possibility before Iris, and found that Iris, too, had been exploring possible avenues of reprieve.

"It isn't likely," she told Caroline, "that any woman could stand Robert for *long*. Perhaps she'll call it off. And perhaps he'll realize, when he starts looking at maps and things, how far off civilization this place is, and change his mind. After all, watching our faces may be quite rewarding for a day, but it wouldn't make up for the lack of any other amusement here. But if he does come — " her voice became gloomy once more — "I don't know what I'll do. You're all right, because you don't get overwrought about anything. You've got a way of staying on a nice even keel and you don't even let Robert ruffle you — much. But he'll drive me out, Carol, or drive me mad — I don't know which. I — "

"You mustn't take him too seriously," said Caroline. "He — "

Iris stared at her sister with her mouth open. "Too seriously?" she said at last, on a high note. "Too *seriously!* Good Heavens,

Carol, have you forgotten what living with him is like? *Have* you?" She sighed. "It's no use, Carol darling. Keep as calm and as placid and as jellyfishish — jellyfishy — oh, well, keep calm, anyhow, but don't make any mistake — you're in and I'm in and we're both in for a peculiar hell of a time."

Caroline rose from her chair. "All right — we are," she acknowledged. "But let's put it aside, or perhaps I mean let's sit quietly and let it — "

" — break over us."

"Yes. I'll go and get a nice hot supper," said Caroline, and we'll stoke up the fire and get books and — Oh! that reminds me. Colonel Brock brought back your magazines and said thank you very much, he enjoyed them."

"Well, that shows I've got a suspicious nature," said Iris. "I never really expected to see them again. Where are they?"

"On that little table," called Caroline from the kitchen. Iris looked on all three little tables, but saw none of her magazines. "They're not here," she said.

Caroline's head appeared round the doorway, and she pointed with a floury finger. "There — that bundle," she said.

Iris walked to the bundle and picked it up, and something in her face brought the rest of Caroline round the door.

"Something wrong?" she asked.

"No, nothing — nothing at all," said Iris. "Only that the magazines you lent the old boy were bang new ones, all good ones and all expensive ones. Right?"

"Well — yes."

"And these — " Iris held them out — "are year before last's, nothing like the ones you lent him, and all cheap and tripy publications." She put them back on the table and turned to her sister, her expression awed. "Golly, Carol," she said, "we've got an artist in our midst."

"Perhaps," suggested Caroline slowly, "he brought the wrong bundle."

"How you *reach* these brilliant conclusions beats me," said Iris in an excess of admiration. "That's just what he's been and done — brought the wrong bundle."

"What shall you do — tell him?"

"No, I shan't," said Iris. "I'm learning. He'll only strike his most soul-of-honor stance and convince me — and, my golly, he *does* convince me, while he's doing it — that those were the very selfsame magazines you put into his hand. No, I won't tell him. But I'll keep my possessions where I can see them and next time we'll let him have a book or magazine belonging to you. Or, better still, lend him something of Robert's and then sit back and watch the Greeks having it out."

"He might," said Caroline, "like Robert."

Iris stared at her sister in the utmost astonishment.

"My dear Carol," she said. "Who on *earth* could like Robert?"

Nobody had ever looked upon the Drakes — Caroline, Robert, and Iris — as a family. Nor had they, indeed, had more than a brief experience of any kind of family life. They had been what Robert now termed "early orphans," and had been sent home from the East after the death of their parents, when Caroline was nine, Robert seven, and Iris a mere toddler. Neither of the parents had brothers or sisters, but there were great-aunts and great-uncles, all kindly and all eager to do what they could for the little ones, and it was decided, after a meeting had been held to discuss the problem, that the most sensible course would be to choose good boarding schools — in the baby's case, a good nursery school — and offer the children happy holidays at the homes of their relations.

Opinions on Robert Drake had, from his earliest years, varied widely. To his sisters, he had always been incalculable. Holidays spent in his company could be pleasant or the reverse, depending upon his moods. He passed through school leaving in his wake a trail of fiercely disagreeing masters, half of whom averred that he was a subject more fit for a reformatory than a normal school and the other half declaring that he was a boy of exceptional merit, promise, and charm. There was no way to account for the contrast between his exceptionally good looks and his frequently astonishingly bad behavior. On only one point was there unanimity — all agreed that Robert Drake was unfailingly sure of himself.

The problem of earning a living caused him, at first, a good deal of thought. He had no objection to working if he felt that the conditions were ideal, the pay adequate, and the prospects bright, but the only offer which seemed to cover any of these demands came from a mine owner in Chile.

To Chile, therefore, Robert decided to go. An air passage was provided for him, but Robert declined it and elected to go by sea. He chose the smallest ship making the Atlantic run and left England on a blustery, exhilarating day in April. Thus a young man, of whom few in his own country — and nobody outside it — had ever heard, became in a little over a month a renowned figure whose handsome countenance figured prominently in newspapers all over the world.

For the ship never reached Chile and never, in fact, came near its destination. Robert, far from finding himself in a mine, came to himself in the cold waters of mid-

Atlantic. The *Sierra Morena*, blown to fragments by the explosive cargo it had carried, was no more than a few pieces of floating wreckage; her crew was nowhere to be seen and four of her seven passengers were struggling to reach the last remaining lifeboat.

With a badly injured shoulder, Robert sat in the swaying boat and coldly surveyed his chances of survival. He thought that they were slight, and the thought made him angry. He had, after much deliberation, chosen a career, and Fate had deposited him in the middle of an ocean. Robert liked the sea, but he had no intention of ending his days in it. He was young and, but for this unlooked-for development, would shortly have embarked upon a life of success and ease.

With the coolness which always succeeded his worst moods, Robert set about cheating Fate. There was a boat beneath him — damaged, untrustworthy, but still a boat. If human hands could repair the damage, if human knowledge could bring it to harbor, to harbor it would go.

Robert fished the other three survivors out of the water and inspected them. The world, he decided, would have been no worse off without them, but they were alive and he needed them. Directing, cursing, bullying, and threatening, he got his crew to work, addressing to the Almighty a stern admonition for God's sake to keep the wind in the right direction. To his inexperienced crew he offered the alternative of a grim struggle for life or a lingering and unpleasant death.

In the dreadful voyage that followed, Robert was master, leader, and finally the sole hope. He brought his battered craft to land, handed his exhausted crew to the rapidly assembled medical authorities, and expressed the hope that he would never set eyes on any of them again.

Robert's skill, his stamina and magnificent leadership would in themselves have made a story, but there were other facts in the adventure which made news. His name, his youth, and, above all, his good looks made him a popular hero, while his dislike of publicity and savage hatred of newspapermen made him even more interesting a subject.

Dodging reporters and refusing to impart any information concerning his late voyage, Robert set about finding his way to Chile. Before his arrangements were complete, however, he received a letter which opened the possibility of earning a livelihood doing the thing which he liked more than anything in the world.

The letter was from an American living in New England. The writer had a family of boys and girls all of whom — and all of whose friends — loved to sail. Would Mr. Drake, asked the writer, consider coming to New England to open a Sailing Club? There was an offer of a generous fee, and a heartening sentence regarding expenses.

The father was not alone. Parents from all over the world wrote to Robert, and it was obvious that the writers felt that the chief factor responsible for the qualities shown by Robert in his stirring adventure was his early training in seamanship.

To the end that every child should grow up with skill, courage, and stamina, Robert Drake began to form Drake Sailing Clubs. The first was inaugurated at the New England bay; later, Drake Clubs began to flourish in places as far apart as San Sebastian and San Francisco. Civic authorities in English seaside towns provided facilities for children whose parents could not afford Club fees; Club members were rescued from the fringes of the North Sea and the Caribbean, taken home and rubbed down, and returned to sail again. International Drake contests were held and Robert made speeches at the prize-givings.

He was very happy. It was work which was always performed at the best season and in the most pleasant conditions. His picture, in a white linen suit, decorated every Clubhouse. He lived in sunshine, beside glittering waters. He seldom visited his sisters and had a marked capacity for eluding all the charming young women who showed themselves eager to be friendly.

Nothing had ever prepared Caroline for the telegram. Her brother's visits had been brief and troublesome, and she had always been deeply relieved when he left. In the sanctuary of Lilac Cottage, with its few comforts, she had felt safe from Robert and had never dreamed of any fiancée. . . .

Of the kind of fiancée he would have, Caroline and Iris from the first entertained no doubt, but both felt, as they finished their supper on the evening the telegram arrived, that it would be best to put the thought of the impending visit aside and go on with their usual routine.

"I'll air the beds," said Caroline, "and if they don't like the rooms, which they couldn't possibly, they'll have to go somewhere else, and then we shall all be happy. They mightn't come at all, and then — "

"Then," said Iris, "we shall be happier still."

CHAPTER NINE

Thursday came, and Robert had not arrived. There was a white covering over the ground, snow which the morning sun quickly melted. The afternoon was cold and dry, and Iris, setting out toward the large, ugly house occupied by Miss Stannard and her sister, sniffed the brisk air and wished the distance twice as much.

She left the village behind and, coming to the crossroads, saw two figures approaching from the direction of the houses. With a friendly wave, Iris walked on, but a loud hail from Mr. Swintzchell stopped her. He put on speed and came up to her, and beside him, walking with long, unhurried strides, was Michael Sheridan.

Mr. Swintzchell came to a halt and waved a sheaf of papers at Iris. He was in the highest spirits.

"See now," he said, "I give you three guesses. Where am I going on this fine, good afternoon? Now where? You shall guess — one, two, three guesses."

"North Pole?" hazarded Iris.

"No, no, no," said the delighted Mr. Swintzchell, "not the North Pole and not the South Pole and not to Brazil and not to Iceland.

Now where? Look all the hints I have told you."

"You're going to give Caroline a lesson," said Iris. "And I'm going to tea with Miss Stannard."

Mr. Swintzchell looked more delighted than ever.

"You go to the Stannards? You, too?" he asked, beaming. "Then there will be two of you, for Michael here, he is also going to tea. He does not wish to go, for he never wishes to go anywhere to take tea or to take supper or to take lunch, but he must go, because now it is his turn. Each time that Miss Stannard has any party, she asks one, two from the School, and Mr. Clunes says, 'Now who will go?' Always nobody wishes to go, but Mr. Clunes says, 'Yes, you must go by turns.' And now it is Michael's turn but, like you, he does not wish to take tea with the two old ladies — and they are such nice old ladies. If I did not go to Mrs. Caroline to sing, I would go willingly to the old ladies to take tea. Now, Miss Iris, you will take Michael and see that he does not escape and go back to write in his notebook about the birds. Now go — good-by, good-by."

Iris walked on, Michael Sheridan by her side.

"Do you really have to do this in turns?" she asked.

"Something of the sort — yes," said Michael. "The Head feels it's good policy to keep in with them, or he feels sorry for them and thinks this keeps them in touch with the School — I don't know which. You know they used to run it at one time?"

Iris nodded. "Yes," she said. "They used to teach the man I work for — but that's no advertisement. Now I'm on my way to wave a teacup in one hand and eat a wafery bit of bread and butter with the other, and I shall arrive in a starving state but there won't be anything but the most delicate fare. And the cups'll be fragile and priceless, and some of them'll be riveted together with bits of tin and might quite well come to pieces in your hand, and the conversation will be about the delightful pension at Villefranche or on the borders of the Lake of Geneva, where you used to stay for an entire season on what it costs to take you there and back these days. And then the whole delightful affair'll come to an end and then we can go home. And you can go on with your notes on the feathered world."

Her words, swift, careless, came to an end, and the two walked for a time in silence. Iris glanced at the man beside her.

"Well, go on," she urged. "Say something."

"Certainly," said Mr. Sheridan. "What about?"

Iris considered. "Well, take them in rotation," she suggested. "Riding for beginners,

French for beginners, bird-watching for — "

"They're not all beginners," said Mr. Sheridan. "Some of the boys speak better French than I do. And young Winter can ride anything from a — "

"You're talking shop," said Iris. "Come off primus and secundus for a moment and try to look at it in a big way. If you can leave the school aside and — "

"Perhaps," said Mr. Sheridan, "I don't want to."

"Want to what?"

"Leave the School aside. I happen to be interested in it, and all the subjects you offered me are inextricably tied up with — "

"With the School. I know," said Iris. "But this is the fourth time I've met you and we don't seem to be getting on. I — "

"I don't think," said Mr. Sheridan in his calm, unemotional voice, "that we shall get on. It's extraordinarily nice of you to want to, but I don't think we've really what you might term any basis for getting on. I take it, from your manner, that you don't care for schoolmasters and I don't know the first thing about the kind of thing you do — which I understand from Mr. Swintzchell is some kind of newspaper work. What are you," he asked, "a lady detective?"

"I'm not even," said Iris, "a woman reporter — yet."

There was a pause and Michael Sheridan

spoke with the first touch of interest he had so far shown. "Are you," he asked, "any relation to the man who organizes all the Sailing Clubs — Robert Drake?"

"I'm his sister," said Iris. "You know him?"

"Not personally," said Michael. "He opened the Strand Sailing Club about eleven miles from my home and I ran into him two or three times during the week he was there. It was really that that got my mind back on the lake in Lord Fellmount's grounds. The school had had a shot at it before, but I came back full of the idea of making the old man, Lord Fellmount, let the school rent it. No go. He more or less threw me out. He's about five feet five and I'm six one, but I believe he could have done it. I never saw a fellow in such a blue rage. I thought once or twice of asking your brother if he'd come down, when he was reasonably near this part of the world, and see what he could do."

"He gets into blue rages himself," said Iris. "He's got a nasty kind of temperament."

"What does his temperament matter?" asked Michael. "He does a pretty good job. There were fifty reasons why the Club at Strand couldn't get running smoothly; the people running it were all at each other's throats and the entire thing looked like packing up the moment the opening ceremony'd been performed. Your brother talked one or two rounds, knocked a few heads together, revised the entire rules, and ironed the thing out. It was a fine piece of organization."

"You can congratulate him personally," said Iris. "He's coming here — he and his fiancée."

"I didn't realize he had one," said Michael.

"Neither did we. And, going by the type of fallen womanhood he's always favored, High Ambo's going to see something. If a large, well-covered lady of doubtful age but certain morals stops you in the village street and asks you where you met before, just get behind the music professor and stay there. Or send for me."

"Certainly."

"And don't keep on saying 'Certainly,' like the man you've just asked to direct you to the haberdashery," said Iris. "Go on about bird-watching."

"You go on," invited Mr. Sheridan. "You talk so much more — fluently — than I do."

"Mr. Swintzchell says you ignore all the approaches that people make to you — I mean, for articles," said Iris. "Is that correct?"

"I send an article to a country magazine occasionally. But I haven't the time to set the notes out properly."

"Why," asked Iris, "don't you bring them to me and let me type them?"

"Thank you, but in the first place," said

Michael, "you're busy on whatever your own work is, and, anyhow, you wouldn't be able to make head or tail of the notes."

"Why not?" asked Iris. "I can read."

"Good," said Mr. Sheridan. "But I doubt whether you've ever heard of — for example — Linnaeus."

"Should I have?" asked Iris.

Mr. Sheridan raised his eyebrows. Even Brown Secundus, at eight and a half, had heard of Linnaeus. Michael wondered, not for the first time, what, if anything, was taught in girls' schools and how so many girls managed to emerge without having absorbed any useful knowledge whatsoever.

"Linnaeus," he explained, "evolved the binomial or Linnaean system of nomenclature."

"Ah!" said Iris. "Now we're getting somewhere. What's the binomial system of nomenclature — what I call you and what your mother calls you, yes?"

"You offered to type the notes," pointed out Mr. Sheridan. "And the thing's quite simple. It merely means the denoting of an organism by two Latin words. The first is the genus and the second the species."

"I bet," guessed Iris, "there's a trinomial system, too."

"Certainly there is. The third Latin name," said Mr. Sheridan, "gives you the geographical or sub-specific one. Take for example,

Pyrrhula pyrrhula pyrrhula — you'll see in the notes, that the name Linnaeus comes after it in brackets. That's the bullfinch. In this part of the country they're more colorful and even a bit larger than the ones in the south, but you see — "

"Yes, I see," said Iris. "It explains an awful lot of things. A man who has to say *pyrrhula pyrrhula pyrrhula* every time he wants to mention a bullfinch doesn't, I can see, have much time left over for normal pursuits."

"What," asked Mr. Sheridan, "would you class as normal pursuits? Or may I guess? Talking trivialities to entire strangers in railway carriages, giving a pretty girl the attention she's obviously accustomed to, getting one's mind off an interesting and constructive job and bringing it to bear on the proper phrases to address to a young woman with too much beauty, too much spare time, and no capacity whatsoever for keeping off the particular and sticking to a general conversation."

"My, my, my!" said Iris in admiration. "You can be fluent, too."

"Certainly I can," said Mr. Sheridan.

"If you say 'Certainly' again," said Iris, "I'll throw one of Miss What's-her-name's most priceless pieces of china at you the moment tea's served. It sounds — "

"I know — haberdashery."

" — and pompous," finished Iris, "and

altogether stuffy. You are, without exception, the stuffiest man I've ever met, but if I can see something of you, I mean, if you'll come down out of the trees in the intervals between taking pictures of the *pyrrhula pyrrhula pyrrhula,* I think we'll get on."

"Must we?" inquired Michael. "I'm a busy man."

Iris waved a hand at the landscape. "This," she said, "is a small place, and people must stick together. I'm only here for a short time and in that short time, I don't see any reason why one of the many young men attached to the School shouldn't devote a little time to keeping me amused. I'm easily amused. I'm stuck in a cottage with a sister who, though charming, is now engaged in giving forth an unending series of Koos and Hoos and mi-mi-mis. I've got a job to do, but I have time off sometimes. Have you?" she inquired.

"I'm a very busy man," said Michael. "But I could give you my holiday address."

There was silence for a few moments, and Iris broke it finally. "About that boy I met in the train," she said, "the one with the ears — "

"Most of the boys," said Mr. Sheridan, "have ears."

"Oh — don't be so idiotic," said Iris. "You know quite well what I mean. That David Carruthers, who went splosh into the middle of the water — I'd like to have him out to tea one day at the Cottage — and his friend Winter, too. I think there's a third. They call him Stuffy, but I don't know what for. Could you," she asked, "send them along one day?"

"Do you," asked Mr. Sheridan, "know their parents?"

"Know their parents? Of course I don't know their parents," said Iris. "What do I want to know their parents for? I want the boys to come to tea, that's all."

"If you don't know their parents, or if their parents haven't given some kind of authorization," said Michael, "the Headmaster can't let them out."

"You mean," said Iris, "that before I can ask them out, I've got to write and ask their parents? Don't be silly. I've been to school and I know all about those rules, and I know that as long as a person's living in the district and well known to the School authorities, the parents are only too glad to have their pets taken out of the cage for a meal or two."

"You're not resident in the district, and the School authorities — are you well known to them?" asked Michael.

"I'll ring up the Headmaster," said Iris, "and I'll tell him that I'm practically a member of the School, or at least Carol is. How could he stop Mr. Swintzchell's pupils from meeting one another?"

"You can ring him up," said Michael

coolly, "and ask him."

Nothing more was said. Iris walked beside the tall, calm, baffling schoolmaster and mused on the strangeness of the species. The learned type, she told herself morosely, floating on clouds of knowledge and looking down contemptuously at those who were walking firmly on the ground of common sense. He thought she was a half-wit and perhaps, admitted Iris to herself, in some ways she was. She'd always thought the things her schoolmistresses had written on blackboards dull, dreary, and pointless. She had got through quadratic equations, been pushed through the ghastly geometry theorems until she stuck, fast and finally, at the frightful one about the — what was it? The hypot — hypoten — well, that. And when they introduced *pi* into mathematics and threw out terrifying hints of an approaching menace called trigonometry, it was time for a girl to get out and give her mind to something that really mattered. If that was education, they could have it. Nobody'd ever taught her how to make a dress for herself or how to cook or how to make a thimbleful of ration into a stomachful of food. Nobody'd taught her how to deal with learned characters — and this afternoon, the technique would have been useful. He . . .

Her companion stopped before a wrought-iron gate and pushed it open. "Here we are," he said, indicating the large, ugly house. He stood aside for Iris to pass and looked down at her, his face breaking into a wide, attractive smile. "Jolly walk, wasn't it?" he said.

CHAPTER TEN

Caroline walked with Mr. Swintzchell to the gate and thanked him for the lesson.

"It is not," said Mr. Swintzchell, "for you to say thank you, but for me. Now you must go inside and you must practice and — "

"Are you sure," asked Caroline, "you won't stay to tea?"

"No, thank you, I cannot," said Mr. Swintzchell. "Already it is late, already I must be with the boys for the Choir practice. But you must be diligent — remember. And you must breathe. Every day, just as I have told you, you must breathe."

Caroline promised to breathe, and Mr. Swintzchell, looking at his watch and, as usual, dashing his hand against his head in a way which Caroline felt must hurt him very much, hurried away as fast as his enormous bulk would allow.

Caroline turned and walked slowly into the house. She would make herself some tea, and while the kettle boiled she would begin her preparations for something extra for supper. Iris had said that she would come away from tea hungrier than when she had left.

Soup, and a little fish — baked, perhaps.

Iris was difficult about fish, but the meat ration never lasted more than two days at the most. It was a pity that the house was so small. It was impossible to keep every trace of food-smell confined to the kitchen.

Her tea over, Caroline went on with the preparations for supper. The soup was simmering; she shut the kitchen door, firmly determined that this time Iris should not open the front door and complain that the house smelt of fish.

Earnest and absorbed, Caroline was deaf to sounds from the front of the house. Putting the fish into the oven, she thought that she heard the front door open but, after waiting a few moments and hearing nothing more, decided that she had been mistaken.

She went on with her tasks and heard, this time distinctly, a knock on the door. Colonel Brock had tried, she thought, to make her hear, had opened the door and entered, and was now trying to attract her attention.

She frowned in annoyance. He had brought back Iris's books, no doubt, but whatever he had come for, nothing could avert the accompanying flow of talk. It was too bad to have to leave things in the middle to go and listen to an interminable discourse on entirely uninteresting topics.

She opened the kitchen door with a quick gesture and moved back to stir the soup. "Do sit down, please," she called. "I'm so sorry I didn't hear you knocking. I'll be out in a second."

There was no reply. Caroline, expecting to hear the Colonel's hearty tones and to see him appear at the door of the kitchen, heard only a gentle cough, timid, apologetic, from the living room.

Caroline, her spoon now still, called a question. "Is that Colonel Brock?"

"N-no."

It was certainly not Colonel Anybody. The voice was young, girlish, and a little frightened. Caroline, abandoning soup and spoon unceremoniously, turned and stepped to the door.

Before her, in the middle of the room, stood a small, slight figure. A girl — sixteen, Caroline thought — in a coat which she recognized as one which Iris would call simply expensive. Brown shoes, brown hair, brown eyes and — Caroline's eyes moved to it and remained fixed — a brown suitcase.

There was a long silence. The girl seemed anxious to speak, and made several attempts, but nothing came of them. Caroline had only one question to put, but it could be put in such infinitely varied ways, and the answer — for she knew the answer — would be so incredible, that she found herself unable to utter a word.

The girl found her voice. "Are you — are you Caroline?" she asked.

"Yes," said Caroline, adding foolishly and childishly, "What's your name?"

"Mary," said the girl. "Mary Andrews."

A plain name, thought Caroline. A plain name for a plain girl. Mary Andrews.

"I'm usually," Mary told her, "called Polly."

Polly. It couldn't be — but it must be. There was no creature, there was no olive hair. There was only Polly.

Already certain, but still unbelieving, Caroline put her question. "Are you," she asked, "Robert's fiancée?"

Polly merely nodded, but a light appeared in her dark eyes and a faint color on her cheeks. Caroline, struggling with her bewilderment, managed to smile and found herself walking across the room to take the girl's hand in hers.

Polly spoke with a little air of dignity. "Robert," she said, "said he'd write."

"Robert," said Caroline, "sent a telegram."

"Oh!"

There was another pause, but Caroline felt her self-command returning. "I'm so sorry to have been so stupid," she said. "I was so awfully surprised. I mean, I didn't expect you, and — "

"We were both coming," explained Polly, "and then Robert said he didn't like awkward meetings and he was — was sure this would be a — well, he sent me by train and said he'd tell you, and he'd follow when we'd

— when I'd met you and — "

" — and when all the awkwardness was over. That," said Caroline, "sounds awfully like Robert, but he didn't write and he didn't let us know. That's awfully like Robert, too."

Polly smiled, a charming smile that made Caroline add a year to her age. Seventeen.

"I'm sorry," said Polly, "about arriving like — like this. I couldn't make you hear when I knocked, and the man who drove the taxi said you were in the kitchen and so he — well, he put me inside and closed the door and went away."

Caroline studied the small, delicate face. Polly's shy hesitancy was leaving her; her manner was growing more assured, more eager, and her sentences began on a little catch, which made Caroline feel that it would be followed by an eager "Oh, please — " like a schoolgirl addressing a mistress. She could only be sixteen, after all.

"Have you," she asked, struggling to be practical, "had any tea?"

Polly shook her head.

"No, but, please — honestly, I don't want any — truly! I can wait. I'm not hungry, not at all!"

"Well — " Caroline, who longed to stand with Polly before her and gaze at her until her overpowering curiosity was appeased, made another effort to appear hospitable. "Come and sit down," she said, "and take off your hat and make yourself comfortable, and I'll see about getting your room ready."

"Oh — no! Please don't bother about me," said Polly, eager and anxious. "It's all Robert's fault and now I've sort of dropped on you and there honestly isn't need to do anything. I can sleep anywhere and I don't mind whether it's a bed or not. I never even notice, so please just don't do anything at all."

"You'll have to sleep on the bed," pointed out Caroline, "because the bedroom's so small that the bed takes up most of the floor."

Polly's manner was once more shy and hesitating. "W-where's Iris?" she asked.

"Oh — I'm sorry. I quite forgot about Iris," acknowledged Caroline. "She went out to tea, but she ought to be back fairly soon." She went into the kitchen and returned with a piece of cake and a glass of milk. "Get this down," she said, "and I'll hurry up supper and we'll have it early. Did you come from London?"

Polly, her mouth full of cake, nodded with energy.

"Do you live there?" asked Caroline.

There was a sound which she interpreted as a negative. Polly finished her mouthful, shook her head vigorously, and uttered four words before biting once more into the cake.

"Don't really live anywhere," she said.

Caroline decided that, until the cake had

been disposed of, it would be useless to seek further information. It would also, she reflected, be better to wait until Iris came back. She hoped very much that she would come soon. The suspense was really becoming —

There was a sound of quick footsteps up the path, and the door was thrown open.

"Hello, Carol!" said Iris from the doorstep. "Anything to eat? All I had there was — "

Iris, banging the door and swinging round to face her sister, found not one but two pairs of eyes upon her. She glanced at Polly and her eyes went inquiringly to Caroline, but before the latter could do more than open her mouth to answer the casual inquiry about the visitor, Iris's expression underwent a series of extraordinary changes. Caroline had no difficulty in tracing reactions similar to those through which she herself had so recently passed.

There was silence for a time. Iris was lost in astonishment and speculation and Caroline and Polly watched her. At last she spoke.

"No!" The word held decisive unbelief. "No, Carol! No!"

"Yes, Iris, yes," said Caroline. "I felt just as you do."

Iris's eyes appeared to be riveted on the newcomer, but her words were addressed to Caroline. "You mean — she really is?"

"Really is," said Caroline.

"Good Heavens!" said Iris in the purest amazement. "Who would — who could ever have believed it? How old," she asked slowly, "would you say, Carol?"

"First," said Caroline, "I thought sixteen and then I said, 'Well, no, seventeen,' but when I saw her stuffing cake into her mouth I said, 'No, sixteen.' "

"Do you think," asked Iris, "do — you — think she has the faintest idea of what she's in for?"

Polly spoke. "I like Robert," she said.

Iris addressed her future sister-in-law for the first time. "Oh, no!" she protested. "You might *love* him. I can imagine lots of women simply going nuts over him, but *like* him? You couldn't. You couldn't, my sweet young — Gosh, I don't even know your name."

"Polly," said Caroline.

Iris made her way weakly to a chair and sat on it. "And that," she said, "is the finish. I didn't believe it before and I don't believe it now." She turned to Polly. "Tell me, Polly," she asked earnestly, "are you sure — are you ab-so-lutely certain that you're talking about Robert Drake?"

Polly nodded, a smile of enjoyment on her lips.

"And you're sure you're engaged to him? I mean, you're certain he proposed to you and that he put the thing into clear words."

"Very clear," said Polly. "Truly."

"Truly!" murmured Iris, aghast. "She even says 'truly.' She looks sixteen, she puts on make-up like an untalented amateur, she looks normal and healthy and spirited, and she says she's going to marry Robert. My dearest little Polly, have you any — *any* relations to guide you?"

"Only Daddy," said Polly.

"Daddy. And does Daddy," asked Iris, "know Robert?"

Polly nodded.

"Are you aware," asked Iris, "that Robert Drake is the most selfish, the most unscrupulously selfish man that ever walked? Do you know that he's got a temper that can blow the top off a boiler, that he shouts when he wants anything and screams when he doesn't get it, that he thinks of nothing but his tropical suits and what he's going to say when he opens the next Club in the next sunlit bay? That he killed off all his old great-aunts and uncles — not that that was any loss, but still, it was his behavior that did them in. That he'll lead his wife — if you really persist in this madness and he makes you his wife — the life of a dog? Do you know all that?"

Polly nodded.

"Robert said," she answered calmly, "that if there was anything about him I didn't know already, Iris would tell me."

"Ah — he did?"

"Yes," said Polly, and Caroline noticed that the shyness which appeared to overtake her when meeting strangers and which had kept her silent when Iris entered, had vanished once more. "He said that you'd probably be surprised when you saw me because the other girls he'd known were sort of older."

"Older," said Iris, "doesn't quite express it. How old are you?"

"I'm twenty," said Polly.

"Twenty. Twenty whole years in which to study men," said Iris, "and you go and choose Robert. Carol, d'you think we can do anything to save her, or do you think she's too far gone?"

"Much, much too far gone," said Polly. "You know — " she put her head on one side and studied Iris with an odd air of absorption — "You know what I think? I think, in some ways, you and Robert are — are — "

"Well, what?" asked Iris.

"Are awfully alike," said Polly.

There was a pause. The stricken Iris spoke faintly. "Carol," she asked, "is there a drink in the house?"

It was not until supper was over that the details which Caroline and Iris longed to know about the new arrival could be pieced together. Polly's information, though freely given, was unexpected, jumbled, and altogether bewildering. The fragments of conversation, however, gathered during supper, could be put together to form a fairly clear picture of her background.

Her mother, she told them, had died at her birth. She mentioned the place in Mexico at which the event had occurred, but it, and innumerable tongue-twisting place-names that followed, made Iris's head ache and drove her to plead with Polly.

"Don't bother to pronounce them," she begged. "Just say Timbuktu each time. It'll mean just as much and won't make my head spin."

In Timbuktu, therefore, Mrs. Andrews had died and Polly had entered the world, and for the next twenty years had wandered over its face. Daddy, she explained, was something to do with finance. When anybody wanted to start anything, said Polly, and they weren't sure how it was going to work out and whether it was going to be a success or not, they sent for Daddy. Daddy examined the project and gave his estimate of how much, or how little, profit could be hoped for. On Daddy's estimate — which was always, said Polly, absolutely right — it was decided whether the scheme should go forward or be abandoned. Daddy was in great demand and received calls from all over the world, and he always took his daughter with him. Polly had been in every continent, in cities new and old; she had lived in flourishing communities and in towns still in their infancy. She had lived on ships and in hotels; she had flown many thousands of miles. She had never been to school for more than eight months at a time and Daddy had never owned a house. In cars, on horses, camels or elephants, Polly had followed Daddy and had never, in the course of all her journeys, known a day's anxiety or unhappiness.

She had met Robert Drake and experienced both these unpleasant sensations at once. He had been, said Polly, on the ship. The ship was taking Daddy on his usual business, this time in Florida; Robert was on his way to inaugurate a Drake Club at Miami. He seemed to like Polly, and Polly loved him very much indeed, but at the end of the journey he had vanished with scarcely a good-by, and with no word of any future meeting. Four months later, he walked into Daddy's suite at the hotel in London, resumed his friendship with Polly where it had left off, and, a month later, asked her to marry him.

"And here," said Polly, "I am."

This fact was brought home to Caroline when, the next morning, she knocked gently on Polly's door and, getting no answer, opened it and peeped inside.

There was no sign of Polly, but there was a bulge under the bedclothes, at the extreme foot of the bed, which reassured Caroline as to the visitor's presence. She gave a glance round the room and, with astonishment and horror which every moment grew greater, saw that, if the appearance of the room was anything to go by, Polly was making preparations for a prolonged stay.

It was clear that in the past ayahs and amahs, bonnes and chambermaids had in turn picked up clothes from the floor and tidied the extraordinary collection of articles lying upon Miss Andrews's dressing table. Polly's suitcase, open and empty, stood in one corner of the room, while on the bed, on the floor, on the chair, trailing from the dressing table or hanging from half-opened drawers, were clothes of great and colorful variety. Caroline glanced at the cosmetics on the dressing table; they consisted of a jar of cold cream, a box of powder, and a battered lipstick. The rest of the table was littered with books, a wire hairbrush, a broken comb, a collection of beautiful silk stockings, and three or four piles of clean handkerchiefs.

It was no wonder, thought Caroline, that Polly had told her, late last night, that she felt completely at home. She certainly looked at home, but if this was what she could accomplish with the contents of one suitcase, it was going to be interesting to see how she disposed of the contents of the trunk which she had told them that Robert was bringing when he came.

Caroline closed the door and went softly downstairs. Iris was carrying the breakfast toast from the kitchen to the living room.

"Is she still asleep?" she asked.

"I think so. I can't see her," said Caroline. "She's either asleep or smothered. She's right at the — "

Iris, reaching for the butter, laughed. "I know. I looked in to see if she was up," she said. "Nice tidy girl, isn't she? What do you think of her?"

Caroline pulled a chair up to the table and began her breakfast, frowning over the double difficulty of answering Iris's question and making a tiny portion of butter spread over several inches of toast.

"I don't know what I think of her, exactly," she said at last. "It's rather like having a nice Upper-Fifth girl staying for the holidays, but then in a way she isn't at all school-girlish."

"I like her," said Iris.

"So do I," said Caroline. "Anybody would. She's sweet. But she dresses in a rather — I mean, did you see the clothes she changed into yesterday evening?"

"Yes," said Iris, "I did. A conglomeration of garments which, on anybody else, would have looked too frightful for words — that gorgeous bright blue Mandarin coat from, presumably, China, and a pair of awful slacks that must have cost a mint when they were new, but were covered with paint marks, and straw slippers from — would it be the West Indies? — and her hair in plaits round her head. I think she dresses by picking up things. First thing that comes to hand goes on."

"It did look like it," agreed Caroline.

It looked even more like it when Polly made an appearance half an hour later. There was a series of thumps from above and Polly came downstairs in impetuous haste, apologizing as she came for her tardy arrival.

She was dressed in a checked lumberjack blouse and a pair of dark blue skiing trousers. On her feet were woolly slippers. Her hair was drawn back tightly from her forehead into a bun on the top of her head and from the bun waved three small curls. On these Iris's eyes remained fixed, and Polly, seeing her glance, put up a hand and fingered the curls exploringly.

"They're sticking up, aren't they?" she said. "Shall I tuck them in? Do they look frightful?"

"It depends," said Iris. "If you didn't know they were there, they look terrible, but if you arranged them like that, they look too cute for words. Going skiing?"

Polly glanced at her trousers. "Oh — these? I packed in a hurry," she said. "I just pushed in the first things I found, but when my trunk comes — "

"There'll be several more skiing suits," said Iris. "Sit down. Carol's making you some more toast."

With a cry of dismay, Polly leapt into the kitchen. "Oh, Carol, don't make toast for me, please!" she cried. "I can make it myself, honestly. I can make toast; I make toast quite well. Do, please, let me do it!"

Polly's earnest desire to be of assistance did not end with toast-making. After two days spent in watching Caroline as she cooked, she begged to be allowed to take over the work.

"I know I can't cook," she pleaded, "but if you'll be patient, I'll learn awfully quickly, honestly I will, Carol, I truly will. If you'll just let me take it over, I'll come and ask you when I can't do it, and this'll be a wonderful opportunity for me to learn how to cook for Robert, because if I'm going to be married, I ought to know how to cook, oughtn't I, because if I ever have to, think how useful it'll be! And then you can practice singing properly and I do love hearing you and I'd much, much rather hear you singing than have you cooking all the time. Do let me try, Carol, won't you? Go on, Iris — do ask her!

And Iris can show me things. Can you cook, Iris?"

"No, I can't."

"Well, then, there you are. We can both learn together. We can go so far by ourselves, don't you see, and then if we can't finish off something, we can ask Carol and she'll show us. It's awfully easy, really—you can follow the book and do just as it says, and they give you temperatures for the ovens and everything. I've seen them. You put the oven onto— "

"Our oven," said Caroline, "doesn't have a temperature."

"Oh! Well, what does that matter? We can sort of guess, can't we? Oh do, Carol, do let's try it, can't we?"

It was agreed that the scheme might be tried. Iris refused to have anything to do with the cooking, but promised, on being pressed by Polly, to give whatever advice she could in times of emergency. Polly, overflowing with enthusiasm, hurried upstairs and returned in a few moments with an armful of magazines.

"Look, these have got heaps and heaps of recipes," she said. "Let's look at them and see what they all say. They're lovely pictures, aren't they? D'you think my things will look like that when I make them?"

The magazines were spread on the floor. Caroline and Iris sat upon chairs and

Polly, cross-legged, sat on the floor at their feet.

"Those are no use," said Caroline. "They're American magazines."

"Well, yes," said Polly, "but they've got much better colors and much better pictures. Look, here's something called Refrigerator Cookies. You — "

"No refrigerator," said Iris.

"Oh! Well, this one — Sugar Bubbles," suggested Polly.

"No sugar," said Caroline.

"Oh! Well, what about this one?" said Polly, undaunted. "Syrup Stand-Ups. You take one and a half cups of syrup — "

"Which we haven't got," put in Caroline.

" — and a cup of heavy cream," went on Polly. "What's heavy cream?"

"What's cream?" inquired Iris.

"And half a cup of butter," Polly read on. "Half a cup — Does that mean you have to melt the butter and pour in half a cupful, or do you have to put in half a cupful of lumps of butter?"

"I can't tell you, but it doesn't make any difference," said Caroline, "because we finished the last lump at breakfast this morning. What else does the book demand?"

"It says press in a pecan and — "

"What sort of dish would a pecan be, and why do you have to press something into it?" asked Iris.

"A pecan's a nut," said Polly. "Don't you have pecans?"

"No — go on," said Caroline.

"Garnish with lemon and — "

"We haven't," said Caroline, "any lemons."

Polly looked gloomily at the appetizing illustrations. "All of them," she complained, "say things we don't have."

"That," said Caroline calmly, "is the great drawback. But you'll find it's stimulating to read recipes of that kind. It makes you remember the names of things you'd forgotten, and it's so much more exciting than being told how to serve a week's breakfasts on the bits of leftover potatoes or that dreadful pale yellow fish which there seems to be so much of nowadays. But at the same time, it's rather dashing to find that you can't make any of the lovely things they make pictures of."

"Aren't the Americans supposed to be a go-ahead lot?" asked Iris. "Why don't they go ahead and issue the ingredients with the magazines? 'Take fourteen eggs (herewith and the cream and sugar inclosed in the pink and blue packets. Mix well and add to the butter given away with this month's issue.' Crumbs! I'd even pay a bit more for a magazine like that."

"Well, it doesn't matter," said Polly philosophically. "We'll just have to cook with what we've got."

Polly cooked. The kitchen, which was scarcely of modern design and could not be said to be well-planned, had always been a place which Caroline found difficult to keep tidy, but after the preparations for Polly's first lunch, during which she refused all offers of help, the room looked as though an explosion had taken place inside it. In the sink, on tables, even on the stove, were piled dirty dishes, saucepans, bowls and utensils of every kind. Almost every article in the room appeared to be stacked, awaiting cleaning.

Great had been the preparations for very little result. The cook, hot, weary, and disheveled, served for lunch, seventy minutes late, some tinned soup and a mess of what might have been meat balls swimming in fat which Caroline had carefully saved during the past weeks. Bread was eaten with this dish, since the potatoes, the cook informed them, had met with an accident. The steamed pudding, in spite of Polly's having followed the directions in the book implicitly, was still looking as it had looked when she put it into the bowl.

When the morning's chaos had been cleared, Iris, who had a healthy appetite and who foresaw hungry days before her, volunteered to give Polly the benefit of her limited cooking experience. Caroline expressed her relief, for Polly had used, for one meal, stores which ought to have been eked out, treasured, and made the most of for days to come. She agreed to leave the kitchen to Iris and Polly, and occupied herself in the bedrooms or the sitting room or at her singing practice, while the two cooks spent their time at the stove.

Cooking, to Polly, was science, art, and amusement rolled into one. It was also an occupation which afforded a series of enchanting sights. What, she asked, could be prettier than milk on the boil, pulsating gently, throbbing, and finally rising in a creamy lather and running in a foaming cascade down the sides of the saucepan? Frying was a constant excitement and she watched fascinated and oblivious to the charred remains in the pan, as the hot fat sent up little dancing spurts — as though, said Polly, it was raining into the frying pan. She opened the oven door to watch the miracle of a sponge cake, once an uninteresting white powder in a packet, rising in a delicate, golden brown curve. Little cakes, put into too hot an oven, soared into brown bubbles and then dropped, crisp little pieces, with interesting thuds, to the bottom of the oven. There was not, she assured Iris, a dull moment, and Iris, hurrying from the meat burning in one place to the potatoes burning in another, agreed. On the fifth day, she confided to Caroline that, while she found herself liking Polly more and more, she felt extremely sorry for Robert.

"That's how I feel, too," said Caroline. "Or that's how I feel at times. I — well, fluctuate perhaps is the word, between feeling sorry on his account and apprehensive on hers. It's confusing, isn't it? Do you think she'll make him a good wife?"

"She won't make a wife at all," said Iris. "She'll just go on being Polly. For twenty years she's followed Daddy round happily and for another twenty she'll tail along after Robert. Where's the difference? They both take her from one place to another. She's used to waking up one day and seeing a Chinese and waking up the next day and seeing a Zulu and waking up the next day and seeing a Mexican. One day she'll wake up and see Robert in her room instead of Daddy in the next room — that's all. She'll put M.D. on her luggage instead of M.A., and I suppose every now and then Robert'll locate her in a tight ball down at the bottom of the bed and wake her up — if anything can wake her, once she's asleep — and make love to her. And I suppose she'll wake up one morning," continued Iris, "and say, 'Oh, look what I've found, Robert — the tweeniest, tweeniest baby and it looks exactly like you.' And they'll engage a competent woman and pay her a huge salary to look after it in between voyages. It's quite simple. Polly'll be happy and the nurse'll be happy and the baby'll be happy."

There was a pause.

"And Robert?" asked Caroline.

"Robert? Robert," said Iris, "will be in charge of the whole circus. And it serves him jolly well right."

CHAPTER ELEVEN

A few days after Polly's arrival, Caroline found herself trying to remember what life had been like for the brief time she had been alone at Lilac Cottage. She looked back nostalgically, thinking of the quiet days when Iris's typewriter had not clattered on the unsteady table, when peals of laughter or the sound of breaking dishes had not sounded in the kitchen, when Polly's light, gay tones and Iris's swift decisive ones were not heard ceaselessly, upstairs or downstairs, in the bedroom discussing clothes or in the kitchen discussing food. Peace, she realized with a sigh, had indeed fled.

Mr. Swintzchell's visits were no longer limited to Thursdays. He had met Polly. He was charmed with the new addition to an already delightful household and deeply interested to hear the long list of failures which constituted, to date, Polly's menus. He went into the kitchen, advised, superintended, and delivered a speech condemning all cookery books.

"When you are proficient," he told Polly, "then you must look into the book and say, 'What shall I cook?' But now, when you know nothing, you must do only the simple things. You must throw away the books, all the books, and you must use your head to cook. I will show you."

Nor was Mr. Swintzchell the only visitor. Colonel Brock called frequently; Iris, seeing him approach, fled upstairs and shut herself in her bedroom; Polly made a brief and polite appearance from the kitchen with Mr. Swintzchell and then, with him, went back to work. It was left to the unfortunate Caroline to sit through the tedious and repetitive monologue.

One afternoon there was a knock at the door and Caroline, answering it, saw before her a small boy with large ears.

"Good afternoon," he said politely. "Please, is Miss Drake in?"

"Come in, won't you?" said Caroline. She went to the foot of the stairs. "Iris," she called, "there's somebody to see you."

"My name's Carruthers," said David.

"Oh — how do you do?" said Caroline. "Won't you sit down?"

David sat down and rose again as Iris came downstairs.

"Oh — hello, David," she said. "How nice to see you. Been swimming again lately?"

David gave a grin. "No, Miss Drake. Twice I got over all right, and the third time, the other day, I nearly got over, but I didn't fall in." He became serious as he announced his business. "I came," he said, "because Mr.

Sheridan sent me. He said that you — well, you asked me and Winter and Stuffy to tea one day."

"I did, and I'd love you all to come," said Iris, "but Mr. Sheridan murmured something, I thought, about — "

Mr. Swintzchell's head appeared round the kitchen door. An arm in a floury coat sleeve waved apologetically.

"I am sorry," he said. "In cooking, I forget. Mr. Sheridan talked to me about your kind invitation and I went to ask Mr. Rawlinson and — "

"Who," inquired Iris, "is Mr. Rawlinson? Is he coming to tea, too?"

"No, no, no," said Mr. Swintzchell. "But it is necessary to ask. Mr. Rawlinson is the — the — "

"He's our Form Master," supplied David.

"Yes — that. And so," continued Mr. Swintzchell, "he said it would be quite all right, and he asked Mr. Plaistow and — "

"He's our Headmaster," said David.

"And Mr. — "

"Allow me," begged Iris. "Mr. Plaistow approached Mr. Clunes. Right?"

"That's it," said David.

"And the Headmaster," said Mr. Swintzchell, "said that you are very kind, and in this case it is not necessary to write to the parents to get permission because you are a friend of Miss Stannard and he has asked — "

"Don't break it too suddenly," said Iris. "but can the boys come?"

"That is it — yes," said Mr. Swintzchell, preparing to withdraw. "What day you fix, the boys can come."

"But it must be at the week end," said David. "We aren't allowed out except at week ends."

"Well, let's make it this week end, shall we?" said Iris. "Will you give my compliments to your friend Winter and and — ?"

"I say, thanks awfully," said David. "He'd like it, awfully, if you'd ask him yourself."

"Well, next time he's passing," said Iris, "I'll be only too — "

She paused. David had gone to the door and opened it. Outside was standing a small boy. He snatched off his cap, smiled eagerly, and stood on one foot.

"Won't you come in?" said Iris.

Alan Winter came in, shuffled his feet — under the impression, perhaps, that there was a door mat under them — and looked expectantly at his hostess.

"This is my sister, Mrs. West," said Iris. "I was just asking David if you'd care to come to tea on Saturday."

"I say, thanks awfully," said Alan. "It's awfully good of you. Thank you. Yes, thank you, I'd love to, awfully."

"Good," said Iris. "And will you bring — well, I don't know his name, but you call him Stuffy, don't you?"

"Yes, that's what everybody calls him," said David. "Stuffy."

"Stuffy," agreed Alan, nodding his head in corroboration. "He — I hope you don't mind — he sort of came along and — "

Iris glanced at Caroline and Caroline, walking to the door, opened it and admitted the waiting Stuffy.

"Ah! Now we're all here," said Iris. "Will you, being now assembled, come and have tea on Saturday?"

There was a chorus of eager assent. Everybody would be charmed to come to tea on Saturday. David turned to Caroline and added a half-shy sentence. "Mr. Sheridan said — well, I'm pretty good at making things," he said, "and I can mend them, too, and Mr. Sheridan said that I was to tell you that if you had any — any — "

"Minor repairs," put in Winter.

"Yes — if you had any, then I can do them," offered David. "I can stay now, if you like, Mr. Sheridan says, and do anything now and then go back with Mr. Swintzchell."

"That's an awfully kind offer," said Caroline gratefully. "Just at the moment, though, I can't think of — "

"Oh, Carol," exclaimed Iris eagerly, "the ironing board!"

"Oh, yes, the ironing board," echoed Caroline. "It gave way in the legs — I don't know how seriously. If you could look at it — "

David and his two friends were led upstairs and shown the ironing board propped against the wall on the landing. After a brief but expert examination, it was agreed that the job would take no more than half an hour.

"Tools?" asked David.

"Well, there's a box of some kind of things," said Caroline. "This way."

She led the boys to the tool box and watched them select the tools necessary for the work. David rose from his knees and gave an order to Winter.

"You go back," he said, "and tell Mr. Sheridan we're working and we'll come back with Mr. Swintzchell, like he said."

"Go on, Stuffy," said Winter. "Leg it."

"But who," objected Stuffy, "will sort of hold things?"

"I will," said Winter. "Go on — push off."

Stuffy's face registered emotions not far removed from despair and Iris spoke impulsively. "I'll go," she said. "I've promised to type some notes for Mr. Sheridan, and this is as good a time to get them as any other."

"I say, will you really?" said Stuffy in an ecstasy of gratitude. "I say, that's awfully good of you. Thanks."

Iris put on a coat and went out of the house and walked to Holly Lodge. She knocked at the front door and Michael Sheridan answered the summons. If he was surprised to see Iris, he made no sign. "Can I come in, or do I have to ask Mr. Rawlinson and Mr. Plaistow and Mr. Clunes?"

Michael stood aside. "Come in," he said. "I see you've met the boys."

"I left them," said Iris, "mending an ironing board that collapsed under the strain of getting the creases out of my brother's fiancée's innumerable suits of clothes. There was a deadlock over who should come and tell you what was going on — can't the poor little fellows go anywhere without being herded? — and I said I'd come and save them the trouble. And collect those notes at the same time."

"Which notes?" asked Michael.

"Pyrrhula pyrrhula pyrrhula," said Iris. "I know you haven't any great ideas about my fund of intelligence, but I'm a newspaper woman and that means I'm a journalist and that means I take a serious view of getting money out of editors — of whatever paper. If somebody's actually asking you to send stuff to them, it hurts me to let some other character cut in and take the business away. Editors don't wait. If you can get your mind off unessentials like French grammar and so on and so on and devote it to the not unpleasant business of trying to make some money, then go and get the notes and give them to me."

"It's very good of you," said Michael calmly, "but — "

"I know. You wouldn't dream of taking advantage of my kindness," said Iris. "For Pete's sake, stop standing there and do go and give me the thing and then I can go away and start on it. Go *on!*"

"There's no hurry," said Michael. "I can give you some sherry if you'd care for some."

"I never," said Iris, "drink sherry. Strange at it may sound, I never drink anything. It's very awkward at parties. I'll have a cigarette if you've got one."

"Sit down," said Michael.

He went to the cigarette box and Iris walked to the writing desk and picked up the photograph she had seen on her last uncomfortable visit to the house. Michael held out the cigarettes and she took one.

"She's like you," she said. "Or you're like her. Do you think she'd like me?"

"I don't know. You're not a very easy person to make up one's mind about," said Michael.

"I'm not?" said Iris in surprise. "I thought I was as — as transparent as — as anything."

"In some ways," agreed Michael. "You don't like schoolmasters."

"How could I like schoolmasters?" asked Iris. "You're the first schoolmaster I ever met in my life, and how do you behave? You sit through a long train journey without so much as looking in my direction. I didn't want you to flow on and on like Colonel Brock, but you could have made the usual remarks about the weather or the scenery, and it would have been graceful — and quite safe — to venture a word or two. Then you caught me trying to be a — a lady detective, and you behaved like a policeman looking for promotion. I meet you on a walk and you despatch me in charge of a small boy, and then, on the day of the Stannard tea party, we go for a walk together and end up nowhere. I made what's really a magnificent offer to copy out your dreary notes, and you act as though you thought I had ulterior motives. All I want you to do," she told him, "is just be normal and friendly and come and see me — and Caroline and Polly, who's practically a unique specimen — and listen to Caroline going Koo Koo and see the cat we've got, the one that drives its claws into everything within reach. If I thought you were really stuffy by nature, I wouldn't go to all this trouble, but somewhere under that unmoved exterior there must — there *must* be a man. What," she asked, "made you be a schoolmaster?"

"My father," said Michael, "was a schoolmaster. My grandfather was a schoolmaster, and his father and grandfather before him were schoolmasters. We've always been schoolmasters. We like being schoolmasters. We're good schoolmasters, born schoolmasters. It isn't just a profession. It's in our blood and — "

"Well," said Iris, "that covers that."

" — and we'll go on being schoolmasters," proceeded Mr. Sheridan.

"Yes?"

"Yes. In spite of the pull of other professions," said Mr. Sheridan, "and the desirability of being, for example, journalists, we shall go on being schoolmasters."

"Fine," said Iris warmly. "Now — "

"My cousins," said Mr. Sheridan, "are schoolmasters."

"Yes?"

"Yes. And my sons," said Mr. Sheridan, "will be school masters."

"You think so?" inquired Iris. "Well, let's by-pass your grandfather and your cousins and go on to you. Where were you born?"

"In Madeira," said Michael unexpectedly.

"Madeira? Ah! Your father was in charge of the Madeira College of — ?"

"No. It sounds a little like the low comedian's stock joke," said Michael, "but I was only born there because my mother happened to be there at the time — on holiday."

"Ah! She shouldn't have gone on the donkeys," said Iris. "Then what?"

"Then," said Michael, "we all went home."

"Where's home?"

"Home," said Michael, "is a house called

Monk's Lodge, at a place called Bishophowe in the county of Kent."

"Father living?"

"No."

"Died of schoolmastering," commented Iris. "Any brothers or sisters?"

"One sister — married."

"And does your mother live at Monk's Lodge?"

"And always will," said Michael.

"What's she like?" asked Iris.

"There's her photograph," said Michael.

"Well, yes. But what's she *like?*" asked Iris again. "Is she impossible to get to know, like you, and deep and reserved and — and — well, would she like *me?*"

Michael considered the matter. "Oddly enough," he said slowly at last. "I think she would. . . . And now I'll get the notes."

He left her for a few moments and returned with a sheaf of papers. "I've marked the places," he said. "You won't change your mind about that sherry?"

"No. You won't change yours, I suppose," suggested Iris, "about my being a man-hunter, a time-waster, a camera-grabber, and a — a lady detective?"

"You put it," said Michael, "very strongly. I do hope," he added, "we can meet during the holidays, when a man has more time."

Iris rose. "Good-by," she said.

"Good-by. It's nice of you to do those

notes," said Michael. "Don't let those boys make nuisances of themselves."

He accompanied Iris to the gate and then walked back meditatively into the house. His mother's picture, he noticed, was in the wrong place. He picked it up and looked at it for a few moments. Beautiful, even now, and gentle. It would be interesting to know what she had looked like at that girl's age, and whether she had a pretty voice and used it to talk about absolutely nothing. . . .

And whether she ran after schoolmasters.

Mr. Swintzchell took off the apron Polly had insisted on his wearing, gave it as his opinion that the cooking lesson had been entirely successful, and prepared, reluctantly, to depart.

The departure was a little delayed, for the boys, having mended the ironing board with a thoroughness for which Caroline was grateful, had found themselves ahead of schedule and, after a search, had discovered two little tins of white paint. With one of these they had applied finishing touches to the ironing board, which now looked very glossy and smart. Caroline, going out to the shed in which they were working, expressed her gratitude.

"It's really lovely," she said. "Thank you very, very much. I'm so sorry, but I think you'll have to hurry off, because Mr. Swintzchell is ready. Don't bother to clear up the tins. I'll put them away."

The three workmen gathered their tools, put them neatly into the tool box, and followed Mr. Swintzchell down the path. Polly, in the hope of meeting Iris on the way, decided to join the party, and Caroline walked with them as far as the village.

"There is one thing," said Mr. Swintzchell on parting, "that I forget. Tomorrow, for the singing lesson, I shall come at eleven o'clock. Is that the same for you?"

"It'll suit me very well," said Caroline.

"You are sure?" persisted Mr. Swintzchell, his head on one side, his look anxious. "The change of hour will not make you any inconvenience?"

"None whatsoever."

"Good! Then eleven o'clock."

It was dark, but the night was starry. Caroline turned homewards and, walking slowly, let her mind dwell on her brother's anticipated arrival. He must come soon, and when he came, things were going to be difficult.

There would be quarrels, she thought. There would be arguments and noise and disagreement. Things were going to be very uncomfortable when he arrived.

Approaching the house, Caroline saw with dismay Robert had already arrived. Outside the house stood his car, looking, in its sleek expensiveness and modernity, quite out of place in the country road. Caroline walked up the path and, entering the house, saw at once that Robert was, indeed, in residence.

Two large suitcases stood in the middle of the room; an overcoat lay across the sofa. On a small chair, and spilling over it, were several expensive magazines and three or four books whose titles Caroline had seen on her latest book list. On the floor beside the thickest book, happily engaged in chewing it to pieces, was a Cocker spaniel puppy.

Before the fire, sprawled in the best chair, with his feet on the mantelpiece, was Robert Drake. Caroline, looking at him, came to her usual conclusion that he was the most selfish young man in England — and the best looking.

Robert made no attempt to move. Reaching down to a plate on which lay the remains of the fruit tart which was to have served as a sweet for supper, he took a piece, put it into his mouth, and ate it with relish.

"It's so nice," said Caroline, "to see you. Please don't get up — if you were thinking of getting up."

"Where's Polly?" inquired Robert

"Is that dog," Caroline inquired in turn, "house-trained?"

"At that age? How could he be?" asked Robert in surprise. "Where's Polly?"

"In the village, and I don't suppose she'll

be long," said Caroline. "That's half the supper you've eaten."

"Bit stodgy," commented Robert. "Could you mix me a short?"

"I could if I had the ingredients," said Caroline, "but we don't keep anything in the house except sherry, and when I knew you were coming, I took the precaution of taking it upstairs and putting it under my mattress. Your dog," she informed her uninterested listener, "is throwing bits of paper all round the room."

"He does," agreed Robert. "Brought him for Polly. Nine champions in his pedigree."

"That won't save him," said Caroline, "if he forgets himself on my — No!" She gave a little scream, rushed to the puppy, and, seizing it by the neck, carried it hastily to the door and put it outside. "Just in time," she said, with a deep relief, "but I warn you, Robert, any mistakes of that kind and — "

"What d'you think of Polly?" asked Robert.

"Exactly what you thought I'd think of her," replied Caroline, "only with feelings of the deepest pity thrown in. I can't imagine what her father, who apparently actually met you, could be thinking of. If you're here, and I can see you are," she went on, "would you hand over your ration book and I'll see if I can get anything for you to eat before the shop shuts."

Robert put out a foot and kicked a piece of coal into place. "My what?" he inquired.

"Ration book," said Caroline. "A buff-colored document with — "

"Oh — that!" said Robert. "It's somewhere. Probably being posted on from whoever had it last."

"And who," asked Caroline patiently, "had it last?"

"Can't think," said Robert.

"If you don't produce your ration book within two days," said Caroline, "I'm afraid — "

Robert twisted himself on his chair and turned an irritated countenance on his sister. "Do you mean to tell me," he asked angrily, "that until I produce this thing which can obtain an infinitesimal quantity of stuff that could fit onto a saucer without hiding the pattern — d'you mean to tell me that until you get it, you can't produce any meals for me? Rot. Absolute and utter tripe. I could put the entire lot into your hands now, and it wouldn't do a farthing's-worth toward furthering your supplies. So, for God's sake, don't yap about shortages!"

There was silence. Caroline knew the futility of arguing. "That," she said at last, "disposes of the food question. Shall I show you your room?"

"I went up," Robert informed her, "and had a look round. I suppose you thought I'd sleep in that bed in the olive green surroundings?"

"Well," began Caroline, "we — "

"Being women," went on Robert, "the mere question of measurement wouldn't interest you. So you planned to put a man of six feet plus into a bed — if you can call it a bed — measuring five feet eight. Half of me, that is, hanging over the end. Well, I'm not going to sleep in the semi-open for anybody, not at this time of the year and in an unheated bedroom, thank you all the same."

"Where," inquired Caroline, "are you going to sleep?"

"In Polly's bed," said Robert, "but not," he added regretfully, "with Polly in it too. Her bed isn't the longest, but I tried the other two and the mattresses appeared to me to be filled with, in one case shingle, and in the other case lumps of earth. Polly can sleep in my room with the underwater décor."

"That," said Caroline, "settles the bed question."

Robert removed his feet from the mantelpiece and put them on the second-best chair. "Tell me," he said, "have you made up your mind about marrying Simon Gunter? I saw him in Town. He sent messages but they didn't sound important. He didn't say that anything was fixed up, so I presume you're still considering the matter."

"Quite right," said Caroline.

"Most women," observed Robert, "would unfold their hands after a couple of years' considering to find the fellow galloping down the aisle with a bride whose thought-processes were swifter. But you're safe with old Gunter — Rock of Gibralter."

"He's thirty-four. Is that old?" asked Caroline.

"It's old compared with what he would have been if you'd married him when he first asked you to, instead of choosing that old fossil Jeffry God-rest-his-soul West," said Robert. "But there's faithful old Simon still panting for you, and don't forget he's a better *parti* — and I mean *parti* with a final *i* — than your last. That grand old house and a nice park all to yourself, and a flat in Town. Think," he advised, "upon these things."

There were sounds of hasty footsteps on the path, and an instant later the door flew open and Polly, pink-cheeked and breathless, burst into the room.

"I saw the car," she said, the words coming out in a rush of excitement. "I saw the car and I *hared*. Oh, Robert darling, how lovely. You've come!"

Whether her brother would have stirred to greet his fiancée, Caroline could not decide, since Polly, with a bound, precipitated herself bodily onto him. Sitting upon him, she took his face between her hands and dropped upon it a succession of light, loving kisses. Robert received the caresses without visible emotion, only putting up a hand now and then to tuck in any stray tendril of Polly's hair that threatened to go into his eyes. Caroline thought that he looked like a man tolerating the enthusiastic greetings of a puppy, while Polly, she thought, looked like a child trying out a new rocking horse.

The second-best chair proved unequal to the double strain imposed upon it and, with a splitting sound, collapsed. Polly slid to the floor and stayed there, while Robert smoothed his disordered hair and turned to look at Iris, who had just entered.

"Hello," he said. "Polly wrote to say you were here. What're you on — holiday, or has old Ernest sent you down here to report on the High Ambo millinery?"

"Both," said Iris. "This is going to be a small house," she commented, "for the both of us."

"I shan't," promised her brother, "be in it long. I merely came to collect Polly."

"Well, leave Polly here," said Iris, "and ask someone to come and collect you. We like Polly."

"I knew you would," said Robert. "She's just the sort of girl that sisters — and mothers, if you've got any — instantly and erroneously assume will make just the right sort of little wife."

"You mean I won't?" asked Polly.

"Who cares?" answered Robert. "I brought you a puppy."

"A *puppy!* Oh, *Robert!*" Polly, with a squeak of delight, looked eagerly about her, under Robert's chair, and among the ruins of the second-best. "No puppy," she said finally.

"Caroline," said Robert, "threw it out into the rhododendrons."

"Oh, no. You *couldn't,* Caroline!" protested Polly, scrambling to her feet. She went outside and returned with the puppy held close to her cheek, cooing as its active little tongue licked her face in joy and friendship. "Oh, look, Caroline, look how sweet he is. What's his name, Robert?"

"Rajah of Singhpatia — or words to that effect," said Robert. "Nine champions, including three Rajahs, in his pedigree, and Caroline hurls him into the rhododendrons."

"Do you think," asked Polly, "that Solly'll scratch him?"

"You haven't, I hope," said Robert with distaste, "got a stinking cat?"

As if to answer in person this monstrous charge, Solly appeared at the kitchen door and, standing in the opening, looked unbelievingly at the scene before him. The puppy, after remaining quite still for a few seconds in order to place the species, bounded from Polly's arms and went into a full gallop across the room. Warning cries, shouts, were in vain; straight toward the waiting claws ran the Rajah, and Solly, taking leisurely aim, landed on the wet, black nose.

There was no doubt that the puppy was surprised. Retreating with a yelp, he sat at a safe distance and, raising a paw, drew it several times across the afflicted organ. Finding that the wounds were, after all, superficial, he sneezed, shook himself, and, crouching low, uttered a series of short, shrill barks, obviously intended to inform Solly that jokes were all very well, but must not be carried to excessive lengths.

Solly snarled.

Rajah approached, but to Solly's disappointment and fury the claw, usually so accurate, missed the puppy as he flew by. Solly sprang round and Rajah dodged. He approached from the fore and from the flank; he leapt, he gamboled; he came at a breathless rush and, applying a system of instant braking, came to a dead stop just beyond the cat's reach. Solly spat and clawed, arched and spluttered, but Rajah was young, tireless, and enjoying himself immensely. It was clear to Caroline that not only her own days of peace in this house were numbered. Solly, too, was to feel the effects of the changes that had come over the once quiet dwelling. It was difficult, remembering the cat's record of malignancy, to feel very much regret.

The evening passed, but its passing was

scarcely smooth. Several disagreeable facts had to be communicated to Robert, and he liked each less than the one before. There was no garage, and his car had to be housed in a shed belonging to Colonel Brock. Having returned from the shed, through a sharp fall of sleet, he found one Miss Stannard installed in what was now understood to be his own chair by the fire. Miss Louisa was on the sofa, and Robert eyed both ladies with equal dislike.

"We didn't," said Miss Stannard, "know that you were coming, but now that you are here, you must bring Miss Andrews one evening and come and dine with us."

"I'm so sorry," said Robert, instantly and firmly. "I shall be leaving almost at once."

"That's a pity," said Miss Stannard. "There's a good deal to see here. Shall you," she inquired, "go up and see the boys?"

Robert raised interrogative eyebrows, and Caroline, to spare Miss Stannard his query as to whether she meant the backroom boys, put in a hasty word. "There's a large prep school here, Robert," she said. "Castle Ambo."

"Never heard of it," said Robert.

This remark, designed to inflict humiliation, had quite the opposite effect. Miss Stannard, becoming pink with pleasure, directed a look of "You-see-my-dear" at her sister.

"Since the Stannards left its direction entirely to the new schoolmaster," she explained, "it has fallen upon sad days, but the site is magnificent — you must go up and see it. And what," she continued, "do you think of this new Government move?"

Caroline, to prevent Robert from telling her, interposed hastily. "Robert is a little out of touch," she said. "He's — he's been in America."

"Really? What," Miss Stannard asked him, "do you think of the Americans?"

Robert considered. "I think," he said at last, "that there are as many fat fools on *that* side of the Atlantic as there are on *this*."

There was a silence as his hearers digested this depressing statement. Miss Louisa appeared to be calculating.

"I take it," she said, "that that gives us a higher percentage of them?"

Robert looked at her with dislike. He was not used to having his barriers of insult passed over thus lightly. He looked at his watch and seemed to be comparing it with the clock on the mantelpiece.

"Don't worry," said Miss Louisa reassuringly. "Just going."

Caroline accompanied her guests out of the house and to the little gate, in the hope of making up for a little of her brother's rudeness. Miss Stannard, she could see, had forgotten all about Robert. She had picked up the wriggling Rajah and was stroking him affectionately. Miss Louisa looked at Caroline and nodded her head toward the house. "What they call temperament nowadays," she said. "But that girl'll cure him."

"Polly?" Caroline looked surprised and incredulous.

"Polly," repeated Miss Louisa firmly. "She'll do it — without knowing, of course. It'll be twenty years before she learns how to make a man comfortable."

"But — "

"Good girl, she is, and as blithe as a bird, too. You can see that she looks on him as some sort of circus performer. And so he is," said Miss Louisa. She watched her sister affectionately as Miss Stannard bent to put down the puppy, and spoke her final word on Robert. "Thinks he's going to have his own way with that girl," she said, "but he's probably picked the only woman in the world who's had more waiting on than he's had. If he wants anything at all done after they're married, he'll have to get down and do it himself. Yes — she'll cure him."

The sisters took their departure and Caroline walked slowly back to the house, to hear Robert's voice from above. He came down a few steps and bent an angry head over the banisters.

"Hey — Caroline."

"Yes?"

"Could you come up here," asked Robert, "and give me a hand? These cases are full of stuff for the laundry."

"The laundry," said Caroline, "only comes once a fortnight, and this isn't its week."

"What!" shouted the horrified Robert. He came downstairs to confirm this incredible information. "I'm talking," he said, "about dirty linen."

"So am I," said Caroline "The laundry comes from Blakely, which is four miles away. They collect every second Monday and bring the things back — well, when they're ready."

"You mean to stand there and tell me," said Robert slowly and incredulously, "that you keep your soiled, filthy, sweaty, unclean clothes in this house for a *fortnight?* You mean you — ?"

Words failed him and he stood glaring at his sister. Caroline opened her mouth to speak, but before she could do so, Robert had recovered his power of speech and was using it with energy.

"You, and the other millions like you," he said furiously, "are the cause of the whole rotten state of things. You're palmed off with a fourth-rate service, you're fobbed off with fifth-rate living and fortnightly cleanings and why? Why? Why? I'll tell you why. Because you stand for it, that's why. You and all the other spineless women all over this foully organized land. Laundry once a month? *Thank* yew. Hardly anything to eat? *Thank* yew. No decent service and no hope of any? No return to the decencies? No more joy, no more fun, no more anything but standing in the ruddy kitchen dabbling in stinking washing-up water? *Thank* yew. That's what you do — just *take* it, just swallow it all, just put up with it because why? Because you don't want anything else? No. Because you're too tired to care? No. I'll tell you why. Because you're too damn lazy and too damn cowardly to make a stand. While you accept a fortnightly service, you'll get it. While you ask for little, you'll get little and what's more, you'll get less and less and go on getting less and less. Upstairs there — " Robert half turned and pointed a finger at the ceiling — "up there I've got shirts. Dirty shirts. Dozens of 'em. And I'll tell you something — I'm going to get 'em washed. Tomorrow. Not this fortnight or next fortnight, but tomorrow. You can tell me where the bloody laundry functions and I shall drive in and I can tell you, here and now, that they will take my laundry, deal with it, and return it to me at the time I wish to have it."

"I believe you," said Caroline.

She did. She had no fear that Robert would not get the best of service — the best, in fact, of everything.

"You think it out," said Robert, going upstairs once more. "Just think it out. You've forgotten how to think, but try it. And you'll find," he told her, pausing at the bend of the staircase, "that you've let things get a bit lopsided. You've got into the habit of paying good money for bad service, and until you stop taking the worst and forking out the best, they'll continue to dish out the kind of living you never cease to grouse at and never do anything to alter. Women!" he ended in a tone of such contempt and loathing that Caroline half expected him to spit over the banisters. "Women!"

He was gone, and Caroline heard him no more until he expressed his intention of taking a bath and found that Polly had used up the available hot water and he would be compelled to wait until the tank had been reheated. When the tumult arising from this incident had died down, there was a lull which lasted surprisingly, all the next day, Robert and Polly having gone to Blakely early and come back at night.

CHAPTER TWELVE

Caroline, on her way downstairs the following morning, found herself held up by Polly who was sitting on the stairs practicing, she explained to Caroline, a new way of going down.

"You sit like this," she said, "and just push yourself off and bump onto the next step. It doesn't hurt if you just let yourself go, Caroline. Come and try it."

"Thank you," said Caroline, "but I wonder if you'd mind if I just went down on my feet in the ordinary way? Is Robert up?"

"No, he's asleep," said Polly, dropping her voice to a hushed whisper to impart this information, and then resuming her normal tones. "I peeped in to see if he was still there. I'm always afraid he'll go away in the night, as if I'd dreamt about him and he wasn't really here. Watch, Caroline — one, two, three, wheeeee!" Polly arrived at the bottom and became entangled with the wildly excited puppy, who had at that moment been brought in by Iris from his sleeping box in the shed.

Caroline stepped round the two wriggling bodies and went into the kitchen feeling that Robert's arrival had not, after all, made very much difference to the household — or to

Polly. The behavior of the engaged couple was, indeed, unorthodox. Polly's affection seemed to be divided equally between Robert and the puppy, whose name had been changed successively to Rex, Poogy, Bodge, Rollo, and last — but not, Caroline thought, finally — to Sam. Sam had done comparatively little damage in the house, for Caroline transferred him automatically to the rhododendrons whenever she came across him. He was showing a tendency to scamper there himself whenever he saw Caroline approaching, but he had, as yet, no idea why she should imagine he liked rhododendrons.

Polly got to her feet, and announced that Sam was a silly name for a puppy. "I'm going to call him Biff," she said. "He likes Biff. I tried it last night and he liked it awfully. You know, Iris, he's getting awfully clever."

"As how?" inquired Iris skeptically.

"Well, he's getting to know everything you say to him," said Polly proudly. "He's beginning to do what you tell him to go and do, too, and he does tricks and things."

"Go on — I'll watch," invited Iris.

"Well — look. Biff, Biff, Biff," called Polly.

Biff was galloping happily round a chair in pursuit of Solly, unaware that Solly had turned and was awaiting his approach.

"Biff! Come here, Biff," said Polly severely.

Biff, with a bound, rounded the chair. The

waiting, vicious claws sank deep into his nose and, with a yelp of rage, anguish, and frustration, he backed away and went up to Polly in order to lodge a formal complaint.

"There — he comes. You see!" said Polly.

"He comes. Next trick," demanded Iris.

"Well, you watch. Biff," commanded Polly, "go and get your ball."

Tongue out, tail wagging, Biff looked happily up at his owner.

"There — you see? He knows exactly what I'm saying," said Polly.

"Well, why doesn't he go and get it, then?" asked Iris.

"He will in *time*, don't you see?" said Polly. "He has to learn what it *is* first, and then after that he learns to do it."

"Wonderful! Next trick," requested Iris.

"Now watch him — he'll beg," said Polly. "Beg, Biff, beg! Up, good dog then, up!"

Biff gave a short, excited bark, ran into the kitchen, seized one of Caroline's shoelaces, bit it, and scampered back to his mistress.

"There — he knows I've said something for him to do," said Polly.

"You didn't say, 'Chew Caroline's shoelace,' " protested Iris. "You said, 'Beg.' "

"Well, he knows it's *something*," said Polly. "That's how they sort of learn, don't you see? You go on saying 'Beg' and 'Beg' and then they do."

"And by that time," pointed out Iris,

"Caroline hasn't got any shoelaces."

Polly snatched Biff, squirming and licking, into her arms. "They don't *appreciate* you, my lamb," she cooed. "They don't believe anything about you, because you're cleverer than that horrid Solly. They're jealous, that's what."

"Who does the cooking?" asked Caroline from the kitchen. "Come on, you two. There's work in here."

The meal over, Iris went to her typewriter and began to copy Michael Sheridan's notes. Polly dried the plates and ran races round the kitchen table with the puppy. Robert came downstairs, demanded hot coffee, drank it, and left the house to see to his car, and Caroline, watching him go, gave a sigh of relief. She wondered why Polly had not seen him off, and went to look for her in the kitchen. The kitchen was empty, but a call came from outside and Caroline, going to the back door, saw with astonishment that Polly was seated, cross-legged, on the damp ground, busily engaged in cleaning a saucepan with mud. She stared at her for a moment, too amazed to speak.

"Good Heavens, Polly," she said at last, "have you gone out of your mind? Do, for goodness sake, Polly, do get up at once! You'll catch your death of cold. Get up and come inside and don't be so — so crazy."

"Look, Caroline," said Polly, rubbing vigorously. "This is the way they clean them in India. I used to watch them. No powder, no anything. Just a bit of wet mud and there you are — look."

"Polly, come *inside,*" said Caroline. "I don't care how they did them in India. This isn't India and you can't sit on wet ground in this country. Come on in."

"I'm not cold," said Polly. "I never feel cold. Look how it's shining, Caroline, and look how you can save lots of money, because you don't have to use any of those powder things. Look — you can see your face."

"I don't *want* to see my face, Polly. Get up and come inside."

Polly rose reluctantly. "Don't you think it's nice and clean?" she asked in a crestfallen manner.

"The saucepan," conceded Caroline, "is clean. Your sleeves, your face, your blouse, and the back of your trousers are all covered with mud and I'm very angry with you."

She accompanied Polly to the kitchen sink and helped her to remove the mud, unmoved by Polly's insistence that it was still an excellent way of cleaning saucepans, and pointing out in her turn that those who had originated the method were unencumbered with sleeves, blouses, or backs of trousers, and had countenances of a shade not designed to show mudstains.

Having seen Polly embark upon her preparations for lunch, Caroline went into the living room and saw that Iris was still typing.

"You're busy, aren't you?" she asked. "Is that work for Ernest?"

"Ernest? Good Heavens, no!" said Iris, without pausing.

Caroline looked at her in perplexity. "But you told me, didn't you, that he was paying you a larger salary. I mean, oughtn't you to be — ?"

"Out on the prowl? Certainly I ought," said Iris, looking up. "But one thing at a time. Ernest told me I had to get to know the people at the School, and I'm getting to know them — like anything. Carruthers, Winter, Stuffy, Swintzchell — "

"And here's another one of them," interrupted Caroline, looking out of the window. "Robert's bringing — come and look — the one who was standing near you at the station when you arrived."

There was a scrape of a chair and a shuffling sound as a sheaf of papers fell to the floor. Caroline found Iris by her side.

"Michael Sheridan."

"Is *that* who he is!" said Caroline. Her voice became anxious. "You don't think Robert'll ask him to stay to lunch, do you?"

Iris, without answering, turned and gathered the papers which had fallen to the floor, and was straightening them as the door was flung open and Robert entered, ushering in Michael Sheridan.

"Come in," he said. "That chair, I think." He indicated the third best. "Most of the others collapse as soon as you sit on them. My sister Caroline, my sister Iris. How about a drink? They only keep sherry here, God knows why. Sit down. How about lunch? Do you have to go back?"

"Yes, he does," said Iris. "Polly's cooking it and he'll get a much better one up at the School."

"You know him?" asked Robert.

"Of course I know him," said Iris. "I do half his work for him. Carol, this is Michael Sheridan. French Master, riding master, bird master — and so on."

"How do you do?" said Caroline. "What nice boys you've got at Holly Lodge. I — "

"Can't discuss boys," interrupted Robert. "Sit down, Sheridan."

Michael Sheridan remained standing and looked at Caroline. "I was walking up," he explained, "to see your brother and ask him if he could find time to look at some of the model yachts — only small affairs, of course — that the boys have built. And also to try to persuade him to have one last try at persuading old Lord Fellmount to let the School rent that little lake in his grounds. We've asked once or twice, but if someone like your brother — with a bit of standing, as it were, in the sailing world —

were to make a last attempt — "

"If you could get a day off," suggested Robert, "I could run you over to see a fellow not far from here who's got one or two fine little models. We could perhaps pick up one or two and bring 'em back with us. He's a good fellow. He's been experimenting on the things for years. He taught me a devil of a lot. How about running over to see him?"

Michael hesitated. "It wouldn't be possible, normally," he said, "but I believe young Carruthers — well, he might have to pay a short visit home in a day or two, and I could take him to the main line and you could pick me up there. But it wouldn't be a very profitable journey from the School's point of view, since we've no water to sail the boats in. If you could have gone to see Lord Fellmount — "

"I'd go up," said Robert, "if I thought it the slightest use. But a stranger couldn't do much if you've already had a couple of shots at it."

"If you *saw* it," said Michael, "if you saw what a fine stretch of water it was. And not too big. In fact, just right. And practically under our noses. But I'm afraid, as you say, nothing would move the old fellow."

"Well, let's get some models together anyway," suggested Robert. "Perhaps the old boy's never seen one afloat. What do you think of the Duralumin masts?"

What Mr. Sheridan's opinion on Duralumin masts was nobody could find out, for at that moment the kitchen door burst open and Polly entered, carrying carefully a glass bowl.

"Look — it's set! It really has set, Carol. Can't you see how it's set? Look, Robert. That's the first junket I've made that ever junked, isn't it Carol?"

"Congratulations," said Caroline. "This is Mr. Sheridan, Polly."

"This is my fiancée," said Robert. "Go and put that infant diet away, Polly, and go and get dressed and we'll all go into the comparative civilization of Blakely and eat a real lunch. Some English clothes," he added. "Nothing Chinese or Scandinavian and nothing bizarre."

"Bizarre?" Polly looked astonished. "My clothes? They're not. They don't match, because I bought them in different places, that's all. And I can't come out because I want you to eat what I've cooked, because if you ever have to, you'd better begin now and then you'll get used to it. Won't he get used to it, Mr. Sheridan?"

Mr. Sheridan looked at the junket and spoke with a certain relief in his voice. "I'm afraid I've got to get back," he said. "But I'll take you up on that offer, Drake, if I can get the time off."

"I've finished your notes," said Iris, "but you can't have them until I've checked them.

If you tell me when you're going to be in, I'll come round and fetch some more."

"Thanks," said Michael. "I'm doing nothing late this afternoon. Will that be all right for you?"

"It'll be perfect," said Iris.

Iris left the house at half-past three and walked slowly toward Holly Lodge. It was a dull afternoon; a thin, sleet-like drizzle was falling and there was a depressing haze in the air.

Nothing, however, could have depressed Iris just then. Her heart was beating quickly and she found it hard work to keep her steps to the slow pace necessary if she was not to get to her destination far too early.

She went through the village and then, hesitating at the crossroads, turned impulsively onto the road leading away from Holly Lodge. She went a little way, struggling to analyze her feelings and to bring her mind to its normal state of clearness and efficiency.

She was on her way, she told herself soberly, to collect some more hieroglyphics from a bird enthusiast. That was all. Her interest in the matter lay solely in getting the notes to a state in which an editor would consent to look at them. Nothing more. There was no occasion for excitement, for this odd breathless feeling which she hadn't experienced since she dived off the top board when she was fifteen. She was a cool young woman; she went out frequently to theaters, cinemas, dances, concerts. Why, therefore, should she feel this unwonted exhilaration at the prospect of going to visit a schoolmaster? She was tripping along like a — like a shepherdess going to meet her swain.

Iris came to an abrupt stop, her head spinning. Taking a deep breath, she walked on again more slowly and, in a few moments, she found her brain clear and in full possession of the shattering truth.

She felt — it was useless to deny it, and stupid not to face it — she felt like a shepherdess. And she wished with all her heart that Michael Sheridan was her swain.

Iris walked steadily, her eyes straight ahead, struggling to marshal the facts in a sensible, straightforward way. She had read a great deal about love at all levels, but she had always felt that the subject had either been dealt with by overexcitable persons, or that she herself was fortunately made of sterner stuff than the average heroine. She had never anticipated falling a victim to the very flutterings about which she had remained so skeptical, and she had never, she told herself bitterly, dreamed of the day on which she would fall a victim to a man she had seen less than half a dozen times and who, as far as she could tell, had never given her a thought in his life.

It was an unnerving spectacle, but Iris forced herself to look straight at it, and, as she looked, something rose and steadied her — a feeling that there was nothing, after all, very much wrong. She knew that she thought swiftly, made swift decisions, and was used to making her own way through life; there was nothing to be worried about if she fell in love quickly. Michael Sheridan was not, Iris remembered with rising spirits, the impulsive type. He had obviously been one of those children who catch things on the very last day of the quarantine. Things, with him, would go in very slowly, and they would go in very deep.

It was all right. What, Iris asked herself, had she to fear? She could lead him gently, and by imperceptible degrees, into loving her. A little patience . . .

Restored to her usual confidence, she paused, took her bearings, and went along a narrow lane leading back to the village. She walked quickly, humming snatches of song and feeling more than ever like a shepherdess.

She turned a small bend and there, straight ahead, walking swiftly and with evident purpose, was the object of her thoughts. No mistaking that tall, athletic figure. She was too early, after all, or didn't he intend to keep the appointment?

Iris felt an impulse to call out and run up to him, but no, she would not run after him and undoubtedly be told she was interfering with a bird hunt. The village was in sight. She would turn off soon and make her way slowly to Michael's cottage. If he was going home soon they would probably arrive at the same time. She looked about for a short cut that would take her directly to the village. When she turned back, to her surprise, Michael was no longer in sight.

Iris frowned. The path was straight. He could not have walked so fast as to be out of sight. It was obvious that he had left the road and taken to the fields. Perhaps it would be nice, after all, she thought, if they walked back together — if she could find him. No point getting there before he did, anyway. Without pausing to think further, Iris walked on, looking to right and left to see at what point he could have branched off. The hedges on either side were thick, but at last she saw an opening and, some distance beyond it, a gate.

She struggled through the gap and found herself in a large field. Crossing it, she went down a steep bank, scrambled up a slope, and found herself in a wooded spot overlooking the road.

She leaned against a tree and looked about her; she could see no sign of Michael, but she felt convinced that he had not gone far.

After waiting a few moments she decided to go on. He might be in the hollow beyond; he might —

At the same moment, there came a shout from above and a sound of crashing branches. From the trees there hurtled a camera, landing with absolute accuracy on the side of Iris's head. In an instant the search was over; all was idyllic peace and charm.

On the ground, unmoving, eyes closed in sleep, lay Iris. Holding her in his arms and regarding his battered camera with infinite regret, knelt the French Master, Mr. Sheridan.

CHAPTER THIRTEEN

Iris hadn't been gone long when Caroline heard a knock on the front door and, opening it, found David Carruthers on the step.

"Good afternoon," he said. "Please, could I see Mr. Drake?"

"Come in, won't you?" said Caroline. "I'm sorry," she went on, closing the door behind him, "but Mr. Drake went out with Miss Andrews just a few moments ago, and I'm afraid they won't be back until this evening."

David's face fell.

"Can I," asked Caroline, "do anything?"

"Oh, no — no, thanks," said David. "Mr. Sheridan sent me with a message. The ground was too bad for games today and he'd arranged with Mr. Raynes — he's the Games Master, Mr. Raynes — that all the boys who had model ships, or who wanted to make model ships, could do their prep now and then listen to Mr. Drake talking to them if he could come and talk to them. But now," ended David, "he can't, can he?"

"I'm afraid not," said Caroline. "If you'd been just a little earlier — "

"It doesn't matter," said David. "He can do it another day, if he's in, and Mr. Sheridan says they aren't a bad collection. Porter's got a jolly fine one. He didn't make it himself, but Mellick made his himself and it's jolly good." He paused and, shifting his weight to the other leg, looked toward the door. "I expect," he said, "I'd better be going." His eyes went to the corner of the room in which Caroline had placed the broken chair. "That bust?" he inquired.

"Well, yes. Mr. Drake sat on it rather too heavily," said Caroline, "and it just collapsed."

David walked across the room and, stooping, examined the damage. "I could mend that," he said finally. "Would you like me to mend it? I'd like to mend it, rather."

"That's awfully kind of you," said Caroline, "but won't you have to get back and tell Mr. Sheridan — ?"

David bent down once more and ran his hands over the break in the chair. When he raised his head, he looked a little flushed.

"As a matter'r fact," he said awkwardly, "I mean — "

The damage claimed his attention once again, and Caroline, puzzled but willing to assist him, tried another opening.

"If we'd had a telephone," she said regretfully, "we could have rung up to ask if you could stay to tea — "

"Yes," said David. "We could've easily. It isn't a week end, but as there weren't any games and as Mr. Drake isn't here and as we've done our prep, it would have been, well, sort of all right."

"Yes," said Caroline. "What a pity."

There was a pause. David cleared his throat. "Yes," he said. "I mean, it could've been all right. I did say to Mr. Sheridan that p'raps Mr. Drake would be out."

"Oh! Well — " Caroline trod delicately over ground that was growing every moment more slippery — "perhaps if you didn't go back, he'd realize that you'd — well, stayed."

"Yes. That's what we told him," said David.

"How nice," said Caroline. "Well, do you think, then, that it'll be all right if you stay to tea?"

"Oh, yes," said David, in a tone of deep relief. "Oh, yes, it'd be quite all right. I mean — " his voice faltered — "I mean, if you could've had Winter, too, it would — "

"Do bring him in," said Caroline cordially.

"Oh — thanks! Thanks!" David hurried to the door and, opening it, admitted the figure waiting on the doorstep.

"Oh — good afternoon, Alan," said Caroline. "We've just been arranging about tea."

Deep relief overspread Master Winter's countenance. "I say — thanks. Thanks awfully," he said.

"I'm afraid I'm the only one in," said Caroline. "Tea first," she inquired, "and then chair-mending, or mending first and tea afterwards?"

David led his friend to the broken chair and looked at it speculatively. "Well, I think," he said, "tea first in case we haven't time to actually finish the chair and have to leave some of it."

"Tea first," said Caroline. "I'll show you where things are and you can lay the table."

"Yes," said David. He glanced at his friend and gave a gentle cough. "I wonder," he said, "if you'd mind — "

"Not a bit," said Caroline. "I'd love it. Do ask him to come in, won't you?"

There was a scamper as the two boys crossed the room together and wrenched open the door.

"Come on in, Stuffy," said David.

It was a happy party that assembled a little later at the tea table. The food appeared to be adequate even for three schoolboys, and nothing remained for Caroline but to break through the thin crust of good manners which prevented the visitors from eating as much as they longed to. Stuffy was clearly under observation, and as the meal went on, Caroline thought his nickname extremely suitable. She felt sorry for him, for in the middle of his largest and most luscious mouthfuls he would look up to encounter the fierce glares of his friends, and have serious difficulty in disposing of the portions in a polite manner. He lacked the technique of the other two, who took enormous helpings with polite murmurs of thanks and, it seemed to Caroline, disposed of them without the preliminary of mastication.

The meal over and the plates cleared, the three boys carried the chair into the kitchen and, in a short space of time, had made an efficient splint for the broken leg. Caroline viewed the work admiringly and declined David's offer to "smack a bit of paint on to finish it off."

"No, thanks," she said. "I think we'll leave it as it is and, anyway, I'm afraid you'd have to leave it in the middle."

"I suppose so," said David. "We could — "

He paused. A series of knocks was sounding upon the door. Caroline opened it and Mr. Swintzchell, breathless and looking extremely agitated, stepped inside.

Caroline's first thought was regret at having allowed the boys to stay without definite permission. They had probably put a garbled request before Mr. Sheridan and obtained an imaginary consent, and now Mr. Swintzchell had come to —

Mr. Swintzchell, however, looked at the boys with nothing more than surprise. "You are here?" he asked.

The boys, no doubt feeling this fact to be obvious, made no reply. Caroline looked at the old professor and he pushed back his white locks and spoke with something of an effort. "It is very kind," he told Caroline, "to ask the boys. They have behaved well?"

"Very well," said Caroline. She wondered what had brought the old man, and she knew that the boys, sensing his agitation, were anxious to stay and find out the cause of it.

Mr. Swintzchell cleared his throat, smiled at the boys in an absent way, pulled down his waistcoat, and addressed Caroline. "I come," he said, "to tell you that your sister is with us."

"Iris? Well, that's awfully kind," said Caroline, puzzled. "But you shouldn't have — "

"Oh, it was no trouble," broke in Mr. Swintzchell eagerly.

"It was no trouble — none at all. Mr. Sheridan said, 'I will stay here and it will be you to go,' and so I came."

Caroline, quite at a loss, thanked him once more.

"And besides," went on Mr. Swintzchell, "Mr. Sheridan could not have come — not possibly. For he, too, needed some attention. You see, he was — "

Mr. Swintzchell stopped, wrung his hands together, smiled reassuringly at Caroline, pulled down his spectacles, and gazed abstractedly over them. A little air of tension grew; the boys waited with well-controlled eagerness. Caroline felt that something must be done to help the hesitating old man.

"Why," she asked, "did Iris ask you to bring a message?"

"Your sister? Oh, no, she didn't ask me," exclaimed Mr. Swintzchell. "She is — as I tell you, it was Mr. Sheridan. He said what to do. He said, 'You go to Mrs. West and I will go for the doctor and — ' "

The color flew from Caroline's cheeks and the faces of the three boys became red with excitement.

"Somebody's hurt!" said Caroline.

"Nobody," said Mr. Swintzchell earnestly, "has hurt nobody. It was just an accident, that is all. Mr. Sheridan — "

"Is Iris hurt?" asked Caroline, her tone abrupt.

Mr. Swintzchell put his head on one side and considered the matter. "Hurt? A little — yes," he admitted reluctantly. "But there is nothing to worry. Not-hing. She is safe in bed. We put her in the room of Mr. Sheridan and she is safe. It fell," he explained belatedly, "on her head."

"What did?" asked the frightened Caroline.

"It fell from the tree. The camera was in the tree and it came down — " Mr. Swintzchell, warming to his story, raised a hand and brought it down swiftly through the air — "it came like this — so!"

Caroline made no further effort to extract

information from Mr. Swintzchell. She ran upstairs, snatched a scarf and coat, and flung them on as she hurried down again. Everybody now knew what had happened. A camera had come out of the trees and hit Miss Drake; the doctor had been summoned; the patient was in bed at Holly Lodge. Caroline was eager to get there as fast as possible to glean further details.

Before the party had been long on the road, the three boys began to draw ahead. Soon they vanished and when Caroline, slowing her impatient steps to Mr. Swintzchell's pace, arrived at the house, David was waiting at the gate with a brief and sensible report.

"She's all right, I think, Mrs. West," he said. "Mr. Sheridan was taking bird photographs and his camera fell out of the tree and sort of hit Miss Drake for six. Mr. Sheridan carried her here 'cos it was nearest and the doctor's waiting for you and says it's all right."

"Thank you, David," said Caroline gratefully.

She hurried inside. Michael Sheridan was standing in the hall and she saw that his shoes and the lower half of his trousers were caked with mud. He looked pale and tired but his voice was as slow and calm as usual.

"I hope you weren't alarmed, Mrs. West," he said. "The doctor says there's nothing to worry about. He's waiting for you."

He led Caroline upstairs and into a large, pleasant bedroom. By the light of the reading lamp beside the bed, Caroline saw Iris lying with closed eyes. The doctor rose from a chair nearby and approached Caroline.

"She's quite all right, Mrs. West," he said, "but if I were you I'd leave her here. She got a nasty knock. It'll patch up, but she'll need rest and quiet."

Caroline felt a little shaky. The sight of her sister, usually so full of life and spirits, lying quiet and still, in the house of comparative strangers, was not a sight on which she could look calmly.

With a murmur of thanks to the doctor, she went across the room and, sitting gently on the bed, took Iris's hand.

"Hello, Carol," said Iris, without moving.

Caroline pressed the hand she held, and asked a gentle question. "How d'you feel, Iris?"

"I feel," said Iris, after painful thought, "like hell." She paused and then went on with a little quaver. "Carol," she asked, "can't I come home now?"

"Well — no. Not just at once, darling," said Caroline. She saw the doctor making graphic signs, and nodded. "You've got to go to sleep," she told Iris.

"You won't go away?" asked Iris.

"Only for a little while. I shan't leave you for long," promised Caroline. "Try to sleep, Iris."

She followed the doctor downstairs and saw Michael Sheridan talking with a man with gray hair and a thin but curiously young face.

"This is the Headmaster, Mrs. West," said Michael.

"How do you do?" said Caroline. "I'm afraid this is going to upset the house rather seriously tonight. I'm awfully sorry."

"All the apologies, Mrs. West," said Mr. Clunes, "must come from our side. I've never had a man on my staff who did anything so ungallant, and the least we can do now is to ask you to let us make you as comfortable as circumstances will permit. How," he asked the doctor, "is Miss Drake?"

"She'll be all right," said the doctor, "but she mustn't move for a day or two. She was lucky. The thing was heavy, but it grazed the side of the head and didn't come down squarely. I don't think there's any concussion, but she'll have to be quiet."

"Should we send one of the Matrons down?" asked the Headmaster.

"Oh no, please!" said Caroline. "If I may sit with my sister tonight, I can do everything that's necessary. Mr. Sheridan loses his bedroom, I'm afraid — "

"Leave all the arrangements to us," said

Mr. Clunes. "And please forgive us."

"Could I," pleaded Caroline, "know exactly what happened?"

"I don't think," said Mr. Clunes, "that anybody's very clear on the subject. What exactly happened, Sheridan?"

"Well — " Michael looked at Caroline — "I've been trying for some time to photograph a nuthatch nesting in a hole in a tree — not a very easy job. I'd had the camera fixed up for some days hoping for a combination of, well, bird and weather and opportunity, but this afternoon I realized it was no go, and so I went up the tree to collect my gear. Just as I'd unleashed it from its mooring, I saw somebody suddenly appear underneath the tree like — like a dryad — " Michael blushed — "and I hadn't noticed anybody following me so I was startled, I guess, and I dropped the thing. It fell on Miss Drake," he concluded unhappily. "I'm sorry."

"I'm sorry, too," said Caroline. "My sister'll soon be all right, but I don't suppose the camera will, will it?"

"Serves him right," said Mr. Clunes. "You'll sleep up at the School, Sheridan, I suppose?"

"Yes, sir."

"That leaves Mr. Swintzchell to keep an eye on the boys. They won't worry you, I hope, Mrs. West?"

"Not at all. They've been very good indeed," said Caroline.

"Good. Oh — by the way, Sheridan — " the Headmaster put his hand into his pocket and brought out a letter — "this concerns young Carruthers."

Michael Sheridan took the letter and looked at the Headmaster with eyebrows raised in inquiry.

"His mother, sir?"

"Yes. What d'you think's arrived?" asked Mr. Clunes with an expressionless face.

Michael hesitated. The Head obviously had a joke up his sleeve.

"Twins, sir?"

"You're getting warm," said the Headmaster.

Caroline looked at him in horror. "You don't mean — could it be triplets?" she asked.

The Headmaster's face broke into an appreciative smile. "Triplets," he said. "Colonel Carruthers calls it a — well, perhaps we'd better not go into that. But young Carruthers is going to have a hard time living this down. Will you break the news to him, Sheridan? His father says he hasn't the courage to write for a day or two."

"I'll tell him, sir," said Michael.

Mr. Clunes, with further instructions to Caroline to make use of anything she needed for the night, took his departure, and the doctor, after looking at Iris once more and pronouncing her to be in a sound sleep, followed the Headmaster and promised to come in the morning.

Caroline found Mr. Swintzchell and the French Master waiting anxiously to do all in their power to make her comfortable. From the stores in the kitchen, Mr. Swintzchell produced sandwiches and coffee; Michael Sheridan stoked the boiler and the boys, tiptoeing, crept to their bedrooms and were seen no more.

Soon Michael Sheridan, with a pair of pajamas borrowed from his massive colleague, went to his temporary quarters at the School, and Caroline, realizing with some surprise that she felt weak and tired, said good night to Mr. Swintzchell and prepared to sleep on the sofa beside Iris. She had got half-way up the stairs when the doorbell sounded.

She turned. Mr. Swintzchell was going to the door, and she waited to see who was there. She heard a familiar voice, and in a moment her brother had stepped into the hall.

"Hello, Robert," she said.

Robert glanced up at her. "What's gone wrong?" he asked. "I put my car away and that old talking machine waylaid me and said something about Iris. She got a knock on the head — is that it?"

"Yes. I'm sorry," said Caroline, "but you'll have to manage by yourself tonight.

I'm staying here with Iris."

Robert frowned. "But she's all right, isn't she?" he asked with some irritation.

"Yes, she's all right," said Caroline, "but I'm not going to leave her tonight."

"Rot — she'll sleep like the dead," said Robert. "You can't expect Polly to — "

"Aaah!" Mr. Swintzchell gave an exclamation like that of a man coming to a late, but obvious conclusion. "Ah, of course, you are right!" He folded his hands across his stomach and gazed at Robert with admiration. "And you are the first to think of it. Here we have been busy, here we have been excited, nobody has said, 'But what of the little Polly and what of Robert?' And you are right. It cannot be expected that you shall two be alone. You see — " Mr. Swintzchell pushed out his lower lip and looked almost reproachfully at Caroline — "we did not think. But look — " he addressed the puzzled Robert reassuringly. "Look, you shall not worry. I myself, I shall come and I shall be the — the — I cannot find the word — yes, the chaperon!"

"Chaperon! Don't be a fool," said Robert bluntly. "We don't want a chaperon. We want a cook."

"I, too — the cook!" said Mr. Swintzchell triumphantly. "You wait five, ten minutes and I shall come with you when I have got my little box for the night."

He hurried up the stairs, passed Caroline with a breathless apology, and disappeared in the direction of his bedroom.

"Look," said Robert angrily, "I'm not going to have that fat fool ambling about a pocket-size house all night. You can tell him to take his prehistoric conventions and go to hell. If I want to skip the marital preliminaries, a ruddy organist isn't going to stop me. When he comes back with his nightshirt, tell him to unwrap it again and mind his own blasted business. I'm going. And if he wants to follow me, tell him to save his feet. He won't get in."

He turned to the door and walked toward it with long, angry strides, but before he could reach it, there was a prolonged ring, a banging on the panels, and an agitated rattling of the door handle. Robert flung open the door and there entered simultaneously a flurry of wind and rain and a huddled, rain-soaked figure. The newcomer shut the door hastily behind him, turned down the collar of his coat, took off his dripping hat, and revealed to the watchers the pinched and half-frozen countenance of Ernest Reed.

"Good Heavens, Ernest!" exclaimed Caroline in the utmost astonishment.

She came downstairs and Ernest Reed surveyed her with an expression in which wrath and pleasure were mingled.

"Hello, Caroline," he said. "I've got to see Iris. It's urgent. Where is she?"

"In bed," said Robert. "Now what?"

"Now get her out of bed," Ernest ordered him peremptorily. "Go on. Don't stand there like a frozen piece of beef. You're not as frozen as I am, not by a long chalk. All the way from London on an important errand and try to contact your confounded sister and what? Not here, not there, not there, not here. I didn't come all this way to run around like a hunted fowl. I came on special business and it's important, it's absolutely imperative, that I see your sister at once."

"Well, that's too bad," drawled Robert.

Ernest glared at him with undisguised hatred. "You keep your damned insulting nose out of this, d'you hear?" he ordered. "I don't like you and I never did and I didn't come all this way to get cold and wet and catch a hell of a chill just to listen to you and your blasted schoolboy cheek." He turned to Caroline. "Look here, Caroline," he said. "I'm serious. I must see Iris right away. I've something to tell her, something which it's very important she should know. Where is she?"

"I'm awfully sorry, Ernest," said Caroline, "but she met with an accident this afternoon and her head was injured, not seriously, thank goodness, but the doctor says that nobody is to disturb her."

"I won't disturb her," said Ernest. "I'll only talk to her, that's all."

"No, you won't," said Robert. "You heard what the doctor ordered, didn't you?"

"You keep your mouth shut, will you?" demanded Ernest.

"You're making a fat fool of yourself," said Robert. "If you stood here yapping all night, you couldn't see Iris. She's had a crack on the cranium and she wouldn't understand a word you said, anyhow."

"Robert's right, Ernest," put in Caroline swiftly. "She's really too dazed to take in anything. If you'll go back with Robert he'll fix up a bed for the night and — "

"He can fix his own bed," said Robert. "I've got — "

He paused. Mr. Swintzchell, a small attaché case held in one hand, was hurrying down the stairs. He looked at Ernest Reed with some astonishment and Ernest, attempting to glare, screwed up his face and gave way instead to a prodigious sneeze.

"You are wet," said Mr. Swintzchell, looking him over. "Tsst, tsst, tsst, tsst, tsst, how wet you are!"

"So'd you be wet," said Ernest, "if you'd come miles in a car and then had to get out of it and walk up this drive and that drive and the other drive to find out where people were. I'm — Atishoo! Atishoo!"

"If you are not careful," said Mr. Swintzchell, "you will take a chill. You must go home and — "

"Mr. Reed is going back to Lilac Cottage for the night," said Caroline.

"He is?" Mr. Swintzchell looked delighted. "Then we two, the two of us, we shall be two chaperons for the little Polly. And I shall be the cook and perhaps Mr. Reed can also be the cook together with me. It will be a happy night together — one, two, three — four people."

"Atishoo!" said Mr. Reed.

Caroline looked at him anxiously. He was, she knew, a man who treated minor indispositions as major illnesses. A common cold drove him to his doctor and aroused in him the deepest apprehensions.

"Can I give you anything, Ernest?" she asked. "I — "

"This," prophesied Ernest, "will settle on my chest. It's on my chest now. I can feel it. I wish to God I'd never set out. I don't see Iris and I get a cold settling right on my chest. When they settle on my chest, they — "

"Enough about your chest," said Robert. "There's a lady present. For God's sake come along and sit in a mustard bath. If that doesn't fix your chest, it'll at least — "

"If you will give me something," said Mr. Swintzchell to Caroline, "I will put it upon his chest and then his cold will go away. Have you something?"

Caroline hesitated. "I've got a tin of anti-phlogistine," she said at last.

"Please?" begged Mr. Swintzchell.

"Antiphlogistine," repeated Caroline. "That stuff that you spread over like paint and it warms and — "

"Ah! Yes, I know," said Mr. Swintzchell. "I cannot say it, but I can put it on. And where is this thing?"

"It's in a little tin in the kitchen cupboard," said Caroline. "You spread it on with a knife."

"In the kitchen cupboard. Come!" said Mr. Swintzchell, gathering his flock. "We shall go. I shall cook and I shall rub on this thing onto Mr. Reed's cold in the chest and it will be better."

"If you come in the morning, Ernest," said Caroline, "I'll take you up and you can talk to Iris."

She watched the ill-assorted trio going through the door, Mr. Swintzchell with one arm thrown protectingly around Ernest. She saw the door close behind them and, drawing a deep sigh of relief, turned toward the stairs once more.

"Thank Heaven," she said aloud, "that I haven't got to be there too."

CHAPTER FOURTEEN

Caroline was up early. She had slept fitfully. She was comfortable on the sofa, but had been impelled to get up at intervals throughout the night to look at Iris.

Iris, however, had slept peacefully and was still asleep when Caroline dressed and went cautiously downstairs.

The boys, she found, had already gone. A jug of milk and some glasses in the kitchen were the only traces of the light meal they had taken before going up to the School for breakfast.

Caroline found a tray, made a milk drink for Iris and some coffee for herself, and carried it upstairs. Finding that Iris had not stirred, she drank her coffee and took her cup back to the kitchen. She washed it and was drying it when she heard sounds in the hall and, going to the door, looked out.

Mr. Swintzchell had just come in, but Caroline saw with dismay that he was not the gay, confident Mr. Swintzchell who had taken leave of her the night before. He was pale; his cravat was disordered and his white locks hung in the wildest confusion. Taking in these details hastily, Caroline went toward him with a sense of foreboding and put a hand on his arm.

"Something's happened," she said.

Mr. Swintzchell looked at her. His gaze was mournful and his mouth drooped, and a little feeling of fear crept over Caroline. Mr. Swintzchell saw her grow pale and hastened to speak.

"No — no. Nothing," he said, "has happened to your brother. Your brother — and the little Polly — they are well."

Caroline's fears vanished. Robert and Polly were well. Mr. Swintzchell stood before her and Ernest was quite capable of looking after himself. She forgot her own feelings in contemplation of the gloomy figure before her and set about finding out what had thrown the good-humored Professor so greatly off his balance.

"You've had a trying night," she said soothingly. "I oughtn't to have let you go. I'm so sorry, but I was worried about Iris and it made me selfish. I don't suppose you had any supper. Polly means well, but — Did you," she asked, "get anything to eat?"

Mr. Swintzchell shook his head. "To eat? No, I think we did not eat," he said. "Something, I think, went wrong with it. When I got there, there was no supper."

"Didn't Robert do anything?" asked Caroline.

"Robert? No. Robert," said Mr. Swintzchell, "was quite sensible and he said, 'There is no supper. I will go out and get some at

Blakely,' and he went, and Miss Polly and I had some — a little — cheese and — and there were some pickles, I think." Mr. Swintzchell paused, passed a hand through his hair, and looked at Caroline with a glance of despair.

Caroline frowned. He was hungry and he had probably had an unrestful night, but that was scarcely reason enough for his obvious distress. She sought further enlightenment.

"Mr. Reed — is he better?" she asked.

A look of anguish passed over Mr. Swintzchell's face. "No," he groaned. "Mr. Reed, he is not better, I think."

"You — you mean he's — he's ill?" asked Caroline.

Mr. Swintzchell put his hands together and wrung them. He looked imploringly at Caroline.

"I did my best," he said. "Everything that you told me, I did. All the night, I ask myself, 'How could this have come to me?' And I answer that the fault was not mine. But, yes — " Mr. Swintzchell smote his forehead in despair — "yes, I was to blame. The light was bad, and I was hungry, so hungry, and I was trying to help the little Polly, and — "

Caroline broke into the recital and, putting a firm hand under Mr. Swintzchell's elbow, led him across the hall and put him into a deep chair.

"Stay there," she said, "and I'll bring you something hot to drink. And then you can tell me what happened."

Mr. Swintzchell seemed incapable of resisting, and Caroline hurrying to the kitchen, returned with a cup of steaming coffee. She handed it to her patient and watched a little color returning to his cheeks.

"Now," she said when he had finished, "do you feel a little better?"

"Thank you," said Mr. Swintzcheil.

"Then," said Caroline, "you can tell me what happened to Mr. Reed. Did his cold get worse?"

Mr. Swintzchell shook his head. "I do not know," he said.

"Then — "

Mr. Swintzchell leaned forward and put a hand on Caroline's knee, speaking in a slow and miserable tone. "I shall confess to you," he said. He leaned back and looked at her. "You told me," he went on, "to find the little tin. You said, 'Go to the cupboard in the kitchen and get the little tin and in the little tin will be' — that thing to rub on."

"Antiphlogistine," said Caroline. "Yes. Did you find it?"

"I went into the kitchen," said Mr. Swintzchell, "and I asked the little Polly 'Which is the cupboard where will be the little tin,' and she showed me. And I took out the little tin and I went upstairs and I said to Mr. Reed,

'Here is the little tin of what Mrs. Caroline says I must put on to you to make an embrocation.' And I put on the light to see, but Mr. Reed said, 'No, put the light out, because it is too much glare.' And so there was only a little light, from the landing outside, and so perhaps it was not my fault in that way. And I opened the tin and with a knife — just as you said to me — I put it on Mr. Reed's chest and then I said, 'Please to sit up,' and I put it onto his back to make an embrocation for the lungs."

"Well, that was all right," said Caroline.

"So far," said Mr. Swintzchell heavily, "it was all right. I put on Mr. Reed's pajama and I took my little tin and I went downstairs and put it into the cupboard and Miss Polly saw me and said — and said . . ."

Mr. Swintzchell's voice died away and he sat speechless, gazing at Caroline in utter misery. Caroline felt a lump in her throat, but there would be time enough, she felt, for crying when she knew what to cry about.

"What," she asked firmly. "did Polly say?"

"Polly said — she said," answered Mr. Swintzchell with an effort, "she said, 'What have you been doing with the tin of white paint . . . ?' "

There was a dreadful silence. Caroline, her mouth opening slowly, stared at Mr. Swintzchell, and Mr. Swintzchell stared back.

"You mean you — you — "

Caroline could say no more, but Mr. Swintzchell nodded in dreary confirmation.

"It was the white paint," he said heavily. "I put it — with a knife — onto Mr. Reed's chest and Mr. Reed's back. . . ."

Caroline took a deep breath. "And when did he — ?" she began fearfully.

"It was not long," said Mr. Swintzchell. "Miss Polly and I waited, and we were frightened, and then we heard some shouting and after a time — for, Mrs. Caroline, I can assure you that although I am not a coward, I did not wish to go up the stairs — but we went up together and Mr. Reed — Mr. Reed — " Mr. Swintzchell took out a handkerchief and mopped his damp brow. "I thought," he said simply, "that he was going to kill me. And perhaps he would not have been to blame. For the paint, it was all over, and paint does not easily come off, and his pajama — and his — his — his everything, and your good sheets and — ach!" Mr. Swintzchell, with a shudder, dropped his head in his hands.

There was a long silence.

"Where," asked Caroline, "is Mr. Reed now?"

"I do not know," he said. "His car was near, and he put on some clothes and he was like a madman and he said that he was going at once, and it was all confusion. Miss Polly put his baggage quickly ready and Mr. Reed said that he would put me into prison and ran out of the house, and we heard him go away very fast. . . ."

The tale was told. Tears rolled slowly down Mr. Swintzchell's cheeks and he made no attempt to brush them away. He laughed when he was happy and he saw no reason why he should not cry when he was miserable. Caroline, feeling strangely helpless, gave his hand an abstracted little pat and went slowly back to the kitchen. Cutting some sandwiches, she carried them, with a fresh cup of coffee, to the weeping man's chair.

"Take this," she said gently, "and you'll feel better. And you mustn't worry. Mr. Reed always made a great deal of his little ailments and I don't suppose there's very much the matter with him."

"He is painted white," moaned Mr. Swintzchell. "That is not a — a little ailment. It is a terrible thing."

"It's probably all off by now and he's on his way back to London," said Caroline. "Put him right out of your mind. I'm quite certain he'll never enter High Ambo again."

"If he comes," faltered Mr. Swintzchell, "with policemen, as he told me — "

"Rubbish," said Caroline, with more confidence than she felt. She wondered whether painting a man white would come under the heading of assault. It was in the same category, probably, as tarring and feathering, but if it was done without vindictiveness . . .

She patted Mr.. Swintzchell's hand again and spoke soothingly. "Forget all about it," she advised. "You did it with — with the best intentions and I'm not even sure that a coat of paint wouldn't do just as well to keep the damp out of his lungs."

Mr.. Swintzchell looked slightly more cheerful. "You think so?" he asked.

"Certainly," said Caroline. "Now — " she stopped, feeling that she could hardly urge him to dry his eyes. Mr. Swintzchell, however, drew out a large handkerchief and wiped his face resolutely.

"If he brings the policemen," he said, "I shall tell them it was a mistake."

"Of course. Now cheer up and forget the whole thing," said Caroline. "I'm going up to Iris."

Mr.. Swintzchell gave his forehead one of the resounding blows which Caroline always felt must be extremely harmful. "Ah!" he exclaimed. "I am so selfish. I think only of what has happened to me, and I do not even ask, 'How is your sister.' How," he inquired, "is your sister?"

"She was still asleep when I came down," said Caroline, "but she had a very good night and I'm sure she's better."

"Good. That is good," said Mr. Swintzchell. "And — " he spoke hesitatingly "perhaps it will not be good for her to hear — "

"I shan't say a word," promised Caroline. "I'll just say he's gone."

"Yes." Mr. Swintzchell looked relieved. "It would be bad to tell her when she is weak. But — " his countenance became almost cheerful — "but there is one good thing. If she should say, when you tell her that he is gone, if she should say that he has gone without taking the papers which she did for him on her machine, then you can say to her, 'Do not worry, for those papers he has.' "

"What papers?" asked Caroline.

"Last night," explained Mr. Swintzchell, "Mr. Reed was sad not to see your sister, but he said as he went to his bedroom, he said, 'Perhaps there are some papers for me that would have been sent by the Post?' And Miss Polly told him that Miss Iris had worked very hard at making the papers, and she gave them to him, in that big envelope which was on the machine."

Caroline stared at him, opened her mouth, and then closed it again. With a murmured phrase which she hoped he would interpret as gratitude, she turned and walked thoughtfully upstairs.

It was going to be a little difficult, she reflected, to answer Iris's questions. It would be inadvisable to tell her that her employer, making a long journey to see her, had left during the night in a coat of paint.

And it would be still less advisable to

inform her that he had gone off with Mr. Sheridan's notes on the Greenshank and the Ring–Ousel.

Iris's inquiries, fortunately, were directed less toward the details of her employer's visit, which seemed to Caroline to make surprisingly little impression, than to the events following the descent of the camera.

"I honestly can't tell you much about it," said Caroline, sitting on the bed and noting with satisfaction that Iris seemed almost herself again. "Everything was rather confused."

"Well — " Iris frowned impatiently, "somebody must have asked Michael Sheridan something about it, mustn't they? Didn't he say anything?"

"Yes. He said you startled him and he dropped his camera."

"It wasn't a good light," pointed out Iris. "And nobody can take photographs in a bad light. What was he doing?"

"He was bringing the camera down," said Caroline. "I don't know anything about bird photography, but I think they tie the camera up the tree — presumably under a shelter, though I don't really know — and then they go away and pull a string — that's attached to the camera, of course — and then they might or might not get a picture before the bird knows what's happened."

Beyond this informative statement, Iris could learn nothing. She got out of bed and, dressing slowly, meditated upon the circumstances attending the accident. Did the sight of her really upset him so? She waited with ill-concealed patience for the slow hours to go by, and longed for an opportunity to talk to the French Master.

The doctor came, gave his permission for Iris's return to Lilac Cottage, and, expressing a jovial conviction that she would live, for perhaps fifty years more, offered his car for the journey back to the Cottage.

"It's very kind of you," said Iris, "but my brother'll probably be along soon, and I'll go back with him."

"Just as you like," said the doctor, "but I had an idea he'd gone."

Caroline and Iris stared at him.

"Gone! Gone where?" asked Caroline.

"I don't mean gone altogether," said the doctor, "but I heard Sheridan saying something to the Headmaster this morning about meeting your brother and driving somewhere to see some model yachts. Hadn't you heard the plan?"

"Well — vaguely," said Iris. "Has Mr. Sheridan gone?"

"I shouldn't think so," said the doctor. "He's got to come here and pack a bag and get young Carruthers ready."

"Ready? What for?" asked Iris.

"Oh, I didn't tell you, Iris," said Caroline. "He's got triplet sisters."

"Good Lord — triplets!" said Iris. "What did he say when they told him?"

"He's a pretty philosophical chap," said the doctor. "He didn't seemed perturbed until he read a note from his mother and learned that the babies were born during a very bad storm and she'd decided to call them Storm, Gail — spelt with an *i* — and Rayne spelt with an *a–y*."

"My goodness!" said Caroline, awed. "How does a schoolboy live down that sort of thing?"

The doctor smiled. "You needn't worry about young David," he said. "He's rechristened them Tempest, Typhoon, and Tornado and he's busy interviewing interested schoolmates three at a time. Sensible sort of woman his mother must be — twelve years' rest and then three at a sitting. You're sure I can't take Miss Drake back?"

"No, thank you. I'm going to wait here for Mr.. Sheridan," said Iris. "He hasn't even apologized yet."

"Don't be hard on him," said the doctor. "He carried you half a mile across mud-logged country. Told me it felt like clasping a thousand-pounder."

With this gallant remark, the doctor took his leave, and less than a quarter of an hour later, Michael Sheridan entered the house.

Caroline was upstairs, putting the finishing touches to her work of tidying the bedroom. Iris, curled up on a deep chair in the hall, looked up as the door opened and waited for Michael to speak.

"Oh, you're there," he said. "I thought the doctor might have run you back. Has your brother gone yet?"

"I don't know," said Iris.

"Oh, well," said Michael, "I suppose I ought to say that I'm sorry I shied the camera. And I am, too. Total wreck. But you shouldn't appear suddenly under trees. You weren't, by any chance, following me?"

"I — "

"You might," said Michael, "have got hurt. I mean seriously."

Iris looked at him in bewilderment. "What do you call a knock on the head that knocks you out?" she asked. "Isn't that being hurt?"

"How," asked Michael gently, "does it feel?"

"How does it look? Do I appeal to you in sticking plaster?"

Michael studied her. "On the whole, I think so," he said after a time. "If I weren't taking young Carruthers to the main line train and going on a short trip with your brother, I should have felt it my duty to ease the long hours of convalescence. As it is, I'm afraid I must pass out of your life and — "

"No, don't do that," said Iris, and added impulsively, "Mike, I *like* you. Can't we be friends?"

Michael waited for a few moments, and when he spoke, his voice and his expression were unchanged. "I think not, Iris," he said. "There seems to be a rather wide difference in our interpretations of the word. Look at it like this — a pretty girl with a lot of spare time on her hands and a busy man with no spare time at all. In London, a line of fellows with time — and inclination — to embark on a mild affair and, at High Ambo, a collection of schoolmasters with no time to embark on any affairs at all."

"But who," asked Iris, "is talking about affairs? That's such a silly word, Michael, and it means exactly nothing except in the kind of novel I wouldn't have suspected you of reading. People don't have affairs any more. Affairs went out with the long waxed mustaches and the delicate complexions. That's what's wrong with you — you've slipped out of your age group. And you're behaving like a terrified male being pursued by a — by a — a pursuing female."

"And that," said Michael, "is exactly what I feel like."

There was a long silence. The words hung in the air and, dying slowly away, left the atmosphere clear and free from doubts and misunderstandings. Iris stared at the man before her and seemed to see him clearly for the first time.

Michael Sheridan watched her, and her

face was easy to read. He saw hurt and then bewilderment, and for a moment he wanted to put out a hand and lay it gently upon hers. It was the devil, he thought, to say a thing like that, but it was true and it was kinder to kill the thing at the start. She was too, far too disturbing in the middle of a busy term. She was too pretty. She was more than pretty, sitting there staring at him with wide, dark blue eyes and those odd, stubby lashes. She was too lovely and she was far, far too much alive. And far too fast-moving. She'd like to put a hand into a man's heart and pull it out to see how it worked. Well, she'd done that now, and she'd found it wasn't working at all. It was hard lines and he was sorry. She looked, sitting there, like a — a stricken deer.

He rose to his feet and Iris looked up at him quietly, waiting for him to speak.

"Good-by," he said.

Iris's voice was tranquil. "I'll see you," she said, "when you come back."

CHAPTER FIFTEEN

Caroline sat at the piano in the little sitting room of Lilac Cottage and, with her hands idle on her lap, stared absently at the keys.

She ought to be practicing. She ought to be running up and down scales and going through the exercises which Mr. Swintzchell had so carefully prepared for her. But it seemed heartless to raise a voice in song while Iris and Polly were going about the house looking, Caroline thought, as though each had suffered a recent and heavy bereavement.

She struck a soft chord and meditated on the change which had come over the house in the three days following Iris's accident. It was easy, of course, to understand the change in Iris; a girl who had been on the verge of promotion and success could not be expected to remain cheerful with her prospects so suddenly and unexpectedly blighted. The slight injury to her head would heal, it was true, but it had been impossible to keep from her the details of Mr. Swintzchell's short career as a nurse and, following close on this distressing disclosure, there had come a letter from Ernest containing the bird notes and an outspoken expression of feelings natural in a man who had been painted white and driven into a nursing home, the charges for which, said Ernest, were to be placed against any salary which Iris might have been expecting for her valueless and no-longer required services.

Yes, decided Caroline, Iris, out of a job, might well be out of spirits. But what was the matter with Polly?

Caroline ran a forefinger absently along the white notes and tried to answer the question. Polly had spent a night in the society of an angry Robert, a terrified Mr. Swintzchell, and a maddened Ernest — a horrid experience, but surely, mused Caroline, not enough to make so deep an impression on a disposition like Polly's. It might be — here Caroline struck a soft, discordant chord — it might be that Polly, after seeing Robert at close quarters, was for the first time beginning to realize what life with him would be like. It was a conclusion which, in the case of anybody but Polly, would have been reasonable but Caroline found it impossible to believe that a girl who had served dreadful food to her fiancé, listened unmoved to his complaints, and urged him to swallow it and pretend it was nice could, in a single night, turn into a woman who regarded him with sober eyes of disillusionment.

Of course — Caroline stabbed thoughtfully

at Middle C — of course, there was the other possibility. Robert might have done something — something . . . unprincipled, only Iris was always saying that nobody used those terms nowadays. He might have done something to frighten Polly . . . though it wasn't in the least likely. One could hear almost everything that went on in all the bedrooms. It wasn't likely that Robert could behave with anything but the utmost propriety with Mr. Swintzchell a mere brick away. Mr. Swintzchell, moreover, had spent a wakeful night. If anything had happened, Caroline told herself, Mr. Swintzchell would have known, and a man with so uncompromising an outlook on the conventions would instantly have made sure that they were observed.

And although Iris didn't agree at all, it wasn't the sort of thing Robert would do. If he wanted to go into Polly's bedroom, and Caroline was sure he didn't, he would do it as he did all his unconventional acts — in the most open and unconcealed way.

No, it was something else, and Caroline wished very much that she could find out what it was. She had never, she reflected, wanted anybody to come and stay with her, and had insisted that she was really happier alone. And this proved it, for here she was, on a lovely cold morning, with two gloomy guests and in such low spirits herself that she was quite unable to do any serious practice. She could not burst into song while Polly peeled onions in the kitchen and pretended that they were what made her cry, and Iris answered questions a quarter of an hour after a person had asked them and when the conversation had turned on entirely irrelevant matters. It was the sort of thing, Caroline remembered, that Iris was always saying she herself did. If it was true, she would try to conquer this habit, for it was a very irritating one.

If Robert would come back, he could perhaps take Polly's mind off whatever it was that was troubling her; and if Mr. Sheridan would come back he could give Iris some more bird notes to copy and that would give her something to do until she had made up her mind about her future.

She heard a sound, and looked up to find Polly at the kitchen door, taking off her apron and sucking a wounded finger.

"Hurt?" said Caroline.

"I burnt it a bit," said Polly.

"It's a cruel sport," said Caroline sympathetically. "Can I do anything?"

Polly shook her head and, to her dismay, Caroline saw that she was near to tears.

"No, thank you," she said. "I'm just — well, I've got some telephoning to do and I may have to go up to London for a bit. I can't explain now."

She went upstairs and, coming down in a hooded coat, carrying a small suitcase in one hand and the puppy in the other, she looked, Caroline thought, as young and innocent as Red Riding Hood.

A few moments later, Iris came downstairs and looked inquiringly at her sister. "Thought I heard the door," she said.

"Yes, Polly's gone out to do some telephoning, and then I expect she's on her way to London. She said she can't explain now. Have you any idea, Iris, what can be wrong with her? Or haven't you noticed?"

"Yes, I've noticed," said Iris. "She's got the glooms, that's all. After a night practically alone with Robert, it isn't surprising. She's probably phoning Daddy to see if he's still in London so she can go back to him."

"Perhaps," agreed Caroline. "Are you going out?"

"Don't know," said Iris absently, staring out of the window. There's not much else to do, is there? Stay in or go out. Aren't you supposed to be filling the house with song today?"

"Mr. Swintzchell can't come. He's fetching David Carruthers back."

"And when d'you suppose the two men'll come back with their toy boats?" asked Iris.

"They oughtn't to be long," said Caroline. "At least, I hope not. I'm getting worried.

What will Robert say when he finds Polly gone? And I'm worried a little bit," she added hesitatingly, "about you, too. You're not worrying about Ernest or about — about another job or anything, are you?"

Iris seemed to consider. "No, I don't think so," she said. "I'm — yes, I suppose I'm thinking about my next job. I'm going for a walk," she went on abruptly. "Coming?"

"Well, no. I don't think I will," said Caroline. "You go and — "

She stopped, feeling that to add "and walk it off" would be thought unkind. She watched thankfully as Iris went up the little path, and, on an impulse, threw a coat over her shoulders and went out into the garden, walking round to the back of the house and staring at the uninspiring collection of bushes and shrubs within view.

She walked slowly along a path, stopping to pull up a straggling little plant here and there and wondering, as she did so, whether she was pulling up weeds or one of the rarer types of flower. Reaching the end of the path, she turned and found Miss Louisa standing at the back door watching her with grim amusement.

"Oh — good morning," called Caroline. "How nice to see you."

Miss Louisa made no reply, waiting in silence until Caroline reached her side.

" 'Morning," she said, with a sardonic

glance round. "Taking up gardening?"

"No. Come inside," invited Caroline, "and let's get nice and warm."

She ushered Miss Louisa into the sitting room and put her near the fire. Miss Louisa loosened her scarf, straightened her back, and refused coffee.

"Can't stay," she said. "Dropped in to ask how your sister is. Head better?"

"Thank you, yes," said Caroline. "But she's out of spirits, a little. I'll hope she'll get over that."

"Not enough for her to do here," diagnosed Miss Louisa. "Not a country type. Needs cinemas and things. The other one — Polly — I suppose she's out of spirits, too?"

Caroline looked a little surprised. Miss Louisa could hardly be expected to know that Polly . . .

"Passed her just now," said Miss Louisa. "Peaked, but can't say I'm surprised. How did she take it?"

Caroline stared at her visitor and, after a few moments, Miss Louisa put an abrupt question. "Not told you?" she asked.

"Well — I don't think — I mean, told me what?" faltered Caroline.

"Her father."

Caroline turned pale. Daddy, who was sweet, who was fun, who was . . .

"W-what? Has something happened?" she asked slowly.

Miss Louisa spread out her gloved hands as if to display their utter emptiness. "Bankrupt," she said.

There was a long silence. Caroline sat and absorbed slowly the implications of the abruptly spoken word, and Miss Louisa waited.

"How did — ?" began Caroline at last.

"Heard two days ago," said Miss Louisa. "Postscript in Sue's letter. No details."

"Bankrupt!" said Caroline slowly. "I know what the word means, of course, but I don't know, well, how *much* it means. Sometimes everything goes and sometimes there's a bit left. Isn't that so?"

"This'll be bad," said Miss Louisa. "You know, of course, how he makes his money?"

"Well, yes," said Caroline, struggling to recall Polly's vague description of her father's activities. "Mr. Andrews advises people on — on projects. Isn't that so?"

"More or less. But he made his money," said Miss Louisa, "by investing in everything he believed in. And as he was always right, he made a fortune. This time, he was wrong. Didn't Polly say anything?"

"No. No, she didn't," said Caroline. "She — I knew there was something worrying her, but — "

"Thought it was your brother. Not surprised," said Miss Louisa. "This affect him, d'you think?"

Caroline shook her head absently and then, as the meaning of the casually spoken words reached her, stared at the speaker. "Affect Robert? Well, no — how can it affect Robert?" she asked in bewilderment.

Miss Louisa looked keenly at Caroline, looked into the fire, and fixed her eyes on Caroline once more. "Offend you," she said. "Can't help it. Always thought — always shall think — he was after her money."

Caroline opened her mouth and tried to say something, but was unable to utter a word. She stared stupidly at Miss Louisa, and then felt the blood rushing to her cheeks.

"Angry," said Miss Louisa. "Thought so. But always so obvious, I would have said. Your brother — and that little thing."

Caroline spoke through a thickness in her throat. "Robert," she said carefully, "loves Polly."

"Never suggested he didn't, my dear," said Miss Louisa. "Who couldn't fall in love with a pretty little thing with a rich father? Quite easy. Anybody. But take away rich father and leave silly little thing with expensive tastes and no money, and then what? No steady job, your brother. No steady principles, either. But a lot of sense. Knows himself, knows the world, knows his own weaknesses. What could he do for a little thing used to luxury all her life? Great expense, great responsibility. Great foolishness. There's a lot of rubbish talked about richer-for-poorer. After marriage, yes, but before marriage, no. One should think twice. That little thing needs a wealthy husband and your brother ought to — and will — think twice. Wait and see. Don't mean to offend you, my dear. Feel myself an old friend and you a niece, like Sue. Nothing against your brother personally."

Caroline sat quite still, her eyes on Miss Louisa and her mind racing with a hundred conflicting thoughts. She felt sick and confused, and she was struggling with a stifling sense of shame and disloyalty. She felt Miss Louisa's little pat on her hand, and knew it was meant as comfort and apology. She longed to open her mouth and affirm, in the most decided accents, her conviction that Robert had never thought of Mr. Andrews' money and that the loss of it would mean nothing more than a necessity to love Polly more deeply and tenderly than before. She wanted to put before her visitor a picture of a man deeply in love and careless of material considerations. But Robert — who could tell what Robert thought or felt? Caroline tried to recall one gesture or one word to his fiancée which could have been interpreted as affection, but she was able to remember nothing save the facts, remarkable in themselves, that Robert had eaten Polly's food, been licked by Polly's dog, and endured all the discomforts of Lilac Cottage, not certainly without protest, but at least without any of his usual violence.

She sat lost in thought and forgetful of her visitor until Miss Louisa rose to leave. She looked at Caroline regretfully. "I've upset you," she said. "Wouldn't have done, but can't understand why you didn't know long ago. Thing happened the morning after your sister met with that accident. That little thing must have known the same day, and your brother — she must have told him. He ought to have told you."

"I wasn't here," said Caroline. "Robert left the house before I came back that morning. He and Mr. Sheridan had planned something and when I got back here, Robert had gone."

"Well, he oughtn't to have gone," said Miss Louisa. "He ought to have stayed here with that poor little thing."

Caroline made no answer. She followed Miss Louisa to the gate, her mind in confusion. With an effort she came back to the present, bade Miss Louisa good-by, and then walked into the house, going back to the fire and standing before it, staring into the flames.

She waited anxiously for Iris's return, and found herself steadier after she had poured the tale into her sister's ears. She was glad to see that the faraway look left Iris's eyes as she listened, and when she spoke, heard with relief the old, quick notes in her voice.

"Of course," she said when Caroline had finished speaking, "if Robert knew, he shouldn't have gone off, but if he wasn't told — only a little idiot like Polly would dream of trying to keep the thing dark. Why wouldn't she tell him, anyhow?"

Caroline found it almost impossible to frame her answer in a way that would convey her meaning without imputing the worst motives to Robert, but before she was half-way through her sentence, Iris gave a brief, derisive laugh.

"Good Lord, can you beat that?" she said. "So that's what she could have been afraid of — that Robert was marrying her for Daddy's money. Is that it?"

"Well — yes," said Caroline.

Iris stared at her sister. "And you're looking pretty worried yourself," she said slowly. "Don't tell me that you — Oh, Carol, you *couldn't* be so — so crazy!"

"I don't think so," said Caroline slowly. "I mean, I don't honestly feel that Robert would do it, but I wish I knew why I thought so. When I try to work it out, I can't find anything in Robert's character or — or history to give us both this faith in his disinterestedness. We both know that he likes good living, that he hasn't got enough money to keep anybody as luxuriously brought up as Polly, and you've heard him and I've heard him say over and over again that if he ever walked up an aisle there'd be a — how did he always put it?"

"There'd be a distinct clink of gold," said Iris. "Well, I know. That's what he said, but then he's always saying things of that sort. It's almost a reflex action. Every time he opens his mouth, somebody's hair stands up. That's why he opens it. But to say he'd take on a proposition like Polly for life just because her father could keep them both in comfort — why, it's rot, that's all."

Little as there was in this speech of any definite proof, Caroline found it comforting. Perhaps Robert did go off without knowing, and when he found out he would go after Polly and everything would be all right. "Are you going back to London?" asked Caroline.

"No. At least, not yet," said Iris. She frowned thoughtfully for a few moments and then put an abrupt question. "Carol," she said, "have you ever heard of a place called Bishophowe in the county of Kent?"

"Never in my life," said Caroline. "What happens there?"

Iris walked to the window and, with an abstracted air, traced the frost patterns on the panes. "Mike Sheridan lives there," she said slowly. "In between terms, that is."

"Mike *who?*" asked the bewildered Caroline.

"Sheridan. Sheridan," repeated Iris, turning to face her sister. "French, riding, birds, and toy boats. That one. He comes from a place called Bishophowe."

Caroline blinked a little stupidly. "I'm sorry," she said. "I don't see any — any connection."

"There isn't," said Iris. "That is — yet."

There was silence. Caroline stared at her sister and tried to piece together the fragments of disjointed information, but could make nothing of them. Mr. Sheridan was that nice young man with the big glasses and the quiet voice. He presumably came from somewhere, but why Iris should be interested in the place — It must be the place, it couldn't be the man, because she only set eyes on him a few weeks ago and she didn't even like him. But if she didn't like him, and if she was only talking about the place, why should a name like Bishop-whatever-it-was, why should it make Iris look a lovely delicate shade of pink, with an expression which . . . ?

Caroline struggled with a fantastic idea for a few moments and then brought out a stammering sentence. "But you — you don't even like him!" she said.

"That's what I thought," said Iris.

There was a long silence. "But you haven't

— you hadn't set eyes on him — I mean, you only met him a few weeks ago!" began Caroline again. "You can't — Iris, you can't be — nobody could be in love with a man they only met a few weeks ago!"

"A few weeks ago," said Iris, "I couldn't have agreed more."

Caroline took a deep breath. "Are you — this really sounds fantastic, Iris, and I'm sorry if I'm — if I'm running away, but are you going to m-marry him?"

"If he asks me — yes," said Iris.

"B-but — " Caroline walked to a chair, sat on it, and felt a little better — "but he will — I mean, of course he'll ask you," she said.

"If he falls in love with me — yes," said Iris.

A shade of anger chased the bewilderment from Caroline's face and she spoke almost sharply.

"You're fooling, Iris," she said. "I don't think it's at all amusing to — "

"I don't think it's amusing either," said Iris. "I don't feel anything like amused. I feel, well, if you want to know, it's pure hell. I didn't imagine," she ended soberly, "that it would feel like this to be in love."

"Love!" Caroline repeated the word slowly and wonderingly. "Love! You mean to say that you see a man a few times, you don't like anything about him — his looks, his profession, his ideas, his habits — and you — "

"I always liked his looks," interrupted Iris.

"I still don't like his profession. If you'd ask me what sort of wife I'd rather not have been, I'd have said, after a bit of considering, a schoolmaster's. His ideas? Well, yes, I do like his ideas. And as for his habits, I don't suppose anybody really finds out about a man's habits before they're married to him, and I should think he's got rather nice habits. I like the way he — "

"But if he hasn't said anything," began Caroline, "then — "

"Ah, yes!" said Iris. "Then what? Do I sit in this room day after day and say to myself, 'One day my love will ride up on a white charger'? He might, too. He'd have quite a choice of chargers. . . . And he'll look at me and say, 'Golly, she's just my type.' But, you see, that's one of the things that's frightening him. I'm not. And what is his type? I bet if he ever thought about it at all, he dreamt about something with muscular calves and a winning way with boys — little boys. With a sensible face and sensible shoes. That's what he'd marry, and think he'd got a prize. If he ever tossed restlessly during the night and dreamt about beauty and passion, she'd give him a cooling powder. Together they'd be one big brain, and their children would be born with big heads and big glasses and be taught about the facts of life in the very latest and most highest-plane way. To look at, it'd be the perfect match. To look at. But *I* don't think so. I don't want to butt in and spoil a perfect union, but I don't think so. Not only because I love him, but because something quite apart from my own — my own wishes, tells me that I'm made for him. I was born for him. I know I was. Why he doesn't know it, too, I can't tell you, but he'll know it soon. He'll come to see that he doesn't have to throw away loveliness and charm and a willowy figure just because they don't appear to fit into the intellectual pattern. He'll learn that I can mean more to him, not only physically but in every other way, than his intellectual types. He'll see that the perfect combination is his brains and my beauty. He'll listen and believe me. He'll — he'll marry me and like it. If he doesn't, I can't be any worse off than I am now, can I, Carol? He's in my mind all day and half the night. I think of his head and his hands and the way his expression stays calm most of the time and the way he walks — no hurry — and his voice. He's got a nice voice, Carol, hasn't he? At first I thought I'd prefer him without glasses, but I wouldn't now. It's all part of the — the set-up. I wake up in the morning feeling all right and then terrible — a wave comes over me and I say, 'I haven't got him yet,' and I get frightened until I think about it and realize that of course I can get him, though I wouldn't try to pin him down if I didn't know it was the best thing he could possibly have — me, I mean. I'm miserable and it's hell, but I've got the most curious feeling that even if I don't bring it off, I'll go to the end of my days being glad I met him. I think he's — I think he's as — as fine as they come."

There was silence. Two tears, unheeded, rolled down Iris's cheeks. She picked up her coat, put it over her arm, and walked slowly upstairs. Caroline sat in her chair, her expression blank, her mouth slightly open and her gaze on the ceiling.

Up there, she thought dazedly, not on the ceiling, of course, but on the other side of it, was Iris, in trouble. The house really wasn't big enough to hold all this emotional upheaval. A week ago, everything had been as normal as possible and the only two vexing questions had been whether there would be any eatable food and whether Polly would make Robert more uncomfortable than he would make her unhappy. Now the air was full of sighs and everybody was thoroughly miserable and it would be worse if Robert had jilted Polly and much worse if Robert found out that Polly had kept something from him. He had always hated secrets and in this case nobody could blame him if he made a fuss. And he would make a fuss — a great deal of fuss. And Iris — Iris, the lovely, sought-after Iris Drake — was sitting up there feeling miserable and . . .

No — the house was really too small, decided Caroline. She went through the kitchen, paused a moment to glance round at the disarray left by Polly, and, with an impatient movement, opened the back door and stepped outside. She felt dejected and curiously lonely. She was surrounded by people working out their own problems and she could do nothing to help, and she felt that this mental distress was, after all, almost worse than the physical distress she had suffered among her husband's relations.

Solly, free from his owner's preoccupations, heard a car stop at the gate and went round the house to investigate. He walked up the path and saw that, from the car, a human was emerging. A human, Solly noted, with trouser legs. Trouser legs . . . and below them, soft, defenseless flesh with a mere covering of light wool . . .

Assuming his mildest air, the cat sprang onto a gatepost. The man approached and, with a mild, "Hello, Puss," put out a hand to open the gate.

Solly sprang, and the next moment the man was nursing his hand and examining ruefully the long, red weals running down it.

"Damn fine reception," he muttered. "Don't know quite what I expected, but — "

There was a little cry and the man, looking

up, saw something which made his heart leap. Round the corner of the house, Caroline was approaching and Simon Gunter saw that she was coming swiftly and eagerly. Her hands were outstretched and a light of welcome shone in her eyes. Miracles, thought Simon, didn't —

"Oh Simon," cried Caroline "Oh, how wonderful! Oh, Simon — I'm so glad — I'm so *glad* to see you!"

Her hands were in his and her face was upturned. Dear God, realized Simon, miracles did —

Thankfully, he bent and kissed her.

CHAPTER SIXTEEN

It was a confused story that Caroline poured out to Simon in the little sitting room of the cottage. Simon, leaning back in his chair, studied the speaker quietly as Caroline beginning with Iris and a case of immersion, went on to Iris and an accident with a camera and switched to Polly, who was keeping important facts from Robert, who would make a great fuss when he found out. The account was tangled, rambling, and entirely unlike the usual slow, calm speech which Simon knew so well.

"You see," said Caroline, after an almost unintelligible statement in conclusion, "you see how worrying it all is."

"Quite," said Simon, and his quiet voice fell soothingly on Caroline's ears. "Quite. But that's all about everything else. Now how about you?"

"No — how about *you?*" said Caroline. "First of all, where are you staying?"

"Four or five miles from here, at a place called Blakely," said Simon. "I've got a room at the 'Queen's Tresses.' "

"This isn't a holiday, is it?" asked Caroline.

"No — it's one of the hopeful journeys I make in your direction now and then," said Simon. "Your letters were getting less frequent and more uninformative and I thought that this would be roughly about the time that Robert would begin to make trouble. How's the singing?"

"Singing? Oh — it was going rather well," said Caroline. "I missed the last lesson but it was just as well. I haven't really felt like practicing, and I didn't feel it would be kind to start a series of trills when everybody was looking so worried."

"When do you expect Robert?" asked Simon.

"Well — soon," said Caroline. "He ought to be back by now, but he never ties himself down to times."

"Well, there's somebody coming," said Simon, who was facing the window. "Quite a lot of people, in fact. An old fellow who looks as though he ought to be that singing professor, and — "

Caroline hurried to the window. "Oh, Mr. Swintzchell!" she exclaimed in surprise. "And the three boys. But in the morning — !"

She went to the door and opened it, and Mr. Swintzchell, removing his hat, entered the room and turned to point to his companions. "See — I bring the boys," he said. "They have to ask a favor."

Caroline shut the door, performed introductions, and looked with undisguised curiosity at the three large bundles which the boys were carrying.

"What," she inquired, "have you got there?"

"That," said Mr. Swintzchell eagerly, "that is the favor. We have all something to ask, but David shall ask first. He has just come back from his visit and — "

"Oh, the triplets! How were they, David?" asked Caroline.

"Fine, thanks," said David. "They're small at present, my mother said, but not as small as some triplets, and they don't look bad. Can I," he went on, turning to more important matters, "show you these clothes?"

"What clothes?" asked Caroline.

By way of answer, the three boys placed their bundles in the middle of the room, opened them, and disclosed a medley of garments made of silks, satins, tinsel, and brocade.

"Good Heavens, theatricals!" exclaimed Caroline.

"Yes, that is it — theatricals," broke in Mr. Swintzchell eagerly. "It is the School Play and see — " he seized a garment or two — "see how they fit! They don't fit! Nowhere, they don't fit. And Mr. Fitzwilliam, who is the master who gives to the boys the clothes for their acting, Mr. Fitzwilliam said, 'You can make them to fit. Take them,' he said, 'and make them to fit.' And how," asked Mr. Swintzchell indignantly, "how can this be done?"

Mr. Swintzchell looked anxiously at Caroline.

"We are asking too much?" he inquired. "If you and the other two ladies will not find the work too great — "

Caroline hastened to reassure him, but felt that the other two ladies, one in London and the other out of sorts, were extremely unlikely to be of much assistance. Without voicing her feelings, however, she promised that the garments would be altered.

"King Alfred and Queen Elizabeth," said Simon thoughtfully. "You're covering a lot of history, aren't you?"

"It's about all the rulers of England," explained David. "And other things, too. It's a sort of — "

"We're doing just the big things," said Alan. "We're having the burning cakes and the defeat of the Armada and how the *Mayflower* pushed off and — "

" — and King John and the Wash and — " began Stuffy.

" — and 'Calais-will-be-found-written-on-my-heart,' and 'When-did-you-last-see-your-father,' and all that," said Alan.

"It's just the big bits," said David. "Meldrum wrote it all and we're doing it ourselves but Mr. Fitzwilliam's being stage manager and Mr. Sheridan's doing the lights and things. Otherwise it's just us. It's called 'This Our Heritage' and Mr. Clunes says that's a jolly good title but — "

" — but we're having it mostly to use up all the costumes we've got, so Mr. Fitzwilliam says it ought to be 'This Our Wardrobe,' " said David. "You're coming to see it, aren't you?"

"First in the queue," promised Caroline.

"And now we go," said Mr. Swintzchell. "But, please — now I come to the other thing which I must ask." He put his hands together in a prayerful attitude and faced Caroline beseechingly. "Please! I have arranged a little piece for you to sing — at the Carol Service. Please! It is the solo part of the 'Song of Noel' — you know it? Of course you will know it, and I have spoken to you of it before, but I have made a new arrangement — a better arrangement. I have it here — " Mr. Swintzchell looked round wildly, slapped one or two of his pockets, and then pounced eagerly upon his hat, which was under a chair. "Here!" He removed the sheets of music from the lining and handed them to Caroline. "You see — the introduction, the organ, the boys singing, and then here is the part, the solo part. Hm hm, hm hm hm hm," he rumbled, following the notes with a fat forefinger. "Hm hm hm-m-m — you see how it comes in?" He pressed the sheets into Caroline's hands. "Please! You will do this for me?"

"Yes, she will," said Simon. "I'll guarantee

it. Regular practice under my eye every day."

Mr. Swintzchell seized the speaker's hands and wrung them in an excess of gratitude. "Thank you, thank you," he said. "That is the two things finished."

With a countenance beaming with satisfaction, he gathered his charges together and moved toward the door. Caroline was about to shut it behind them when Iris ran downstairs and put out a restraining hand.

"Half a minute," she said. "I'll go out to the gate with them." She flashed a greeting at Simon. "Hello," she said. "I saw you arrive but I was changing. See you in a minute."

She snatched Simon's coat from a chair and caught Mr. Swintzchell up at the gate, walking slowly beside him while the boys, with swift steps, drew rapidly away in front.

"You will catch cold," said Mr. Swintzchell, looking at Iris's uncovered head.

"No, I won't. I'm going back in a moment," said Iris. "I came out to ask you when Mr. Sheridan's coming back."

"Michael?" Mr. Swintzchell looked at her half in surprise, half in speculation. "He is back already. He and your brother went to the School. Your brother is to lunch with the Headmaster and afterwards he will go to see the lord, the bad-tempered lord, and say to him, 'For the last time, will you let us come inside your place and sail the little boats on the water?' I think it is no use. We all say that it is no use, but he says he will go after lunch before going back to the little fiancée." He paused and walked a few steps in silence. "It is to find out about your brother," he stated tentatively, "that you say when is Mr. Sheridan coming back — no?"

"If I want to know anything about Robert," said Iris, "I'd ask about Robert."

"I see." Mr. Swintzchell gave the matter his entire mind for the next few steps and then put his conclusion to the test.

"You like Michael?" he asked.

"Yes."

"Ah!" There was simple satisfaction in the word. "That," went on Mr. Swintzchell, "is very sensible, to like Michael. He is a good man, a very, very good young man. Many young men today are not so good, so when you see one who is — "

"Yes, I know," said Iris. "What I wanted to ask you was, how does one meet schoolmasters out of class? I can't call on you at Holly Lodge — the Headmaster'd think there was something going on. And I can't go to the School. So how — ?"

Mr. Swintzchell turned his head to study his companion, tripped over a large stone, and was regretfully compelled to look where he was going. But it was sad, he mused, for he would have liked to look more closely at this pretty girl who seemed to employ such simple and direct — such sensible measures. Here was no coyness, no —

"Well?" said Iris.

"It is difficult in the term," sighed Mr. Swintzchell.

Iris frowned. "But," she said, "schoolmasters get time off, don't they? I mean, they like to have fun, don't they, like everybody else? *Don't* they?"

"Fun. What do you call this fun?" inquired Mr. Swintzchell.

"Oh — " Iris waved a hand — "just fun. Music and dancing and — and that sort of thing."

"Dancing? Well, that is perhaps fun for some," admitted Mr. Swintzchell. "In my own young day, I danced — but in the air, you understand. I loved to go to every festival and dance, and that was very good. But in a little room, where everybody breathes air over and over and there is too much noise — no! I do not think Michael would like that, and I feel glad. Besides, he cannot dance, in or out, because he has no music. In him, you understand. He is tone deaf and — "

"Stone deaf?"

"*Tone* deaf. He hears no melody, he feels no beat, he can not move in time to what is played. To him, it is all the same — Beethoven, Bach, Britten, rubbish, jazz. Everything sounds to him the same. And to see people — he likes that, but again, not in a little room with everybody standing up and shouting with a little wine glass and not able to hear anything, even if what is to hear is good. No. Michael likes to meet those who are like himself, and he is a thinker, you understand, a student, a — I cannot find any words, but you will never make him waste his time in little things that are of no account. And what," asked Mr. Swintzchell, "are these friends you like to meet? When I was young, my father used to frighten away all my friends. One or two he agreed to, but many — no. He said to me, 'Karl, what do all these friends do? They will waste your time, they will fill your mind with useless things, they will talk and talk about nothing and soon the time will be gone and what will you know? What will you have accomplished?' " Mr. Swintzchell turned to Iris and raised a fat forefinger. "When you have children," he said, "do not let them waste all their days. You must feed them and make them laugh, and you must find out their talents and make them work, too. Ah, God!" asked Mr. Swintzchell, raising his eyes to Heaven, "how many children begin with great gifts, and how many, a few years after, can say what has become of this gift or that gift? The great artist — how many could there be, and how few, dear God, come to their full powers? Make your children practice, Miss Iris, and do not get a husband who will dance with you in a little room. Choose one who has eyes to see what is going on in the world — not the world of foolish men, but the world of Nature, the world of science. Leave, I beg you, all the little men who dance all the time, and get a man who is seeking, seeking, learning, a man who will show the world something new."

Mr. Swintzchell came to an end, sighed, and, with a shake of his head, recalled himself to the present. He stopped and turned to Iris. "You must go back. You will be cold," he said. "But I will tell you something. This afternoon the School will be out in the fine snow and the sunshine — it will be like Switzerland, no? — on the mountain behind the Castle. They will all go down in their toboggans — " Mr. Swintzchell, with a fat hand, described the swift progress of a toboggan down the hillside. "You must come there," he said. "You will be — " he put a finger on his nose and winked solemnly — "you will be taking a walk and you will see the fine sports and you also will wish to sport. Is that not so?"

"Thanks," said Iris. "Look out for me."

She turned to go, but Mr. Swintzchell put out a large, detaining hand. "Please," he begged. "I have to say something."

Iris waited, but it was some time before Mr. Swintzchell spoke. He seemed to be searching for the right words.

"Young men," he said slowly at last, "are

not always — sometimes they are not always clear to understand." He peered at her anxiously over his glasses. "You understand?" he inquired.

"Well, no — not quite," said Iris.

Mr. Swintzchell sighed. "It is not easy to say," he said, "but I will try to tell you. It is about Michael."

He paused and Iris prompted him gently. "Yes?"

"Yes. You see," went on Mr. Swintzchell, "he is a little different now. Once he used to talk to me, but now he no longer talks. He goes to his room and he walks."

"He — ?"

"Yes. Up and down, all the time," said Mr. Swintzchell, moving an arm to and fro. "He is absent in his mind, and he frowns and he does not look too happy."

He stopped and looked appealingly at Iris, as if begging her to understand the import of his words. Iris, however, shook her head uncomprehendingly.

"You don't understand?" he asked.

"No."

"Well, listen," said Mr. Swintzchell, "and I will make it more clear. I know Michael. For a long time I have seen him, and I know what he is thinking."

"And what is he thinking?" inquired Iris.

"He thinks," said Mr. Swintzchell, "that you are a very nice girl. He has seen nice girls before, but they have not interfered with his work. Now he cannot work — he only walks in his room. If this was another young man, and not Michael, he would come to you and he would tell you that he — that he likes you. But Michael will not. Do you understand?"

"Why won't he?" asked Iris.

"Because he does not think that pretty girls and busy schoolmasters can fall in love together," said Mr. Swintzchell. "He is wrong, but he is stubborn and he will not see." He came nearer and addressed Iris in a conspiratorial tone. "Now if *I*," he said, "could be the pretty girl who liked the schoolmaster, you know what I would do?"

"No — what?"

"I would see — " Mr. Swintzchell brought out his words slowly and carefully — "I would be sure that the young man knew what I thought. I would not be afraid. I would say loudly, 'Here we are, two, and I like you very much.' "

"I said that," Iris told him, "and it didn't do anything."

"Then," said Mr. Swintzchell, "you must tell him again and tell him more loudly. Dear Miss Iris, I know him so well and I tell you this: he will not follow after you. You," he ended earnestly, "you must follow after him."

He took her hand and patted it, and Iris

turned, thoughtfully, and went back to the house. Mr. Swintzchell stood looking after her in admiration. She was beautiful. She was young and strong and any young man would . . .

Well, amended Mr. Swintzchell, perhaps not any young man. . . . This Michael, for example . . .

CHAPTER SEVENTEEN

Robert Drake entered Lord Fellmount's grounds by the West gate, passed the empty lodge, and drove slowly along the avenue of magnificent beech trees. The road, at first level, with open ground on either side, became gradually steeper and presently went through a wood so thick as to make Robert feel that he was driving through a tunnel.

The drive swept round in a wide curve and Robert saw that he was on flat, open ground once more. Another sweep and Fell-Mount, a large and somewhat grim mansion, appeared before him.

Robert slowed his car to walking pace and studied the house. This, he mused, was what they called a noble pile. It must, in its day, have been pretty imposing. The old days — the spacious days.

Well, for himself, he liked things the way they were. They moved more quickly, for one thing. But it was hard lines on any surviving old boys or girls who weren't sufficiently adaptable to shrink into the new setting. This old boy, f'r example. . . .

At the thought of Lord Fellmount, Robert's musing took another turn. This was going to be an unpleasant interview, and it wasn't likely to be a successful one. Sheridan — and the Headmaster too, for that matter — were reliable fellows, and if they hadn't succeeded in working on the old boy, it wasn't likely that a stranger was going to do it. But the School wanted the lake and he was here to try to get it.

Robert drove under an archway and stopped before the massive oak door. Getting out, he walked through the open door into a narrow hall, through which he could see the main hall and the domed corridors beyond.

He had a little difficulty in finding a bell, but having found and pressed it, he had to wait some time before any sound was heard in answer. Robert lounged against the arm of a long carved bench and waited patiently. There was no hurry; he had all the afternoon and there was no point in getting rattled yet. Time enough for that when the old boy started on him.

There was a distant sound of shuffling and Robert raised his eyebrows. Old retainer coming to let him in? Old boy himself coming to throw him out?

The thin, bowed figure of a manservant came into view. He opened the inner door, gave a slight, stiff bow, but made no motion of invitation.

"Good afternoon, sir," he said.

"Good afternoon," said Robert. "Could I see his lordship?"

"I'm sorry, sir," answered the man firmly. "His lordship never sees anyone."

Robert subdued a rising impatience. "I know that as a general rule he doesn't," he said, "but this is the only opportunity I shall have of meeting him to bring up a most important matter. Will you tell him that," he went on, breaking into the man's sentence of regret, "or shall I be driven to the discourtesy of making a tour of the place and finding him for myself?"

"I'm extremely — "

"Let's keep this," suggested Robert, "on a sensible level, shall we? Will you — " his voice became hard — "will you go and find his lordship and tell him that I'm perfectly willing to be thrown out — if he does it himself. My name," he added, "is Drake, and if I can get this thing done — with your cooperation — without wasting an entire afternoon over it, I'll be very grateful to you."

The old man raised his eyes for a moment and studied the visitor. After a moment, he gave a little sigh and stood aside for Robert to enter. It was clear that he had summed up Robert's potential nuisance value to an accurate degree. He was well used to weighing up callers, and he knew that this young man had come prepared for trouble and wouldn't be satisfied until he got it. It was a hard choice, but he would rather face his master's familiar rage than stir up the fires he saw smoldering in this young stranger's eyes.

He led Robert into the inner hall and Robert felt a chill strike through his thick tweed jacket and woolen sweater. All marble, he saw with a shiver, and the heating permanently out of action. He ignored the seat to which the old man motioned him, and, left alone, walked restlessly round the hall, examining with faint interest the life-size figures and smaller pieces of statuary which, cold and white and in most cases nude, seemed to him to make the temperature drop another ten degrees.

He looked sourly at a naked little boy with a dog and felt sorry for them both. Stuck forever in this below-zero atmosphere, and —

There was a loud banging of doors somewhere beyond the corridors, a confused rumbling, a sound as of furniture being overturned, and then firm and threatening footsteps. Robert turned slowly, his eyes on the spot at which his lordship might be expected to appear.

The sounds, he found, were a little deceptive. His lordship emerged from a doorway only a little beyond the point at which he was standing, and Robert, turning his eyes in that direction, met a glare more malignant than any he had ever encountered.

"Get out," shouted his lordship. "Get out of here, whoever you are. Gerrout — go on, go on — gerrout."

This speech of welcome concluded, Lord Fellmount raised a bony forefinger and pointed to the door. "Gerrout," he added, to prevent any misunderstanding.

Robert felt that this was not the time for subtle approaches. "Are you," he inquired, "using your lake next summer?"

His lordship, who had opened his mouth to issue further directions, left it open and stared at Robert for a moment in an attempt to take in the meaning of his words. Then, as the cool insolence of the question penetrated his heated brain, his face became an alarming purple and the breathless manservant, shuffling through the door in the wake of his master, looked at him in alarm and made a little sound intended to sooth and quieten. Lord Fellmount turned to him in almost inarticulate fury.

"Gerrout. Gerraway from me," he shouted. "And you — " he looked once more toward Robert — "gerrout, you. Now! Gerrout and stay out. Get off my property and stay off it, you and all those other damned impertinent schoolmaster johnnies, too. The whole lot of you, d'ye hear? You and your confounded boys and their confounded boats. You'll keep off, and if I catch one, just one of your damned little whippersnappers with a confounded boat on my land, I'll throw him off with my own hands."

He raised his clenched fists and shook them before Robert to demonstrate their capabilities. Robert looked from them to the small shriveled figure and noted the contorted purple countenance.

No use prolonging it, he thought without regret. It had been a mistaken errand, and if he kept that snarling little terrier in this temperature any longer, he'd catch his death and so would the old henchman. Waste of time, the whole thing, but he'd put in his effort and he'd always feel he'd done what he could.

With a polite inclination of his head toward his host, Robert turned and walked away. He heard a satisfied grunt and the agitated shuffling of the servant struggling to catch him up and show him out. Without waiting, however, Robert opened the door, closed it behind him, and walked out to his car.

He drove under the archway, hesitated for a moment, and then decided to take a different route out of the grounds. If he came out of the gate nearest the School, he could go up and tell Sheridan that the whole thing had been a frost. Frost was the word. Marble and cold statuary. A morgue couldn't have been colder. . . .

This, he noticed, was a less good road.

He'd have done better to stick to the one he had come by. But if the road was worse, the scenery was a good deal better. That rolling bit over there, treeless, looked like a bit of the South Downs, and now that the sun had come out, the resemblance was even more striking. Woods approaching—this must be the other part of the wood he'd gone through. . . .

Entering the wood, he found himself under an archway of trees far less thick than those under which he had passed previously. The sun came through the branches and cast confusing patterns on the path, and overhanging limbs made driving difficult. A car with more headroom would, in one or two places, have found it impossible to pass.

The road became better and Robert was able to take his attention off it and look about him. It had turned, he discovered, into a perfect afternoon. There might be time to pick up Polly and run out to one of the local beauty spots for dinner. He'd —

Robert, looking ahead, frowned and stared at something which seemed to flash and sparkle immediately ahead.

"Water!" His foot came down on the accelerator and the car bounded forward. In a few seconds Robert had driven out of the wood and was on the road which circled the lake.

He stopped, switched off the engine, and, looking at the prospect before him, drew a deep, appreciative breath.

This! He hadn't, he told himself, guessed it was anything like this. He'd imagined, well, a stretch of water such as he'd seen in many other parts of the country. Natural lakes, ornamental lakes, but never anything approaching the beauty, the perfection of this one. For this one, Robert realized, viewing it with a professional eye, had everything. High, open on three sides, innumerable natural launching sites — an absolute Paradise for any fellow with a taste for . . .

And exactly the right size. By gosh, thought Robert, it was a good thing he hadn't seen this before he'd gone up to the old boy. If he'd known, up there, with defeat almost a certainty — if he'd known what the School was losing, he wouldn't have come away without a struggle.

Leaning back in the car, he lit a cigarette and sat, contented and relaxed, watching the wind ruffling the surface of the water. An ideal day, an ideal wind . . .

On an impulse, Robert got out of the car and, going round to the back, opened it. He put out a hand and lifted, lovingly and carefully, the little yacht lying in its box. He ground his cigarette underfoot and, with an expression of utter absorption on his face, walked with the little boat down to the water's edge.

He stood still for a few moments, backed away, and walked a few yards along the road. Once more he walked to the edge of the water and this time he stooped and, setting the tiny sails, held the little craft for a moment between his hands. The sails lifted and Robert released his hold; the beautiful little model swayed, steadied, and went its graceful way over the dancing waters.

It was, as Robert had known, a perfect day and a perfect wind. Forgetful of his distasteful errand to go to the School and inform Mr. Clunes and Michael Sheridan of the failure of his mission, forgetful of his plan to take his fiancée out, forgetful of the damage inflicted on his shoes and trousers by water and mud, Robert launched his craft, urged it, guided it, and once or twice rescued it, and time went by.

Lord Fellmount could never afterwards decide what took him down to the lake that afternoon. He had spoken his mind — a proceeding which always gave him pleasure; he had got rid of an unwanted visitor — a more pleasing circumstance still. It was usual for satisfaction to have a restful effect upon his lordship, but on this keen, pleasant afternoon, back in his own rooms after having watched Robert's departure, he felt restless and unable to return to his chess problem. Sitting at the little table, he studied it gloomily. White to play and mate in five moves. Five moves. . . . Where was he? Bishop to — where the devil was that solution? Bishop to — well, of course. Now Black'd have to shift his King. . . . That damned impertinent puppy had soon put his tail between his legs. He'd like to have seen himself at that age, frightened off by an old man. Bah! Damned weaklings, all of them, nowadays. Filled 'em with cod liver oil and things called vitamins and thought that made men of 'em. Pah! If he'd been fool enough to take a wife, and she'd been woman enough to bear him an heir, he'd have liked to see her shoveling in stuff out of bottles. Look at that young pup — as fine a physical specimen as he'd ever seen, and good-looking into the bargain, if he hadn't looked so damned frightened; fine specimen, and not a shred of guts. None. All cod liver oil and vitamins and soft food and soft upbringing. Take those ninnies of schoolmasters up there, with their toy boats . . . on his lake? He'd see 'em drowned in it first, and their toys with 'em. If he caught one of 'em inside his grounds he'd carry 'em to the lake personally and throw 'em into it.

It is not possible to say whether Lord Fellmount walked down to the lake to picture this plan in action, or whether he went in order to assure himself that no ninnies were in sight. He pushed his chessboard aside with a petulant gesture, drummed an irritable tattoo on his knees for a few moments, and then, with a sudden movement, stood up and walked out of the room. He changed his greenish tweed jacket for one of brownish tweed, placed upon his head a soft hat of a Sherlock Holmes type, and marched with firm steps out of the house.

Nice day. Sort of day he used to enjoy when there was a bit more blood in his legs. No blood in any legs now. Young men's veins full of petrol, bah.

Lot of fallen timber here. Nobody'd think that this rutted bit of road used to be the favorite drive for carriages in the old days. His grandmother always used to insist on coming this way to have a look at the water. There it was, with a bit of sun on it. Gave it a glisten. Nothing like a bit of sun on water. Nothing like —

His lordship's musing ended abruptly as a small object came into view, slid gracefully along the short stretch of water within sight, and disappeared, it seemed, into the trees. Lord Fellmount, his eyes starting from his head, stood still and stared at the empty water, blinking now and then as if to clear his vision.

Must be seeing things. Bit of white paper, perhaps, blowing across his line of vision. Looked like a sail, almost. Peculiar.

He moved forward a few paces and stopped

again, this time with realization and rage flooding his heart. There, on his water in full view, by Jupiter! Under his very nose . . . in the teeth of his emphatic refusal to the young puppy that very afternoon, in the —

By thunder, and there! The young pup himself, crouching there by the lake's edge, hiding, no doubt, the confounded craven. No, worse — bending down with a hand outstretched to draw in the boat and to — He'd kick him in, by Jupiter.

What the devil, wondered his lordship, would he be doing? Adjusting the sails. As if adjusting the sails on a trumpery little toy like that could —

It was away again, and at what a pace, my word! And what an angle! In another second the thing'd be over — there! No, it wasn't; it was steadying and making for — What did that damned young pup think he was doing, walking in *that* direction? Any fool with half an eye in his head could see that the thing was making straight for *that* shore. For — well no, dammit, it wasn't. It was turning and it was — Upon me soul, it was making straight for that pup there. It was nearing him . . . he'd got it. Now he was twiddling away at it again. Now steady — steady there! It was off. By thunder! what a pace. What a pace, what a sight! Little white thing dancing there in the breeze as proud as you please and — now then, now then, steady up there or you'll be over. . . . Good! Good little fellow, then. Coming this way, by Jingo. Ought to land just about on that piece there by the steps. Yes, about here . . . come on, then, come on. No use that young pup scuttling round. He'd got here first and he was going to do the twiddling this time. Another few yards . . . another foot and —

"Look out, you old fool!" shouted Robert.

It was too late. Lord Fellmount had gone in head foremost and was struggling in three feet of water. Robert, cursing fluently in terms particularly directed against elderly gentlemen who appeared from nowhere and cast themselves into muddy water, waded in, seized the submerged nobleman by the collar, and dragged him ashore.

To his surprise, the old man appeared reluctant to leave his watery bed. Unable to speak, but using the little breath he could command to resist Robert's firm pull, he stretched out a scrawny hand and made several stabs in the direction of the water.

"Come on, you," directed Robert.

His lordship, unaccustomed to this inattention to his needs, put his feet together and leaned back like a jibbing mule, and Robert understood, from something more than a stutter but less than a sentence, that he wished to go back for the yacht, which was floating a little forlornly toward the middle of the lake.

"You're not stopping for salvage operations," said Robert firmly. "Come on."

"Gerrout," choked Lord Fellmount.

"I'm getting out," said Robert, "and so are you. For the last time, come *on.*"

"Gerrout," said his lordship.

Without wasting any more words, Robert stooped and lifted the old man. Putting him across his shoulder, he made his way to the car, slithering up the sloping bank and making loud, squelching sounds as his feet reached firmer ground. He got to the car, fumbled for the handle of the door and placed his burden gently on the seat. Hurrying round to the other side, he got in and turned the car in the direction of the house.

He was seriously alarmed. The old man beside him, though still able to swear, was wet through and almost completely covered in mud. His teeth were chattering and the little Robert could see of his face was blue and pinched. If the rest of the house up there, he reflected, was the same temperature as the hall, there was little chance of restoring the old boy to blood heat. He'd probably die on his hands and they'd say he'd pushed him in on purpose, and the next thing, he'd be facing a Coroner's inquest.

He took the car along as fast as he dared,

bumping over obstacles which he had carefully avoided on the way down. Skidding round the last bend, he came to a stop before the massive door and, getting out, came round to the other side of the car and assisted his passenger to alight. After one glance, he picked him up once more and went swiftly into the house.

This time, he went straight into the inner hall and through the door from which his host had previously emerged. Through a door on the other side of the room he entered, he saw the old servant, pale and agitated, hurrying toward him.

"It's all right," said Robert. "Case of immersion. Bedroom?"

With admirable promptitude, the man led the way through corridors, up stairs, and along more corridors, and Robert, his heart beginning to beat faster than was comfortable, hoped that the noble bedchamber would soon be reached. He saw with relief that the panting manservant had stopped before a small alcove, and through this, Robert saw a plainly furnished suite of rooms.

"Blankets and hot water," he ordered, passing the man with his burden. "And brandy. And a suit of pajamas."

In a moment, the man had spread a heavy rug on the bed and Lord Fellmount was lying on it. He put up a shaking hand, wiped some mud from his eyes, and looked at Robert.

"Gerrout," he ordered.

"Presently," promised Robert.

With gentle but dexterous movements, he undressed the old man, rolled the rug round him, and began a firm kneading movement, his hands moving over the chilled, bony frame and bringing the blood back to the half-frozen limbs. His lordship, inert, looked up at him with a malignant stare but Robert was intent on his massaging and scarcely noticed it.

In a very short time, the old man, cleaned with a warm sponge, clad in comfortable pajamas, and fortified with a stiff dose of brandy, lay in his bed. Robert stretched his weary arms, drew a deep breath of relief, and looked round for his coat.

Lord Fellmount studied him. The pup was going. If he thought he hadn't heard all those things he called him when he pulled him out of the water, he was mistaken. Every word. Every strong and uncomplimentary word. Brought him in like a sack of coals. He'd go back and tell a pretty story to those other ninnies and —

He was at the door.

"Hey, you," called the old man.

Robert turned. The old boy looked better. He'd send the doctor up to look at him later, but it looked as though the warmth and the brandy were soon going to have their effect — the old geezer looked half asleep.

Lord Fellmount made a strong effort to combat the drowsiness overtaking him. "That boat," he said. "Buy it off you."

"Sorry," said Robert.

The old man eyed him with strong dislike. "Damned puppy," he said.

Robert inclined his head.

"Blasted insolence," proceeded his lordship.

Robert frowned suddenly and Lord Fellmount studied him with a new interest. Handsome fellow and dangerous-looking. Wouldn't like to trust him with a knife and that look on his face.

"You Games Master?" he inquired.

"No," said Robert.

"What d'you teach, then?"

"I don't teach," responded Robert. "I don't teach and I'm not at the School and I'm not interested in the School or in the boys or in you or in your ruddy lake. You ought to rent it to the School and I came here to tell you so. You can fall in it and stay in it next time, as far as I'm concerned. I didn't come here to play Tiny Tim; I don't give a damn what you do with your property; you can dance round the edge of it howling at trespassers as long as you please."

He turned and walked to the door.

"Hey!" said his lordship.

Robert looked over his shoulder.

"How d'you get the thing to turn by itself?" inquired Lord Fellmount.

"Know anything about sailing?" asked Robert in his turn.

"I'm asking you, you young fool," said his lordship savagely.

Robert raised his eyebrows. "Thing called a beating guy," he said smoothly. "Hooked onto the weather side of your craft and the tension of the elastic adjusted so's when the wind stretches it out fully the sail pulls on the ordinary beating sheet. The guy hauls the mainsheet closer and your boat luffs into the wind and goes about. You hook the jib sheet on the lee side of the — "

"How much," broke in his lordship, "those little boats cost?"

"They needn't cost anything," said Robert. "The boys can make 'em themselves — under supervision, of course."

"Rent 'em the water," said his lordship, "on one condition."

Robert turned slowly and faced the speaker. He gave a keen glance at the lined, flushed face and spoke calmly. "It's the brandy," he said.

Lord Fellmount raised his voice. "Pertwee!" he called hoarsely.

"Your lordship?"

"Listen t'me," commanded the old man. "Get that fool of a lawyer up here tomorrow.

And you — " he turned to Robert — "you, you young puppy, you go back and tell that Headmaster to come up in the morning."

"What," inquired Robert, "is the condition?"

"Myself," said his lordship.

That, he was pleased to observe, had shaken the pup.

"You mean — " began Robert.

"I'm going to sail 'em too," stated his lordship. "I can do it. Matter of simple observation. Put up a kind of boathouse — boys needn't carry the things back and forth. I'd keep m'eye on 'em."

"I'm sure you would," said Robert.

"Go on — gerrout," said his host. "Meet the Headmaster tomorrow at noon and get it in order. And you keep off my land, d'you hear?"

"From now onwards," said Robert. "Good-by."

"Gerrout," said his lordship, in farewell.

Robert went out and closed the door. Holding his wet coat, he ran swiftly down the stairs, taking them four at a time. He got into his car and drove rapidly away, deciding that, wet and cold though he was, it would be better to go up to the School without going to the Cottage to change first.

He entered the School and made his way through the hall. From the shrill, confused sounds emerging from the dining room, he judged that the boys were at tea. The Head would be in his room.

He found the Headmaster bending over a sheaf of papers, with Michael Sheridan standing beside him. Mervyn Clunes gave a glance of concern at Robert's muddied trousers and soaked shoes.

"Did he throw you in?" he inquired.

"No," said Robert.

"I'm sorry you went," said Mr. Clunes. "He's not a pleasant man to have dealings with."

"You'll have to overlook that," said Robert. "He wants to see you at noon tomorrow."

"Great Scott!" Mervyn Clunes stared at Robert unbelievingly. "You mean — has he actually — ?"

"He'll probably try to push you up to a pretty stiff figure," said Robert.

"I don't like it much," put in Michael slowly. "If he feels like throwing the boys out, he'll do it, and papers and agreements won't stop him. Perhaps it would be better to stay off altogether." He turned to the Headmaster. "There's some sort of catch in it, sir," he said.

"There is," said Robert. "You can have the water, but you'll have to swallow the old boy, too. He's taking to model yachts."

There was silence for a few moments as the two listeners digested this piece of news. Then Michael spoke slowly. "You mean —

he's sort of bitten with the sport?" he asked.

"He'll be on your tail," prophesied Robert, "looking into hull design and fin positioning before you know where you are. But it's either that or no water. If he gets really troublesome, you can push him in. He won't stand many more immersions."

"Well, we're very grateful to you," said Mr. Clunes. "Especially as one of the parents, the father of a boy named Harfield, is down here to discuss his son's immersion. The boy was thrown in at the end of last term. There might have been trouble. The father's brought one of his newspapermen with him and we had a troublesome session the other day, but this'll clear the matter up. I'll tell him we've got the lake and his son will come back and fall in as often as he likes without any complications. I don't know how Sheridan will tack yet another subject onto his curriculum," he went on. "Tack! That's a nice professional term. I must be getting yacht-minded, like his lordship."

Robert took a brief leave and walked outside with Michael Sheridan. The Headmaster came to the door and spoke a parting sentence. "I was sorry, Drake," he said, "to hear a day or two ago about your fiancée's father."

Robert halted, turned slowly and looked at the speaker. "My fiancée's — ?" He paused inquiringly.

"That bankruptcy business," said Mr. Clunes. "Damn bad show."

Robert's face was expressionless and his voice, when he spoke, was even. "Quite so," he said.

"How," inquired the Headmaster, "is Miss Andrews taking it?"

There was a slight pause. Robert flicked an imaginary spot from his coatsleeve and looked up.

"I'll just," he said quietly, "go home and see."

CHAPTER EIGHTEEN

Caroline and Iris lunched alone.

"D'you think," Iris asked, "Polly left a pair of slacks that I could borrow? I'm going out on what I think will be a rough party — sliding downhill with all the little boys. The School's holding its winter carnival or something."

"You'll find anything of hers a bit small, won't you?" said Caroline. "But I'll go see what's there."

She walked into Iris's room a little later with a pair of skiing trousers over her arm.

"Here," she said. "Very elegant — navy blue waterproof gabardine. Try them on."

Iris tried them on and took a few careful steps to and fro.

"Tight fit," she announced.

"You could pull them down a bit more at the ankles," suggested Caroline. "They'd keep the snow out."

"If I keep the snow out *that* end, I'll get the draft in *this* end," complained Iris. "Do they look all right?"

"They'll think you wore them when you were younger, and you've grown out of them," said Caroline. "They'll be all right if you keep walking. But if you sit down, then — "

"Kkkkrrrrr!" said Iris. "Quite so. Well, we'll hope for the best."

She wrapped herself up warmly and went out, going briskly up the road and through the village. She took a steep upward path and sniffed appreciatively the clear, frosty air. The sun shone, the snow sparkled, and if the birds were wondering where their next meal was coming from, nobody would have guessed it from their gay twittering. Iris lengthened her steps as she felt the day's exhilaration and shortened them again cautiously as her trouser seams began to protest.

She scrambled up to a point from which the Castle and the slopes beyond were clearly visible, and saw that the landscape was dotted with figures, some moving slowly upwards and others rushing swiftly down. It was a scene of gaiety and movement, and Iris paused for a moment to enjoy it.

She admitted to herself, standing there, that though the School had, in her opinion, a great many structural and geographical disadvantages, there was no doubt whatsoever that it was the finest school in the country for tobogganing.

To green caps, she saw as she drew near, were now added warm green mufflers, worn in a variety of ways — some wound closely round the owner's neck, some thrown on carelessly and waving cheerfully in the breeze, and some — very sensibly, Iris thought — tied over caps, keeping them in place through the most unexpected of spills.

Iris was warmly greeted by her friends. Mr. Swintzchell hurried to meet her, inadvisedly crossing a little frozen puddle which a dozen boys had worked zealously to bring to the smoothness of glass. His greetings, begun from the perpendicular, ended, a little breathlessly but with unabated cheerfulness, from what Smithfield primus termed the heavy horizontal.

"Good morning, good morning. *Gott in Himmel!* Now I am on my back, but never mind, never mind. Thank you, thank you, boys. Yes, I am all right, thank you, but you must put some little flags to show where are your slides, like the little flags on the golf course that warn of the holes. Look, here is Miss Drake come — welcome, welcome! Is this not pleasant, and so fine a day?"

"I've come to join in," announced Iris without wasting time. "Any toboggans on hire?"

There were, it appeared, several owners of toboggans who were only too happy to give Miss Drake a ride. Michael Sheridan left a group of boys and came across to inspect the varieties offered for Iris's inspection.

"Not that one," he called. "Cockran, take away that green one. Its underside is coming away. Smythe, that one's too light for Miss Drake. That one's all right, Winter."

Winter drew his property away from the rest and with a wave of his hand offered it to Iris. She moved toward it, but a cry from behind halted her.

"Wait a mo, Miss Drake," shouted an eager voice. "This one — this one. I made it. She goes like a wizz and she steers, too — look!"

David Carruthers, with cheeks that looked as though they were on fire and with clouds of steam issuing from his mouth to heighten the illusion, came gasping to Iris's side. He was too breathless to do more than point to his toboggan, and Iris studied it dubiously.

"It's all right, truly," said David, recovering his breath. "I've been down five times with Stuffy and she goes like a wizz. You steer — " he demonstrated — "this way."

Mr. Sheridan bent to examine it, and Iris frowned. "Look, I don't have to have special safety devices installed when I slide down a hill," she said. "I just want to sit in something and go down — that's all."

"Well, this'll go down," put in David eagerly. "She goes down like a wizz, and if there're two of you, she isn't very heavy to pull up again. Try it, sir!" he begged. "Miss Drake can be in front and steer, and you can be behind. If you bend over when you go round that bend, she goes like a wizz, doesn't she, Stuffy?"

"Come on," said Iris. "There's a lot too much talking here and not nearly enough traveling. You coming?" she asked Michael, "or are you frightened?"

There was laughter from the boys at this ludicrous suggestion, and Mr. Sheridan, without further words, drew the toboggan to the edge of the slope, put out a hand to help Iris into the front seat, and took his place behind her. Iris sat down and remembering, a little belatedly, Polly's trousers, was pleasantly surprised to find that, far from being tight, they were roomy and comfortable.

An enthusiastic crew laid hands on the toboggan and, but for a sharp check from Mr. Sheridan, would have overturned the passengers before the journey began. In obedience to his orders, however, the start was orderly and uneventful.

"Steady," he said. "And not until I say, 'Go.' Hold it. Now — Go!"

They were away. The toboggan gathered speed and Iris gave a joyful squeak as she felt the air rushing past her face.

"Hang onto those ropes," came Michael's voice. "Get ready for the bend. Now!"

The toboggan flew at the curve, rose to it and round it. Iris gave a yell of triumph. They were round.

They were also, unfortunately, over. Iris had let the ropes go, and in an instant the toboggan had swung to the opposite bank, climbed it, and launched itself over the edge. After a few moments of movement too rapid for sensation, Iris found herself lying half in, half out of a deep snowdrift and, floundering and struggling to reach firm ground, discovered that she was clutching an unfamiliar blue and white woolen scarf.

She made a difficult way through the snow and, finding a fallen tree, brushed the snow from it and sat down, looking about her.

There was no sign of Michael Sheridan, and no sign, moreover, of any part of the gay scene of which, only a few moments ago, they had been a part. Voices could be heard, yells and laughter, but there was nobody in sight. Iris raised her voice and called: "Michael! Where are you?"

There was no reply, but Iris heard a grunt and, turning, saw Michael Sheridan making his way toward her through a small wooded patch. His face was scratched and his hair stood wildly on end; one of his hands was cut and his spectacles had vanished. He sat down beside Iris and frowned at the scarf in her hand.

"So that's where it went?" he remarked. "Next time you spill a man out of a machine, perhaps you'd refrain from trying to choke him, too."

"How did I get this?" asked Iris.

"You got it," Michael informed her, "by the simple process of hanging onto it until it came away in your hand."

"You mean I sort of clutched it?"

"You were holding it all the time," said Michael with resignation. "You were steering with it. And when the toboggan didn't respond to the pull on the muffler and we went overboard, you hung onto it and pulled me half-way down, choking, by the neck. Then it came off, thank God, and you did the rest of the descent by yourself."

"Where's the toboggan?" asked Iris.

"It's practically where we left it," said Michael. "About eighty feet up, I'd say. It certainly went like a wizz."

He stopped speaking and seemed to be looking for something. He took the scarf from Iris's hands and examined it.

"What're you looking for?" she asked.

"My glasses," said Michael. "I can't see very far without them."

"That's all right," said Iris reassuringly. "I won't go far. I've always wanted to see you without them."

"Got 'em!" exclaimed Michael. "I knew they'd be there, if they weren't smashed to pieces."

The glasses were, indeed, caught on the scarf. He disentangled them carefully and, taking out his handkerchief, polished them. Iris put out a hand as he prepared to put them on.

"Please!" she said. "Just for a few minutes. Just so's I can see you without that schoolmaster look."

"There's nothing wrong," said Michael, putting on the glasses, "with a schoolmaster look. If I had to look like anything in particular, I'd rather look like a schoolmaster than like most other things. What, exactly," he inquired, "have you against the profession?"

"It makes men think too much," complained Iris. "It makes them think all the time, and I think that the more they think, the less they — well, the less they feel."

"What," asked Michael in a tone of mild interest, "do you think they ought to feel?"

"I don't quite know," said Iris. "But even if you do pretend to be an entirely detached, cold sort of person you must sometimes — "

"I don't," said Michael, "pretend to be anything. I rather gather that I don't come up to scratch in a lot of ways, but there are more fellows like me than you seem to imagine. A good many of us can get along quite happily without dances and night clubs and drinking parties and theaters and cinemas. And girls. And it's a good thing, too," he added, "since a lot of us couldn't afford all those delights even if we wanted them. I," he ended calmly, "don't want them."

Iris turned and looked at him incredulously. "You mean that all you want, all your life, is little boys?" she asked. "*Je suis, tu es, il* or even *elle est, nous* what-is-it, *vous* something or other, *ils sont?* Just that? For years and years, for the whole of your life?

Sit down Smith minor, get up Brown major, silence you cads, file out in line, *asseyez-vous, levez-vous, asseyez-vous,* until you're old and dead, until you're gray and bent and — and finished? That's all? No home, no love, no woman, no passion, no — no anything?"

"No anything," said Michael.

There was a pause. Iris's eyes were fixed on him, and there was a look of bewilderment in them.

"I don't understand you," she said at last. "You can't be as no-anything as you try to make out."

Michael smiled. "You," he told her, "are a little difficult to understand yourself."

"Explain, please," said Iris.

"Certainly. You're fairly intelligent, for a start," said Michael, "and yet you believe this imbecile, hackneyed fiction about men — highly trained, clever, useful men — being quite unable to live normal and unfretted lives without being torn with what I presume you'd term desire. That's point one. Next, you're a nice girl and you know the value of modesty and restraint, and yet you like to feel that every time you come near a man you whip his blood to fever heat. You have a job, a flat, friends and amusements of your own, and you waste a good deal of time looking for something in a stray schoolmaster that isn't there. Then you — "

"All right," broke in Iris. "You needn't go on. But I'd like to explain something now that we've started on it."

"Need we?" asked Michael.

"Yes, we need," said Iris. "I do know the value of — of modesty and restraint, but I don't think they'd be much use to any girl who tried to get through your concrete fortifications. I came down here, I saw you, and I quite liked you. And if you'd been friendly, we could have had heaps of fun — and I mean fun with lots of modesty and restraint. I've never looked twice at any man in my whole life. I've been brushing them off since I was seventeen, and I don't know why I had to come down here and pick on a — a sort of panjandrum of outdoor sports for boys. All I wanted was to meet you sometimes and go for a walk, or take a bus into the next village or even sit at home and listen to Caroline trying over her arpeggios. I liked the way you looked and I liked your voice and I didn't even mind your glasses though I often wondered how much they'd get in the way if you ever kissed me — with modesty and restraint, that is. I liked you, and all you had to do was to be friendly and laugh and have fun and enjoy things together. All I wanted was just a little plain, honest friendliness. I never imagined that I'd come to — well, to this."

Michael looked at her. "To what?" he inquired.

"Love," said Iris. "After years of dodging brilliant journalists, ambitious undergraduates, successful actors, and starving playwrights. It's odd isn't it? But when you're old and lonely, and no girl will look twice at you, you'll remember this morning — and perhaps you'll wish you were back on this tree trunk, with a beautiful girl telling you what might have been."

"Couldn't I," suggested Michael, "have found myself a beautiful girl in the meantime?"

"No," said Iris. "I'm not conceited and it doesn't matter much to me, but at least I know this — you'll never get a girl who's nicer to look at, or who can put on her clothes to more effect, or who has a more perfect figure or a more perfect skin."

"You've set," admitted Michael, "a pretty high standard."

"I've set it. You try and reach it — if you can," said Iris. She looked at the man beside her, gave a little sigh, and rose to her feet. "And talking of reaching it," she said, "hadn't we better do something about trying to reach that toboggan?"

Michael, rising with her, took her hand and held it lightly in his own. He glanced down and, the next moment, gave a violent start and clutched her arm.

"What's the matter?" she asked in bewilderment.

Michael appeared to be choosing his words. "Your trousers — I mean — " He stopped and tried again. "Is there any part," he asked, "in which you feel particularly chilly?"

Iris, staring at him blankly for a moment, gave a wail of dismay and made a desperate clutch at the seat of her trousers. She could feel nothing but the softest of silk.

"Oh, gosh!" she moaned. "*That's* why I could sit down. Is anything," she asked fearfully, "is anything sh-showing?"

Michael gave a hasty glance. "Only pink. Pink silk," he added hastily. "But there's rather — I mean, it's a pretty big rent."

"Now what?" asked Iris. "Do I walk backwards all the way home?"

"Well, it's awkward," said Michael. "We'd probably get as far as the toboggan without meeting anybody."

"And after that, what? Sit in the toboggan and get towed all the way home?" demanded Iris.

"Well, don't get angry with me. *I* didn't tear your pants," pointed out Michael.

"No," admitted Iris. "Well, go on. Lead me to the toboggan, and I'll sit in it with modesty and you can pull me with restraint."

"You can come up to the School by toboggan," said Michael, "and I'll get hold of a car and run you home."

"A day in the life of an ex-reporter," said Iris.

"Ex-reporter? Aren't you," inquired Michael, "a lady detective any more?"

"Sacked," said Iris. "My Chief came down to see me, couldn't, caught a chill, got painted with white paint by your Mr. Swintzchell, and went off with the notes I'd typed for you."

Michael walked a few steps in deep thought. "I'm sorry," he said. "Perhaps he'll — reinstate you. My mother seemed to think that being a lady detective was — "

Iris uttered an exclamation and, halting, turned to face her companion. "You — you wrote to your mother about — about me?" she asked in amazement.

"Certainly," said Michael.

"What did you say?" asked Iris.

"I said — let me see — I said — well, I gave her a brief description of you," said Michael slowly, "and she said you sounded quite an interesting type and well worth studying. She suggested — "

"Well, what?"

"I forget," said Michael. "Now we've got to get back. But before we go — " he put a hand on Iris's arm and drew her gently toward him — "before we go, we'd better clear up your point."

"What point?" asked Iris.

"Your point," explained Michael, "as to whether my glasses would get in the way."

Slowly and firmly and with an unexpected expertness, he put his arms round her and bent his head to hers.

"This," he paused to explain, "is purely experimental."

Iris entered the house and found herself in the midst of a charming domestic scene. The tea table was drawn up by the fire and round it, eating toasted scones, sat Caroline and Simon.

"Well," Iris said, "Polly's skiing trousers are no more. You can't see the damage yet, because I borrowed Mike Sheridan's coat, but there's a rent from here to there and — "

"It doesn't matter," said Caroline. "She's got lots more. Did you have fun?"

"I had more than fun," said Iris. "Is there anything left to eat? Simon, you pig, you've just taken the last scone. I saw you."

"Yours are keeping hot," said Caroline. "I'll go and get them."

"Any sign of Robert?" she asked Iris.

"None when I left the School, but Mike Sheridan said they're expecting him to call and tell them how he got thrown out on his ear by Lord Fellmount."

Tea over, the table was cleared and the

party prepared to close round the fire once more.

There was the sound of a car stopping, the click of the gate latch, and a moment later the door opened and Robert entered.

"Nice to see you," said Simon.

"Did you get thrown off the site?" asked Iris.

Robert took no notice of their remarks and ignored Caroline's inquiry as to whether he had had tea.

"I've just heard," he said, "some news. Interesting news. About Polly's father. You, of course, were informed of the sad fact that Mr. Andrews had hit a rock?"

Caroline and Iris nodded silently and exchanged pleased glances. He hadn't known.

"And since everybody," Robert continued angrily, "was freely informed of the incident, I can only conclude that there was a very special reason for keeping it from me. I'm here to find out what that reason was. Where's Polly?" he concluded abruptly.

"Polly went to London, with no explanations. We heard the news later," Caroline told him calmly.

"You let her go?" Robert said incredulously. "You merely let her pack and — and just go — is that it?"

"We couldn't stop her, could we?" said Iris reasonably. "You should have left instructions."

"No, you couldn't," said Robert bitterly. "No — of course not. You couldn't tell her not to be a damn fool, and you couldn't tell her to wait until I came back, could you?"

"But we didn't — " Iris began.

"I suppose you all wondered," Robert went on, his fury rising, "if perhaps a swine like myself mightn't have built up a lot of hopes on Daddy's money?" He glared at them for a minute, then, turning on his heel, walked to the door and opened it.

He was outside. The door closed with a crash behind him. The car door banged, the engine came to life, and with a roar and a grinding of gears, Robert was gone.

CHAPTER NINETEEN

The three days following Robert's departure were, for Caroline, the most unhappy period she had ever spent in her life. She went about her household tasks as calmly as possible, and emptied the larder to provide tempting food for Iris.

Through these days, Simon Gunter was a constant support to the two women. He came early every morning, performed a number of indoor and outdoor tasks, and listened to Caroline with unfailing interest and sympathy.

The house seemed empty without Polly. Caroline, worried and depressed, felt grateful for the sewing which the three boys had brought. With cooking and cleaning, sewing and altering and looking over her solo for the Choir Service, she found little time to brood. Iris helped with the sewing, typed notes for Michael Sheridan, sent them off to the appropriate magazine editors, and spent a great deal of time at Holly Lodge trying, she explained carefully to Caroline, the altered garments on the boys.

The day of the Play arrived, misty, wet, and cold. Caroline opened the door to take in the milk, shivered, saw the postman coming up the road, and waited to take the letters.

"Anything interesting?" asked Iris, as she brought them in.

"Nothing. At least — one for you," said Caroline, handing it across the breakfast table. "And two for me — my mother-in-law and a brother-in-law. What's yours?" she asked.

Iris made no reply. She read quickly through her letter, read it again slowly, folded it, and put it beside her plate.

"Bad news?" asked Caroline, looking at her sister's serious face.

"No — not bad news." Iris hesitated. "It's — well, from Ernest. Something that might be called an apology for his previous communication and — "

"Your job back?"

"If I want it," said Iris slowly, "yes."

Caroline found that her appetite had suddenly left her. She crumbled her toast, looked at it distastefully, and replaced the little piece of butter carefully on the butter dish. She felt, for no apparent reason, gloomy and apprehensive. There had been far too much heart trouble, and there might be some more. If Iris's plans were working well, why did she sit there looking at Ernest's letter as if it — as if it could make any difference — as if . . .

It would, she knew, be more delicate to allow Iris to speak or be silent. But delicacy was all very well. Caroline resolved to be delicate at some other time. At this moment she wanted reassurance and she was going to ask for it.

"Do you," she inquired, "intend to—to take the job again?"

Iris looked up, and Caroline, her fears mounting, saw that there was hesitation and doubt in her sister's manner.

"What does 'intend' mean?" asked Iris. "How can I 'intend' anything at all? If I knew how—how matters stood, I'd know whether I had to take Ernest's job or whether I could write and—and tell him to keep it. But—"

There was a pause.

"But what?" asked Caroline. "I'm sorry, Iris," she went on, "to seem so—so inquisitive about things I shouldn't poke into, but, well, there's been so much of everything, I don't want to feel that you—that your—What I mean is," she ended in desperation, "are things going all right between you and—and Michael Sheridan?"

Iris waited for some time before replying. "I don't know," she said at last. "Sounds odd, doesn't it, after all my—my bombast of the other day. I was going to—what was I going to do? Wind myself round his heart. Blast my way into his affections."

"And—and did you?" asked Caroline.

Iris pushed her chair back and stood up. "I don't think so," she said. "I'm sorry to sound like a woman scorned, but I—I don't really know. You can't tell what he's thinking."

"But you can't — " began Caroline reluctantly.

"I know. I can't go on indefinitely waiting for a man who requires all that encouragement. You needn't tell me, Carol. I've known for days. And I don't think I ever really believed I could, well, manage it. I could only hope that he'd see — that he'd understand that I was really in love. And I think he does, and that's as far as a girl can go, and that's ninety per cent of the way." She picked up the letter from the table and pressed it slowly into small, neat folds. "This," she said, "is a nice return to realities."

"You're going to — you're going back to work?" asked Caroline.

"After the Play," said Iris, steadily. "I'll tell Mike I've had the offer. If he wants me to accept it, then, well then, I will."

Caroline opened her mouth to speak and closed it again. There was, she realized, nothing more to say.

Up at Castle Ambo, the Headmaster looked out at the thick mist and wondered how many visitors would be able to arrive in time for the tea which was to be served before the Play. Trains would be late; cars would be held up.

The scene in the Great Hall in the afternoon, however, showed that a large proportion of the expected crowd had arrived punctually. Hungry parents, exercising a difficult self-control, hovered near tables upon which were spread a tempting array of good things. Simon, in response to an urgent appeal from Caroline, struggled to make his way to the little cakes with pink icing — a sight which Caroline asserted she had not seen for years.

Behind the stage, those responsible for the production were busy putting the finishing touches to the setting and the properties. Small boys worked, big boys directed, and Mr. Sheridan and Mr. Fitzwilliam moved about in the wings.

Iris, furious because she had not succeeded in wringing from the reluctant Michael permission to sit beside him and assist with the lighting, climbed down the stairs at the side of the stage and made her way slowly and aimlessly along a corridor. The sounds of the speeches died away and she could hear nothing but an occasional burst of laughter or applause. She found herself at the door of a classroom and, going inside, sat down listlessly at one of the desks and looked about her. Desks. Desks with ink spots and scratches. A small platform at the end of the room and another desk on it. That, she thought, was no doubt where the Master said *levez-vous* and *asseyez-vous*. No—she glanced round at the large pictures on the walls, pictures of village life, colored representations of the seaside, drawings of foreign-looking children running after hoops. And underneath them, words in large black type. What language was that? Not French. Not German. Must be Spanish. Fancy stuffing little boys with Spanish. *Un Accidente en el Hielo.* An accident in the something or other. Ice, probably, if that boy disappearing down the crack meant anything. Girl in bed, and a man. *Visita del Medico.* Well, as long as it was only the Medico. . . . *En el Banco. En el Restaurant.* It was chilly in here, but it mightn't be the room. It might be the cold feeling she'd had all day, as if something awful was going to happen. But the feeling was still there. Gamblers must feel something like this when they were pulling off their shirts and preparing to put them on the last possible hope. Here she was, and before she left this school, if there was any opportunity at all, she was going to tell Mike about the job — and then wait. . . .

El Naufragio. What was that? Something nautical, judging by the sea scene. Did children abroad really wear those long black stockings and comic hats? *En el Huerto.* That was a nice peaceful scene in the orchard. Peace was something that came from inside. Her inside didn't feel peaceful at all. How far could a girl go when she was in love with a man and he didn't seem to . . . Well, yes, he loved her. There was something below his calm manner and his deliberate avoidances and his lack of response. It wasn't her imagination. It was there; she knew it was there. But if he wouldn't admit it, if he felt that she wasn't the kind of wife who'd fit into a setting like this—inky desks and lessons pinned on the walls — if he thought she wouldn't do, if he felt he'd rather stick to what he imagined was his own type . . .

He couldn't. He loved her; she was quite, quite sure he loved her. But that fact, which would have been the end with any of the other men she knew, was only the beginning with this one. He glanced off love and came to rest on all kinds of unrelated matters — suitability, vocation, self-abnegation, dedication. He thought that a man and a woman needed a good deal more than love. Well, perhaps, they did, but they could work it out together afterwards, couldn't they? They could get married and then grow together, couldn't they? Couldn't they, Mike? Couldn't they?

How long she sat in the bare classroom, Iris never knew. Lost in thought, deep in dreams, she took no note of the last prolonged applause, the brief silence during the Headmaster's congratulations, and the notes of the National Anthem. She sat at the desk, her chin on her hands, elbows resting on the ink stains, and wished with all her heart that it was tomorrow. Tomorrow, when she would either be speeding to London and putting piercing memories resolutely away, or tomorrow, when she would wake up knowing that uncertainty was over and she and Michael . . .

She was roused by the switching on of a light and Michael's voice of amazement.

"Good Lord, is this where you'd got to? What on earth," he inquired, "are you doing in here? Taking up Spanish?"

"Is the Play over?"

"Long ago. The Play's over and the parents are saying good-by and in a little while the school will be closed to visitors. Your sister's walked home with Mr. Gunter and left his car for you to use."

"Good. Want a lift?" asked Iris.

"Me? Good Lord, no! I've got a couple of hour's work yet," said Michael. "But I'll see you to the car."

Iris rose from the desk but made no move to depart. She was going to do it and she was going to do it quickly. Here it was.

She faced Michael Sheridan and spoke lightly. "Look, Mike," she said, "I've got something to ask you."

Michael's eyes looked keenly at her for a moment and then became calm once more. "Fire away," he invited.

"I had a letter today," said Iris, "from old Ernest. You know who old Ernest is?"

"I suppose," said Michael, "he's asking you to go back."

"That's it," said Iris. "Apologies — and my job back."

"I see," said Michael. "Are you going to take it?"

Iris fought back a desire to move closer to him, to plead, to argue, to fight. She spoke steadily.

"That depends on you," she said. "I don't want the job. I want to write and tell him he can keep it — forever. But I wanted to ask you about it first. You see, I don't want to embarrass you, but I've been trying to — to make you see what a wonderful — well, all I wanted to ask was whether you thought I ought to take the job or — or not."

There was silence. Michael's face was white, but Iris, seeking desperately, could see nothing behind the usual quietness of his manner. She felt her heart thumping suffocatingly and waited until she could bear the silence no more.

"Well, Mike?" she asked.

"I think, Iris — " Michael Sheridan's voice wavered for an instant and then went on firmly — "I think you'd better write and say you'll take it. I — you see, I — "

"Don't say it!" broke in Iris sharply. "Don't say anything more, Mike. Please!"

"I must, Iris," said Michael quietly. "You see, it — it wouldn't do. You're lovely and you're — you're gay and sweet and nothing I can offer you would — If you could see yourself now, in this setting, you'd understand a little better. . . . You look so beautiful, and so utterly out of place. You need an altogether different background, you could never merge into this one, and I'm not sure that I'd want you to. You're lovely as you are. You belong to a far less serious society; you want a far more colorful setting. You don't — you couldn't fit in with this kind of thing — bare boards, plain desks, successive classes of students and dull, engrossed schoolmasters. Nobody — nobody, Iris — would feel it was right to put you there. And so, darling Iris, you must go back again. I'll remember you all my life, and I'll be grateful to you all my life, but you couldn't, you could never, my darling, be a schoolmaster's wife."

Silence fell in the large, bare room. The lighted windows threw a confused beam out into the darkness. A long way away, boys' voices could be heard, and the thump of noisy feet.

Iris drew a deep breath, looked round the room as if she was committing its details to memory, and faced Michael.

"It's been, on the whole, an instructive visit," she said. "Perhaps I'll even make a better lady detective after it. . . . I'm off tomorrow, Mike, so this is good-by. Do you ever come to London?"

"No, Iris, never," said Michael.

"Then this *is* good-by. Well — good-by. No, don't come with me," said Iris, putting out a restraining hand. "I'd like to leave you here — bare boards, plain desks, and learning on the walls all round you. " 'By, Mike. God Bless."

She was at the door. Michael Sheridan spoke thickly.

"Look, Iris — "

"No, Mike. Good-by. I mean — " Iris threw a glance round the room and gave a small, wry grin. "I mean — *Adios.*"

She was gone. Michael Sheridan stood in the middle of the room and stared at the open door.

CHAPTER TWENTY

The school term was almost over. The trunks had been brought up from the baggage room and were being placed in their appropriate dormitories. The end-of-term examinations were mercifully over and the results would be known only by the expressions on parents' faces as they drew the Reports out of their envelopes in the New Year. The Leaving Boys — not numerous, since this was but the first term of the school year—had held their Party; Mr. Fitzwilliam, who was leaving to be a real producer on the real stage, had held a Levee in his study and received the boys' farewells. Nothing remained but the Choir Service this afternoon and the ordering of the Blakely buses to convey the boys to the station the day after tomorrow. School was, to all intents and purposes over, and minds could be safely directed to plans for the Christmas holidays. Spirits were rising, and Mr. Swintzchell, roaming round the corridors in search of missing choristers, was heard to observe agitatedly that everywhere in the air was a smell of Santa Claus.

Simon called at the Cottage soon after lunch and waited while Caroline went upstairs to dress. He thought the house looked empty. Since Iris's departure it had even looked a little gloomy. It was wrong, he thought, for Caroline to spend the winter here alone, but if she wanted to, if she refused once again the proposal which he had resolved to make after the Carol Service, there was little that he could do in the way of persuasion. He drove slowly up to the School, Caroline beside him, both of them deep in thought.

The Chapel was not large, and could not, in its original state, have afforded room for Mervyn Clunes' steadily increasing flock, but this difficulty had been overcome by enlarging the existing Choir gallery and building a smaller one for the Choir. The masters and the Senior school sat downstairs and the Juniors occupied the large gallery. Those whose view was not totally obscured by the high railing could look across at the Choir, and a system of bush telegraph had been developed, with great success, between the singers and the Junior school and greatly enlivened the tedium of the Chaplain's sermons.

Caroline took her place against the St. Mark window and, sitting quietly on her bench, looked about her. Close to her was the organ, at which sat Mr. Swintzchell, now sorting sheets of music and passing them across to the Choir. The Choir, in spotless white surplices which made the smaller members look, Caroline thought, like cherubim in clean pinafores, fidgeted in their stalls and leaned over the railing to watch the School assembling.

The Juniors clattered into the large gallery; the Seniors filed into the pews below. Masters, entering at intervals, took their places at the end of the rows, and soon the visitors from High Ambo began to arrive, taking their seats in the two back rows.

Simon had received permission to listen to the Service from the Choir gallery, and Caroline could see him, quiet and withdrawn, beyond the restless Choir. He leaned back on his bench, arms folded, and watched the scene with interest, smiling as his eyes met Caroline's.

The air was full of whispers and shufflings, with occasionally a heavy tread or the thump of a prayerbook falling to the floor. Paper rustled and boys fidgeted ceaselessly.

There was a hush, so unexpected and so deep that Caroline felt as though the sound machine at a cinema had suddenly ceased to function. She saw that all motion, too, had ceased. She could not see the assembly below, but the Juniors were still, the Choir was almost rigid. Mr. Swintzchell's fingers were poised above the manual.

A few moments' dead silence, and then a momentary confusion of sound as the entire

School rose to its feet. Caroline heard steady, even footsteps and knew that the Headmaster had entered the Chapel. A moment later Mr. Swintzchell saw the Chaplain, and his hands descended upon the keys. As though he had plunged his hands into a sea of sound, the deep pulsating harmonies rose and filled the lovely building.

The opening prayers were short, and soon the entire assembly was exhorting all Christian men to rejoice. It was a happy moment for the Juniors, who did their best to outdo the Choir at each "Re-joy-hoy-hoyce." Smythe secundus, who had only joined the School in September and knew as yet little of its traditions, found himself growing so excited that he exhorted his neighbor to swing it, and received in return a pinch which brought tears to his eyes and taught him that departures from the orthodox in Church music were strictly limited.

There was no Address, and the School settled down to listen to the Choir's rendering of a famous setting of "Come ye, worship at this Manger." It was an ambitious project, but Mr. Swintzchell looked calm and confident as he came to the end of the opening phrase and nodded to the attentive singers. Caroline picked up a sheet of music and, following it, was moved to admiration at the ease with which the singers performed the difficult passages, watched the organist, and used their brief rests to throw glances of bored contempt across at the Juniors.

The music ended; the School knelt to hear the Chaplain reading the School prayer. Caroline thought it a singularly detached petition, for it asked little for the School and went on to crave blessings upon the poor and needy, upon parents and upon the Royal Family, all of whom, it was clear, were considered by Mr. Clunes to be in far greater need of Heavenly care than those within the confines of the well-appointed and well-regulated Castle Ambo.

It was Caroline's turn. Mr. Swintzchell gave her a nod and a smile, and she rose. He played the introduction, and the Choir sang the story of the Star of Bethlehem and of the Kings who followed it; of the shepherds and of the Manger. The music soared to a pitch of loud, triumphant sound and, at its climax, dropped to a soft, plaintive chord.

Gently and sweetly, Caroline took up the melody. Simon watched her, fair and serene against the narrow stained-glass window, and thought she was like the angels before which she stood. Mr. Swintzchell reached the same conclusion at the same moment, but he was not looking at Caroline. He was listening to the lovely voice, pure and passionless — the voice of the angels.

Mary, Mother of God
By the holy cradle kneeling . . .

sang Caroline.

The diminutive new boy, Marshall, about to put a piece of chocolate into his mouth, paused. He had not enjoyed the term; he disliked games very much; he disliked lessons even more, and he had composed a speech to be delivered to his parents requesting them to find for him an establishment at which these two occupations were given less prominence in the curriculum. He looked now at the white-robed Choir opposite, standing still and attentive, their eyes on the sheets of music held in their hands. His gaze wandered round the beautiful, softly lit Chapel and came back to the faces of his companions. He saw that their expressions, which could be leering and vindictive, were at this moment calm and, though it seemed an extraordinary term to apply to Harrison and Ginger Gale, almost kind. The speech, which had a moment before seemed a reasoned and reasonable composition, faded from Marshall's mind. This was *his* School. A chap, he reflected, had to go to school; it was a pity, but it was necessary, and this, come to think of it, was a pretty fine School once you got used to it, if you could get used to it. It was a pity about the games and the lessons, but perhaps a chap could get used to those, too. Come to think of it, this wasn't a bad sort of place, and he wouldn't say what he'd been going to say to his mother and the old boy. . . .

Mervyn Clunes, listening to the clear, effortless notes filling the Chapel, reflected that he was a lucky man. He was doing the thing he loved best; he was doing it well and he was making a success of it. It was constructive work and he was, he knew, lucky in his staff. They were, on the whole, a brilliant crowd. Young Sheridan had looked like succumbing to the Drake girl — a beauty, Clunes acknowledged, but not up to Sheridan's intellectual level. Women were pretty persistent; it would have been a pity for a man like Sheridan, whose life ought to be spent among boys, to be derailed almost at the beginning of his journey, because of course that girl — what was her name? — Iris would have ideas above schoolmastering. Perhaps a word or two wouldn't have been out of place. She had some kind of intelligence. Perhaps she could have been made to see the fineness of the schoolmaster's calling. . . . It might have been worth trying. . . .

The music slowed; Caroline rose to a high, sweet note and held it. Then the sounds died away and the throb of the organ ceased. There was a moment's stillness and the School, with an almost visible start, came to itself. Marshall raised his chocolate to his mouth and found, to his surprise and disgust, that he had crushed it to pulp.

Simon sat quietly on his bench and Caroline, looking across at him, realized that a climax had been reached in their relations. He would, she knew, ask her to marry him, and this time he would expect a definite yes or no.

Caroline stared unseeingly at the Choir, now sorting and collecting music sheets, and brought herself to the conclusion that it would have to be yes.

She liked him. Perhaps she loved him. She could scarcely tell. She bent her head as the Chaplain began the words of the Blessing and tried to find in herself some strong feeling which could be interpreted as a desire to marry or to remain as she was. She could feel nothing, however, but a conviction that she would be equally happy either way. She would be happy married to Simon, but she would be equally content to live in this cottage at High Ambo, doing little, seeing little, enjoying the small changes brought by each day. She knew that such a life would be regarded by most of her friends and relations with distaste, but she herself found in it the things she liked best in life—

peace, quietness, a complete absence of hurry or confusion.

But she had learned something in the past few weeks. She had found that, with Simon to listen, to comment, to advise, the turmoil and unhappiness which events had roused in her had been greatly eased. Before his arrival, she had been worried and unhappy; Simon had steadied her, and she was grateful. It was this, she reflected, that people called having something, someone, to lean on. If this was leaning on Simon, it was very restful. Would he, she wondered, mind being married in order to be leaned upon?

Driving home after the Service, he gave her his own answer and Caroline appeared to find it convincing.

"Well, in that case, Simon," she said, "I will. I'm awfully grateful to you for asking me, and I'm — well, thank you for having been so patient."

"Do you," inquired Simon quietly, "love me?"

Caroline answered honestly. "That," she said slowly, "is what I've been asking myself, and all I can find out is that I don't know what I would have done in the last week or two if you hadn't been here. Every time things got too bad, I said to myself, 'I'll tell Simon,' and I felt absolutely all right again. But that isn't," she ended, "quite what you want, is it?"

"It'll do," said Simon, "for a start. Coming from you, it's almost a declaration of passion. And it's on an infinitely higher plane than many of the reasons which make women remarry. My cousin Jean, for example, told me that she got over her husband's death, cured herself of loneliness, got used to managing things for herself, and had no great urge to fill the empty bed beside her. But she did marry again."

"Why?"

"The thing that drove her to it," said Simon, "was having to get up in the middle of the night and put the cat out. Or let the cat in. She came to the conclusion that she must have a man. And she's very happy and so is he. And so," he added, "is the cat."

"Solly," said Caroline thoughtfully, "stays in at — "

"I wouldn't," said Simon, "lay hands on that animal if it mewed prayers at me all night. But I love you, Caroline, and in time you'll love me, and we're going to be very, very happy. When we get to the Cottage," he said, "I'll sit in a chair by the fire and you shall get me a good meal and we'll start being happy at once."

The plan, pleasant as it was, was doomed to frustration. From the Cottage lights were blazing as they approached and, at the gate, stood Robert's car.

Caroline looked anxiously at Simon.

"He's back," she said. "Do you think Polly has — ?"

She opened the door and saw that there was no sign of Polly. But on every chair, on every table, strewn on the floor and suspended from doorknobs, were Robert's possessions. Robert was standing before a suitcase, folding and packing garments. He looked up briefly as Caroline and Simon entered and then bent once more to his task.

"Where's Polly?" asked Caroline without preamble.

"Polly," said Robert, fitting a pair of shoes in neatly, "is with her father in London. Where the hell are my trousers? I've looked in every blasted room and — "

"They're hanging up. I'll get them," said Caroline. She brought the trousers and stood watching her brother as he went on silently and efficiently with his packing.

"How's things?" asked Simon.

"I needn't," said Robert without looking up, "ask you that. I presume the years of waiting are about to be rewarded — right?"

"Correct," said Simon. "We shall be brothers."

"Fine." said Robert. "Chuck me over that shirt there, will you? Oh — Caroline — Where the hell's Caroline?"

"Here," said Caroline from the kitchen.

"The old buzzard called," said Robert. "Old Brock. Came in to tell you your singing made him leave the Chapel."

"Too deeply affected to stay, I presume?" said Caroline.

"Didn't ask him. He thought he was going to wait until you got home, but I opened the door wide — a sort of hint — and went on with what I was doing. So he pushed off."

"I see," said Caroline, from the door of the kitchen. Her eyes became fixed speculatively on a shabby gray overcoat lying over a chair near the door. It didn't look like . . .

"Could you come out of your coma," asked Robert, "and put a few things into that small case? Just shove 'em in. I'm in a hurry. I want to drive all night and get to Town by the morning. No — let Simon do that," he amended, "and you go and get me something hot—and some sandwiches of some sort for the road. Something eatable, for God's sake."

Caroline packed some sandwiches, brought in some hot coffee, and saw that Robert was almost ready. He drank his coffee impatiently, standing by his suitcase and giving a final glance round the room. Caroline found courage to put a question.

"When are you — when do you — I mean, when are you going to be married?" she asked.

Robert put down his empty cup, snapped his suitcase shut, and swung it to the floor. "I am not," he said, "going to be married."

There was silence. Caroline handed over the small case, gathered a bundle of clean handkerchiefs, and tucked them absently into a corner.

"Not there — not there," said Robert irritably. "I want the things where I can get at them. Give 'em to me."

Caroline obeyed.

"Why," she asked after a few moments, "aren't you going to be married?"

Robert shut the small case and handed it to Simon.

"Take that out for me, will you? I'll bring these." He turned to Caroline. "I'm not going to be married," he said, "for the simple reason that I'm married already."

Caroline drew in a fearful breath and let it out hopefully. "P-Polly?" she asked.

"Naturally," said Robert, looking round in search of something. "Where's my blasted overcoat gone?" he asked angrily. "It was there, near the door. Now where's it?"

Caroline and Simon looked at the gray overcoat on the chair.

"Isn't that it?" asked Simon.

"That? What sort of clothes," asked Robert incredulously, "do you think I go about in? That? I thought," he added tactfully, "that that was yours."

"I suppose — " Caroline kept her voice carefully casual — "I suppose Colonel Brock made a mistake and — "

"That's it—curse him," said Robert. "Well, I'm not going to stop for it now. I've got to get going."

"Where," asked Caroline, "did you find Polly?"

"Find Polly? Where would you find Polly?" asked Robert. "She wasn't with you and she wasn't with me. That only left one place she could be. With Daddy. So I looked up Daddy and there she was. There they both were. Promising to stand by each other. All very pretty and all very, very impractical. I sent Daddy away to pick up the bits he'd broken and try to piece them together. And I married the girl. And I suppose you're full of morbid curiosity about where we spent our honeymoon, and how?"

"Yes, please," said Caroline.

"We spent it in Iris's flat," said Robert. "I told the caretaker she'd given me permission. It was cramped, but we managed. Polly slept on the bed and the dog slept on the bed and I slept on the bed. We all slept on the bed. Any comments?"

"I knew," said Simon, "that you couldn't be the fool we all thought you."

"Well, let me out of here," requested Robert, "before Caroline starts draping herself round my neck. Embrace *him*," he told Caroline. "He'll enjoy it. And go round and get my overcoat back from that old Brock, will you? It's a good overcoat. It cost me something pretty steep in dollars. Give him back his imitation Harris and tell him to buy himself a stronger pair of glasses. Good-by. Mind that thing, Gunter, will you? Oh — " he glanced back at Caroline — "Polly sent some messages. Can't remember what."

"Shall we," asked Simon, handing in the cases and shutting the car door, "see you at our wedding?"

"Can't say. Send the invitation to Iris's flat," said Robert, "and if we remember, we'll call for it. S'long."

The car had gone; the road was empty. Caroline walked thoughtfully back to the house beside Simon.

"The overcoat," she said, indicating it as they entered the room. "I'm afraid — "

"Total loss," summed up Simon. "Don't worry. Robert'll never give it another thought."

"He won't show his feelings," said Caroline, "but I'm sure he was happy, aren't you?"

"I'm sure, and I'm happy — whichever you meant," said Simon. "Are you happy?"

"Yes — very," said Caroline. She frowned and gave a little sigh. "I'd be quite, quite happy in every way," she said, "if only I could feel that Iris — "

Simon took her hand and held it against his cheek. "Don't worry, Carol," he said. "I'm sure—I don't know why—but I'm quite sure Iris is going to be all right."

CHAPTER TWENTY-ONE

At noon on a clear, fine day, less than a week later, a woman stepped from a bus at Piccadilly Circus and gave a keen glance to left and right. Tall, white-haired, with a beautiful face and a calm, almost regal air, she stood and pursued her usual logical line of argument.

Those people crouching on her right were no doubt waiting to cross. They were watching the lights; probably, she reflected, the lights would, in time, become some other color and everybody would scamper across in a flurried and apologetic manner.

Well, one couldn't wait forever. One could no doubt find gaps between the vehicles wide enough to allow the passage of a still slim figure. Ah! There.

With the utmost calm, she stepped off the pavement into the steady flow of traffic, moved round a double-decker with a purple-faced driver, steadied for a second beside a single decker whose driver's eyes, she noted, bulged curiously, slipped between a Rolls-Royce and a Daimler — the chauffeurs of both vehicles, she thought, showing the strain of driving in London traffic — and stepped up onto the opposite pavement.

Quite simple. One merely required a

steady head. Now where? The street should be quite easy to find. One had no need to stop these people — how they all rushed, to be sure! — in order to put useless questions about roads which were there for anybody to find for themselves. One looked up the place in one's London guide before setting off, and came to it without difficulty.

Quite so — Shaftesbury Avenue on that side — quite correct. That was where the theaters were, of course. Now across here — that was probably it. Yes.

Which building would it be? Nothing seemed to be numbered. This? No. This, perhaps? No. That was a curious shade of green, the door. Perhaps women's clubs always painted their doors . . .

Yes. Here it was, without the slightest difficulty. Charming old staircase. What a beautiful sweep, and how well-placed those windows were!

Very well-dressed, some of these women, but not, perhaps, warmly enough clad. December wasn't midsummer — in England, at all events. It would be Christmas in less than a week and it didn't really look seasonable to see women in lightweight coats and skirts.

There would, of course, be a Secretary of some kind. Quite so. A very neat, well-kept little Office. The visitor approached it, stood in the doorway, and smiled charmingly at the girl at the desk. The Secretary, to her own astonishment, found herself rising to her feet.

"May I — ?" she began.

"Good afternoon. What a beautiful building this is, isn't it?" said the visitor. "I do hope I'm not disturbing you. Would it be possible, I wonder, to see somebody called Miss Drake? I understand she lunches here every day."

"She does — yes," said the Secretary. "I think she'll probably be in the restaurant. Won't you come into one of the lounges and wait?"

The visitor inclined her head. "Thank you. I wonder," she said, "if you have a rather private lounge? I've come a long way to see Miss Drake on some important business, and — you understand?"

The Secretary studied the calm, beautiful face for a few moments. "I've got a private sitting room of my own just along here," she said. "Nobody would disturb you there."

She led the visitor along a short corridor, feeling a little dazed. Her own sitting room — what was she doing letting a complete stranger into her own, private, precious room? She must be off her head; it must be this — Well, anyway, here it was.

"In here," she said. "I'll tell Miss Drake. Would you," she inquired, "care for some lunch?"

"It's very kind of you, thank you, but I've already lunched," said the visitor.

"Then I'll send Miss Drake up. What name," inquired the Secretary with real curiosity, "shall I say?"

"Will you say — ?" The visitor paused, and a smile of quiet amusement came to her lips. "Well, she doesn't know me. Would you, please, just say that a lady has called?"

The Secretary went downstairs, walked across the restaurant to Iris's table, and, pulling out a chair, dropped into it.

"A lady's called," she said.

Iris, listlessly crumbling the remains of a sponge pudding on her plate, looked up without interest. "What lady?" she asked.

"Didn't say. Direct descendant of the Queen of Sheba, I imagine," said the Secretary. "Made an entrance like Sarah Bernhardt, addressed me like Queen Victoria stopping to say a kind word to a loyal subject, and hypnotized me into giving her my sitting room. Says you don't know her."

Iris put her chin on her hands and frowned into space. "Tell her to go away. Tell her I've gone," she said. "I don't want to see anybody."

The Secretary looked across at her keenly. "What's gone wrong with you?" she asked. "A few months ago, you used to be quite refreshingly alive. Now you go about like a duck — sorry, Drake — praying for rain. Would it be love?"

"No."

"I see — just something you've eaten. And, judging by the look of him these days, poor Ted Harris has eaten it too. Well, pop along to the anteroom. Her Majesty's waiting."

Iris rose slowly. "She'll be another of those West End milliners," she said irritably, "wanting me to boost her blasted hats. I've told them I'm not allowed to advertise anything."

"But they just want you to slip their name in by accident — I know," said the Secretary. "Well, I don't think this one's a milliner. Her hat's pure nineteen-fourteen, but it's funny, — you know — I didn't notice it at the time. It's only just come to me. See what I mean?"

Iris opened the door of the private sitting room. A tall, black-clad figure was standing looking out of the far window. Iris shut the door behind her and, at the sound, the visitor turned.

For a full minute, there was silence in the room. The tall woman's eyes were fixed on Iris with a keen, anxious scrutiny which changed, in a few moments, to relief and pleasure.

Quite so. One shouldn't have entertained the slightest doubt. One should have trusted, had faith. Nobody but a girl of this sort could have raised such feelings in —

"I — I k-know you," stammered Iris. "I — I — your photograph — in the frame." She came a step nearer and found herself clutching the visitor's hands. "I — I'd have known, anyway. I — you're the same. I'd have guessed. I'd have known you anywhere — anywhere. I — "

"Quite so," said the visitor gently. "Quite, quite so."

She was patting Iris's hands with a slow, soothing gesture, and Iris's faltering speech died away. The visitor led her to a sofa and, sitting beside her, pulled out a handkerchief, shook its folds open, and dabbed gently at the tears which coursed down Iris's face.

"There, there. You mustn't, you really mustn't cry," she said gently.

Iris gave a sound between a sob and a gulp and looked directly at the woman before her. "Did — did Mike send you, Mrs. Sheridan?" she asked.

"Lady. Lady Sheridan," corrected the older woman gently. "My husband was knighted just before his death for his work on — well, you're too young to have heard about it. No," she ended, "Michael didn't send me."

There was a pause. Iris made an effort at self-control; she produced a handkerchief of her own, wiped her eyes resolutely, blew her nose angrily, and pushed her hair off her forehead.

"If he didn't send you," she said, a little shakily, "then — "

"It's rather a long story," said Lady Sheridan. "May I tell you in my own way?"

Iris put out a hand, grasped one of the black-gloved ones, and found herself feeling a great deal better. "Go on," she said.

"Michael," began lady Sheridan, "hasn't written to me since he told me you'd gone away. I waited — anxiously, as you can imagine — but I heard nothing. I was unhappy, because I felt that he was unhappy, and I was sure that you were unhappy. But there didn't seem anything to be done. Until yesterday."

Iris waited.

"Yesterday," went on Lady Sheridan, "I had a letter, a most extraordinary letter, from a gentleman with a most extraordinary name."

"Mr. Swintzchell!" said Iris instantly. "What did he say?"

"He said a good deal," said Lady Sheridan, "the most roundabout and garbled way. I haven't really fully deciphered it yet. But his letter didn't really matter. What mattered was the one he enclosed."

She opened her bag, produced a torn, crumpled sheet of notepaper, and held it for a moment.

"He enclosed this," she said. "You shall read it in a minute or two, but I must tell you how Mr. — "

" — Swintzchell — "

" — how he got hold of it. He must," Lady Sheridan interrupted her story to observe, "be an amazing man."

"Yes," said Iris. "Go on."

"When you went away," said Lady Sheridan, "he was more unhappy, I think, than all of us put together. He wanted to say something to Michael, but he couldn't think of any suitable English words, and he didn't think that Michael, in any case, would have heard them. Michael was what Mr. — "

" — Swintzchell — "

" — what he called deaf to the outside world. He went about his work in the ordinary way, but he wasn't eating and he wasn't sleeping. Mr. — "

" — Swintzchell — "

" — wasn't sleeping either, because Michael walked about his room all night, his own room, and it's not easy for anybody to sleep when a friend is in great trouble. Then, late one night, Mr. — "

" — Swintzchell — "

" — saw Michael at the desk in the hall, writing what was obviously a very difficult letter. He was very pleased. He felt certain that Michael was writing to you, that he would send the letter off by the morning post, that you would take the first train back the morning after, and — and so on. But as he stood on the landing looking down at Michael, he saw that he wasn't, after all, going to finish the letter. He saw him put his head in his hands, throw the pen down, crush the letter into a ball, and throw it into the wastepaper basket and then go upstairs to walk about his room once more."

Iris put out a hand and clutched the letter which Lady Sheridan held. Lady Sheridan let her take it, but put out a restraining hand.

"In a moment," she said. "That was the letter Michael was writing. You can guess how this kind Mr. — "

"He took it out of the wastepaper basket and sent it to you," said Iris.

She bent her head and unfolded the crumpled sheet with unsteady fingers. There was silence in the room as she read the few lines of hasty writing. She saw them, at first clearly, and then through a mist, and finally not at all, but her eyes remained fixed on them and her heart went out to the man who had penned the words.

"My dear," said Lady Sheridan gently, after a long interval, "you're getting it rather wet."

"Y-yes." Iris mopped the letter, mopped her eyes, and looked apologetically at the older woman. "I'm sorry. I never c-ry and I c-can't think why I'm c-crying now. But — " she strove to speak clearly — "but why didn't Mr. Swintzchell send *me* the letter?"

"If he had," said Lady Sheridan, "would you have — well — acted on it? It tells you all you want to know, true. It tells you that Michael loves you and that he finds he can't, after all, do without you. But would you have gone back to him and said, 'Your letter was found in the wastepaper basket and, well, here I am'? Would you?"

"No," acknowledged Iris with difficulty. "No."

"The German professor is a very wise man," said Lady Sheridan. "He realized that *you* couldn't act on it, and that *I* could. And did. For you see, Iris, my dear, here I am," she went on. "As soon as I read Michael's letter, I decided at once that I would do it."

Iris looked at her. "Do what?"

"Give you to Michael for Christmas," said Lady Sheridan. "We haven't a great deal of time. He'll be home in two days. If we get a taxi and call at your flat to collect some things, we can catch a late afternoon train. When Michael arrives, there you'll be, and it'll be a lovely surprise."

"You — t-think so?" asked Iris.

"It'll be a surprise, anyway," said Lady Sheridan. "I would have said that my son would have conducted his wedding arrangements a little more skillfully, but — Will you come, my dear?" she asked.

Iris opened her mouth, shut it again, and then spoke with an effort. "I — I — do forgive me for saying this," she said hesitatingly, "but I must say it. If you do take me with you, and Mike finds me there, all ready for him when he arrives, then won't he — don't you feel that he'll feel a bit — a bit hag-ridden?"

She looked anxiously at Lady Sheridan and found to her relief that she was looking extremely amused.

"Does Michael," she asked Iris, "strike you as being the kind of man who would allow any woman to run him?"

On this point, Iris knew, there could be no doubt. "No," she said. "I know — well, no."

"Quite so," said Lady Sheridan. "You see, I reasoned on these lines: the issue, if I may use the phrase, was never in any doubt. Michael would have come home tired, unhappy; he would have tried to make my Christmas the usual jolly affair and it would have been like having a haunt in the house. A little later, he would have told me that he had to come to London; he would have come to you and the thing would have been done just as it's being done now, only with a great deal more fuss and argument. And besides that, my dear Iris — " Lady Sheridan smiled a little shyly — "I had other very good reasons. I always liked the sound of you. Michael's letters were more revealing than he realized; and now I like the look of you. When you came in at that door, I said to myself, 'He's going to marry this girl.' "

Iris felt memory stirring. She'd heard those words — well, not those words, but something like them — not so long ago. What were they? Yes! She'd said them herself, to Caroline. "He'll marry me," she had said, "and like it." . . .

She heard Lady Sheridan's voice.

"Don't you agree, Iris?" she asked gently.

Iris looked at her and spoke firmly. "Absolutely," she said.

Lady Sheridan rose. "Then we'll go," she said. "Will you get your things while I thank that charming Secretary for lending me her room?"

"I'll meet you at the top of the staircase," said Iris.

At the staircase, a few minutes later, she saw Lady Sheridan extending a gracious hand to the wide-eyed Secretary. She gave a smile to Iris and a brief glance of amusement at Iris's hat.

"Extraordinary!" she murmured.

She inclined her head toward a woman who stood aside to let her pass, glanced down the stairs at a woman who was about to mount and who, suddenly changing her mind, stepped down again and waited for Lady Sheridan to descend.

"Now a taxi," she said.

Iris thought of the first of the thousand and one things she wanted to say. "Look, Lady Sheridan — " she began.

"Please," begged Lady Sheridan, "don't call me that. Just call me — "

She stepped toward a taxi which a busy commissionaire had, with infinite difficulty, that moment procured for a waiting client.

"How kind — how very kind," she said gratefully, stepping into it and making room for Iris. "Will you tell him where to go, my dear? And don't," she resumed, "call me Lady Sheridan."

Iris looked at her. "Then what — ?"

"Just," begged Lady Sheridan, "call me Mother."

The employees of G.K. Hall & Co. hope you have enjoyed this Large Print book. All our Large Print titles are designed for easy reading, and all our books are made to last. Other G.K. Hall Large Print books are available at your library, through selected bookstores, or directly from us.

For information about titles, please call:

(800) 223-2336

To share your comments, please write:

Publisher
G.K. Hall & Co.
P.O. Box 159
Thorndike, Maine 04986